I0723531

THE BILLIONAIRE'S MARRIAGE PLEDGE

MELODY ARCHER

BOOK REVIEWS

"This is a wonderful billionaire romance. I love the story, and the whole fairy tale vibe! It is sweet and fun to read, and the characters are very endearing..." -Marianne

"Suspense, intrigue, betrayal and love. This book has it all. As the last book in the series, I thought there would be a lot of family repeat. But there is not. Great book. Loved it!" - Serina

"I really enjoyed this book. I've never read anything by Melody Archer but I will follow her. This book was clean and very romantic. I would highly recommend it to anyone." -Connie

WANT MORE SWEET ROMANCE?

Eliza and Daniel Stevenson's Love Story is waiting for you to enjoy. To grab your copy of this FREE Sweet Romance go here: https://www.melodyarcher.com/ free-book/

"Once there was a Princess… and she fell in love. Anyone could see that the Prince was charming. The only one for me…" Snow White *(from the movie)*

CHAPTER ONE

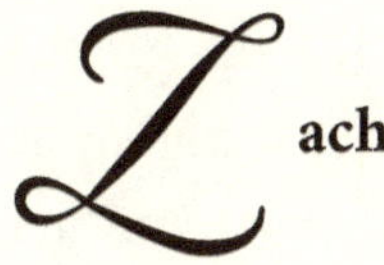ach

"TONIGHT, it's my honor to be the first to take the microphone and introduce my grandson." William Stevenson sent the crowd a side-ways look and winked at Zach.

Soft chuckles could be heard from the many folks who had gathered in the large showroom space that was hosted in one of Zach's massive buildings as part of his company, *Stevenson Sea Adventures*.

Zach's grandfather continued. "But in all seriousness, I couldn't be more proud of my grandson. Since he began this business, *Stevenson Sea Adventures* six years ago, Zach has won numerous awards for his boat designs. He's gained a reputation as a builder of watercraft that meets the highest standards of safety and durability. And tonight's announcement is no different."

The grey haired man turned to Zach. "However, today's news is his to tell. Ladies and gentleman, to share with you his latest project welcome my talented grandson Zach Stevenson."

Zach hurried to the front of the room, a big grin lighting up his face as his gaze met the shiny blue eyes of his grandfather.

His grandfather pulled him into a quick embrace before turning to walk off the stage.

Swallowing nervously, Zach scanned the large crowd. His grandfather had returned to stand beside his grandmother, Catherine Stevenson. His mom wore a big smile as she stood together with William and Catherine and her four sons and their wives.

He was very thankful he could always count on support from his family. The only person missing was his late father.

Zach glanced heavenward. Maybe it was wishful thinking, but he couldn't help but hope that somehow his dad was catching a glimpse of a few of the important moments in his life, like tonight.

He exhaled a long sigh filled with a mixture of nervousness and excitement as he looked over the crowd.

Gratefulness swelled inside his chest as his gaze swept the crowded room filled with business acquaintances as well as childhood friends from Paradise Lake and Seattle. They were here because they had accepted his invitation.

Swallowing once more, courage rose up on the inside and at last he found his voice.

"Thank you everyone for accepting my invitation to tonight's event." Zach grinned. "I was quite vague about the details in the invitation you received. I've since heard many of you ask me, 'What's your big surprise?'"

He paused and the room grew silent. "My secret project is a new line of Motorboats."

Intense pleasure filled him as applause broke out in the room. Seeing smiles on the faces of people he knew who loved boats like he did filled him with a warm glow of happiness.

"Before we unveil the new motorboats, I wanted to share the inspiration behind this new project." He tensed, holding raw emotions in check. Memories that haunted him for years swirled in his mind.

He took a deep breath, forcing himself to relax.

"This project was inspired by the memory of a really good friend of mine. During my teenage years, we spent many summers on the lake together enjoying the water."

"Sadly, when he was only sixteen, Koda died in a motorboat accident." As he spoke, it seemed like the weight of the life and death of his friend was heavy upon him. Zach swallowed back emotions that threatened to spill over.

He hesitated a moment before continuing. "An investigation into what happened revealed that the accident could have been prevented if only my friend had been piloting a safer motorboat that day."

"Since that day, designing and building safe and durable watercraft has become my passion and my life's work."

Loud applause broke out in the crowded room.

Zach paused for a moment until the room was quiet again. "Today we are happy to share with you my friend's story and we're pleased to present the newest line of motorboats dedicated to his memory."

He nodded to a handful of employees who stood in the back beside the covered up new motorboats. His nod was the signal to remove the cover off the two new motorboats at the back of the showroom.

"Ladies and gentleman, introducing our newest production line of watercraft: *The Koda Lightfoot motorboat series.* I hope you take some time to take a look at these new watercraft and that enjoy what you see."

The crowd broke into a round of applause as they turned to see the new motorboats being unveiled. Excited gasps, sighs and many *ohs* and *ahs* could be heard around the room.

Zach grinned as he saw the wide smiles on the faces of family and friends. There were many who had come to support his new venture, for which he was grateful.

He was surprised that some folks from the town council had turned up as well as others like the small town barber and the family doctor.

Eyeing Doc White's familiar wrinkled face and grey hair, Zach took a second look when he noticed the young woman standing beside him.

Thick dark hair hung in long graceful curves over her shoulders. Large dark-framed glasses that were perched on a small straight nose, looked out of place on her delicate, oval face.

Her clothing appeared rather lackluster and oversized on her slender body.

Suddenly she looked up, her large violet eyes connecting with his.

Zach made no attempt to hide the fact that he was watching her. Nodding slightly he held her gaze as an easy smile played at the corners of his mouth.

Her cheeks stained pink at his bold gaze and she swallowed. Lowering her thick dark lashes, she broke eye contact.

He regarded her with a somber curiosity.

There was definitely something about this woman that charmed Zach.

As he stepped off the stage, he was determined to find Doc White and ask for an introduction to the young woman at his side. Was she a new assistant or nurse? Whoever she was, he definitely wanted to meet her.

He weaved his way through the crowd, his mood buoyant after the pleased response from everyone.

Searching the room brimming with people, he had a good vantage point to view the room from his six foot three inch height.

Finally, he caught sight of Doc White and the woman on his arm. Zach moved through the maze of people to catch up with them, but he was too late. Before he could reach them, the two of them had opened the door and exited the building.

Zach stood motionless, his broad shoulders heaving as he sighed.

"I hope all that sighing is because you've been impatient to talk to me." Zach turned to see the beautiful Felicity Kingston walk up to him, slowly curling her hand around his arm. His muscles tensed under her fingertips.

"I'm happy I finally found you. I was looking every-where for you."

He clenched his mouth tighter in annoyance. He really didn't want this conversation tonight.

"This evening is especially busy for me, Felicity. But, like you said, you've found me."

A tinkling sound accompanied her laughter and her well manicured fingers squeezed his arm. "Yes I have, and I'm glad. I wanted to ask why I haven't heard from you since we saw each other at the charity gala last month?"

His eyes widened slightly and his lips thinned in exasperation. "I thought you understood me when I said 'it's over between us.' I haven't changed my mind since that night." Zach shot her a penetrating look at the reminder.

"I thought you were teasing. I was sure you didn't mean it." The beautiful socialite batted her big eyes with their long lashes at him.

"But, I did mean it, Felicity." Zach's voice, though quiet, had an ominous quality. Gently but firmly, he peeled her hands away from his arm.

"I won't be in a relationship with a woman who uses photos of me or of the two of us to line her pockets by selling them to magazines or anywhere else. If there's no trust, there's no relationship."

Betrayal of any kind was something Zach wasn't going to stand for, especially when it hurt others.

Memories haunted him of how his father had been betrayed. It wasn't only because of the fact that his Dad's business partner Simon Black had stolen the money from their accounts. The betrayal went much deeper than that.

Zach had only been ten years old that day years ago

when he stopped by his Dad's office. But, he could still hear the angry woman's shrill voice as if it were today.

"Even if Simon Black stole that money, the fact remains that you were business partners with a crook. Simon Black was dishonest with a lot of people. So, how can we trust you -- his business partner?"

"The truth is, we can't. You are a thief and a liar, Mr. Stevenson and I will tell everyone I know, that I don't trust you and that they should avoid having any association with you."

Zach's cheeks burned in remembrance of that day and the effects of that day in the weeks that followed.

His dad had a heart attack and died. That woman spread vicious lies about his father and mother.

Soon after, his mom stopped seeing anyone in town and in her grief she was so depressed and humiliated for weeks afterwards.

Zach told himself back then, he would never allow betrayal to ruin his life.

Looking at his beautiful woman standing in front of him now, he was repulsed by her actions. She had beauty, but the fact that she was dishonest, sickened him.

Felicity's mouth turned downward into a familiar pout. "But, I..."

She was about to explain when they were interrupted.

"Zach, could you explain the details of this motorboat design?" Zach heard his brother Adam's voice.

Relieved at the interruption, Zach turned back to Felicity. "I need to go. Don't worry Felicity, I have no doubt there are plenty of other men who would be happy to have you by their side. But, it won't be me. Have a good evening."

Zach nodded and quickly walked away.

Mentally, he shook off the irritation he felt at having to repeat the same conversation he already had with Felicity at the charity gala. He didn't think she really understood the fact that she had violated his trust.

If she were willing to sell pictures of them together now, if they married what other information about him would she sell to the highest bidder?

No, he wasn't willing to take the chance.

Nevertheless, he hoped that at last she would finally leave him alone.

Adam stood next to the new sleek dark red motorboat, surrounded by many other onlookers.

"Ah, here's my brother. He can explain the details of this incredible new boat design." Adam grinned and slapped him on the shoulder.

The crowd clapped and listened eagerly as Zach explained how he had designed and built the new line of motorboats with durable and lightweight materials.

"I hope some of your questions have been answered." Zach spoke to everyone who was gathered around the newest motorboat. "If you have any other questions, please ask our Motorboat Division Manager, Manuel. He can also help you place your order."

As Zach walked away, Manuel began answering questions. He needed a little break and some fresh air. Opening the door to the beachfront area, he was surprised to hear his brother Adam's voice behind him.

Adam spoke in a low voice. "Zach, I'm impressed with what you've done with your company. It seems to have doubled overnight."

"Thanks. I'm pleased it's done so well. " Zach smiled as he looked toward the waterfront of his company property, *Stevenson Sea Adventures.*

"Your introduction to this new line of motorboats named after your friend was truly inspiring." Adam's smile widened in approval. "If Koda were alive today, he would be incredibly touched by the gesture. Zach, you amaze me. I'm proud to be your brother."

Zach swallowed back emotions that flooded him at Adam's words. As his oldest brother, Adam had been the closest thing he had as a father figure after his own father passed away. He had always looked up to his oldest brother and was thrilled to hear words of praise.

However, the memories of his best friend's death when they were teenagers were never far from his thoughts, and neither was the guilt that still haunted him to this day.

Deep inside, Zach yearned for Koda's death to leave behind some impact for good. He hoped the newest production of motorboats named in honor of his friend would have meaning to other motorboat enthusiasts.

He shrugged off the thought and turned to face his oldest brother. "Thanks Adam. It means a lot to hear you say that."

"Just speaking the truth." Adam walked to stand closer to him. He pulled out his smartphone and showed Zach a picture of him beside the new motorboat. A big grin over-took his features.

"I love your new design. It's beautiful, sleek and it's also large enough for Elle and I to take our family and some friends with us. I'll take it."

Zach grinned. "I thought you'd like this one. I'll ask

Manuel to sort out the details for you." He took out his smartphone and texted his motorboat division manager.

Each of his four brothers bought their boats from Zach and they consistently told him how happy they were with his boat designs. He was thrilled.

He led Adam towards the waterfront. *Stevenson Sea Adventures* was located along the Southern waterfront of Paradise Lake.

From the very start when he bought this land and built the large boat manufacturing building, Zach's vision had been to design, build and test the boats all in one location.

To do that, having waterfront property was essential. He loved this little stretch of beachfront property along the shores of Paradise Lake.

In fact, Zach liked it so much that at the same time he'd bought another twenty acres of beachfront property in an area around the lake where it was quieter, so that he could enjoy the beauty of the lake.

He had always been happiest enjoying the serenity of the water.

"Looks like you'll be needing more room for all the new boats you've built." Adam commented as he looked around the beachfront.

"Yeah. It is a little crowded, especially during weeks when we are ready to test them." Zach studied the waterfront. Yachts, sailboats and motorboats all filled the beachfront area.

Adam stopped mid-stride and turned to face him. "Walker's Cove Marina would be a great place to bring some of the new boats and you would also create more interest in what you have to offer."

"It makes sense, especially since you'll be inheriting Grand's Marina soon." His brother studied him, a look of expectation in his eyes.

Zach shrugged. A knot tightened his belly as he thought of missing out on his inheritance.

He furrowed his brow and looked farther down the stretch of waterfront and toward the Marina, which was almost two miles away.

How many times had he looked in the direction of the Marina and longed for those beautiful fifteen acres of land to be his? It had been too many times to count.

"Zach, tell me you aren't thinking of giving up on receiving your inheritance from your great grandfather?" Adam stepped closer and blue eyes so similar to his own, probed into his very soul.

Slipping his hands into the side pockets of his navy blue Bermuda shorts, he sighed heavily. "Maybe."

A wave of tension hit him like it always did whenever his thoughts returned to the inheritance he was supposed to receive from Grand when he reached his twenty-seventh birthday.

"Come on, Zach. You've wanted Walker's Cove Marina for as long as I can remember. You can't give up now. Not when you're so close to making it your own."

"You're forgetting one small detail. In order for me to receive my inheritance I have to marry by my twenty-seventh birthday. That particular deadline is only three weeks away." Zach ran a hand through his hair, as reality hit him stronger than ever.

All five of Walker Stevenson great grandsons were told

they must marry by their twenty-seventh birthday to receive their inheritance.

To say each of them were frustrated by the conditions in Grand's will, was an understatement.

Yet, despite the fact that his older brothers hadn't wanted to marry, in the end, each of them had entered into a marriage of convenience with beautiful women. And his brothers had surprisingly fallen in love with their wives.

Including his brother Adam.

"It's not going to happen." Zach knew it would take a miracle for him to find a woman who would agree to marry him in that short amount of time.

"You're kidding me." Adam spoke with a significant lifting of his brows. "Are you telling me you've decided to give up?"

Coming from his oldest brother, those were fighting words. The Stevenson brothers never gave up on themselves or each other. *Ever.*

Throughout his childhood and into adulthood, Zach had known two things for sure: his family loved him and nobody in the Stevenson family would ever give up on each other.

He mumbled a response. "I haven't given up, I just haven't found a woman I like well enough to marry."

"I saw you talking earlier with Felicity Kingston. I thought things were getting serious with her."

Zach's gaze came to rest on his brother's questioning eyes.

He shook his head. "We dated a few times, but I ended

it last month. Turns out, she's a pretty face but is not to be trusted, much like all the other socialites I've dated."

"I've come to the conclusion that if a woman is beautiful, her plan is to use you for her own purpose and then toss you aside like yesterday's news." Zach rubbed the back of his neck.

Adam shook his head, and was silent for a moment. "Not all women are like that Zach."

"Maybe. But, it seems the women I've dated so far have matched that definition."

"Well, perhaps you need to find a woman who is down to earth, humble and kind to the folks around her." Adam's steady, earnest gaze sought his.

A cynical chuckle escaped Zach's lips before he could stop it. "And a woman who isn't wrapped up in her appearance. Sounds like that might be an impossible task."

Adam shook his head. "That's just your bitterness talking. I think you've been looking in the wrong places for a potential wife. My advice is that you keep your eyes and ears open wherever you find yourself."

"You might be surprised to discover the perfect woman for you is right under your nose." At his brother's words, Zach couldn't help but remember the woman at Doc White's side earlier. He quickly shoved that thought away.

He wasn't looking for anything permanent. His past experiences with women had taught him they weren't to be trusted.

No, what he needed was a temporary arrangement. "Just so you know, what I'm looking for in a woman is someone who will agree to be my *fake* wife for a few months. That's all."

"Speaking from experience, sometimes what we originally plan to do can turn out a whole lot differently than what actually happens." Adam's blue eyes held a dreamy look and Zach knew he was thinking about his wife. "But, if I had to do it all over again, I wouldn't change a thing."

Zach sighed. "Yeah, but the difference between you and me is that I refuse to let myself fall in love."

"However, if I find a woman I can tolerate, I will consider asking her to be my fake wife. This will be truly a marriage in name only, because I won't let my heart be crushed again by another beautiful woman." Zach wouldn't budge on that point.

Adam made no response except to speak calmly. "Well, keep me posted. I'll be interested in hearing if you find what you're looking for."

"I don't think it will happen, so don't hold your breath, Adam." Zach grimaced at his brother.

"Oh, ye of little faith." Adam shook his head and chuckled at Zach's look of resolved determination to stand his ground.

He was still smiling as he glanced at his wristwatch.

They walked together along the beach.

"I love this view." Adam stared out along the lake. "I can't wait to take the new boat out on the lake with Elle and the children.

As Zach watched his brother smile with happiness, his belly clenched with a familiar discomfort.

He knew this ache for what it was: *longing.*

Deep inside, Zach yearned for what Adam had.

His brother had found a woman who believed in him and loved him with all her heart. Zach was convinced that kind of love would never happen for him.

At that thought, a deep sense of loss nearly overwhelmed him.

Sighing heavily, he shook off the heavy feelings and turned, his gaze scanning the beachfront area of *Stevenson Sea Adventures*. He was proud of the business he'd been able to build here.

It looked like that would need to be enough for him. Shaking off a deep sense of disappointment, he looked along the waterfront.

Adam stopped and pointed a finger along the beach area along Paradise Lake. "Is that a fire? It looks like it's near the Marina."

Zach got up from his crouched position and with one hand adjusted his sunglasses. Peering out across the shimmering blue water of Paradise Lake, he looked in the direction of his great grandfather's Marina.

Black smoke curled towards the blue sky, just above the tall poplar trees near the Marina.

Zach's jaw clenched.

"Something's wrong." Adam placed his hand above his eyes to shade them from the late afternoon sun as he peered over the water.

Zach nodded in full agreement and swallowed hurriedly.

It was a little over two miles as the crow flies from *Stevenson Sea Adventures* to the Marina.

"I was thinking the same thing." Zach could sense

something was wrong. He turned to Adam. "I'm going to head over there to see what's going on."

Zach ran to his motorboat, quickly unwrapping the rope that anchored it to the pier.

"I'll call the Fire Department." Adam called after him, already on his phone.

As he revved the engine, the motorboat sped across the lake toward the Marina. Billowing black smoke twirled in the sky above the Marina and seemed to get larger the closer he got.

A wave of apprehension swept through him.

Troubled thoughts swirled around in his mind as he thought of losing Walker's Cove Marina.

He simply couldn't lose this place.

Ever since Zach's great grandfather had begun taking him to the Marina as a young boy, he had fallen in love with the place.

The Marina was aptly named Walker's Cove, as it was a sheltered and sandy inlet on the Northern corner of Paradise Lake.

As a ten year old boy, it had felt like his own private haven just off the shoreline. He remembered sitting there for hours on the rocky crag that overlooked the lake to watch the white-capped waves.

Sitting there shaded by the tall trees all by himself, this place had become his own little place on God's green earth where he could forget about the pain of his beloved father's death.

After his Dad passed away, Grand found him many times at the edge of the sandy Cove. He would play there for hours at a time, in another world. The day came when

Grand asked Zach if he would like to inherit Walker's Cove Marina when he was older.

Without hesitation, he had enthusiastically said yes.

However, after Grand passed away a few years ago and his lawyer revealed the terms of the will, Zach and his four brothers realized their inheritance came with an unusual clause.

It seemed Walker Stevenson had found a way to force them into marriage even from beyond the grave.

Yet, despite the fact that his older brothers hadn't wanted to agree to the terms of the will, in the end, each of them had agreed to a marriage of convenience with beautiful women. To top it off, each of them had surprisingly fallen in love with their wives.

Today's conversation with Adam only served to remind him of the short amount of time he had left to meet Grand's demands.

He really longed to own Walker's Cove, as he'd come to call it.

His gut clenched into a ball. He couldn't lose the place he loved so much.

But, it would take a small miracle for him to find a wife in three weeks.

At least he didn't need to worry about falling in love. He'd made a decision the last time his heart was trampled on that he wouldn't fall in love. He wasn't about to get caught in that trap again.

If dating socialite Felicity Kingston had taught him anything, it was that most beautiful women were after what they could get from you. And if you didn't give it to them, they smeared your reputation and good name in petty revenge.

No, this time around he was determined to protect himself when it came to his relationships with women.

Slowing the motorboat to a stop, he threw the rope around the bulky wood post at the end of the pier. In quick motions he tied the rope, before hurrying towards the Marina buildings.

His gaze was focused on the ever widening black smoke and red flames that hovered over the tops of the trees near Walker's Cove Marina.

His belly tightened in panic and he was out of breath by the time he reached the old Marina building.

This first building was the one Grand had built when he started the Marina many years ago. It was this old and slightly crooked building that held the best memories.

A few years ago, it had been re-made into a coffee shop.

Today, all he could see was one side of the building now engulfed in flames.

Workers hurried to pour water on the flames, hard at work to get the fire out.

As far as Zach was concerned, this was the building they couldn't afford to lose.

He looked around and saw people were hurrying back and forth from the Marina to the neighboring property. Zach wondered what was going on.

Spotting his friend Ollie Hapfield who worked at the Marina, he hurried toward him.

"Ollie, I see the fire and black smoke at the coffee shop. And I also see folks carrying buckets, running over to the neighbors property. What's going on?"

A large furrow formed on Ollie's forehead and he set down the large bucket of water he held in his hand. Zach reached out a hand to steady him.

The older man's normally happy features were tight with strain and his words were rushed. "The fire here at the Marina's coffee shop came as a shock. But we're getting it under control. I asked around and no one seems to know how it started."

"I'll get the police to investigate." A deep groove formed between Zach's brows in worry. What was going on? He pointed to the black smoke rolling upwards above the sky over at the neighbors yard. "What's going on over there?"

"A portion of Mrs. Crandell's home next door has gone up in flames. I'm just getting more help and supplies and going back." The older man hurried toward the Marina buildings.

Zach hurried after him as memories came back of Mrs. Olivia Crandell from his childhood. She had always been generous and involved in helping the Paradise Lake community.

Her husband had been a Town Councilor for many years before he died of a heart attack seven years ago. The kind widow already had so many tough things in her life and didn't need a fire to deal with now too.

"What happened?" Zach asked his friend as he turned to look at the large cloud of billowing smoke.

Ollie picked up a bunch of buckets holding them under each arm. "It seemed to me like the older woman was in shock. But, I did overhear Mrs. Crandell explaining to her daughter Emily that she was trying to boil water in her stovetop kettle."

"She was adding more wood to her wood stove as usual, and one of the burning wood pieces must have fallen to the floor without without her noticing. The fire got out of control." The older man shook his head, worry on his lined face.

Zach gathered more buckets as he pressed his lips together with concern. "Sometimes it's the small things that cause the biggest problems."

"You got that right." Ollie shook his head. "I'm going to hurry back now, maybe some of this will be of help. Has someone called the fire department?"

"My brother Adam and Mrs. Crandell's neighbor called not long ago."

Zach's gaze swept the area.

Workers were scattered all along the wide open space. Some were helping customers and some were working hard on maintenance for the rental boats and other equipment.

Zach found the long-time Manager of Walker's Cove Marina standing near the rental boats.

Donald Haffsburger was a grey haired man that had been a teenager at the time Grand hired him to work at the Marina decades ago.

Over the years he had become Walker Stevenson's right hand man and after Grand's passing, he became the company's CEO and overseer.

Donald ran a shaky hand through his grey hair. "Zach, I'm glad you came. As you can see we're a little scattered at the Marina right now. We're trying to get as_many people as we can spare to help put out the fire."

Zach nodded, while he also noted that the older man could be overwhelmed. "I'll make an announcement to everyone, and hopefully that will help."

"By all means, please do." Donald nodded with a weary smile.

Zach jumped up on the wood deck, grabbing the portable microphone they sometimes used.

"Hey everyone. I've got a quick announcement. If any of you can help put out the fire next door, we'd be grateful. Ollie over there has all the tools you need. Thanks." Zach jumped down to the ground and quickly placed the microphone back on its stand, before he hurried toward Ollie.

Suddenly within a short while, a whole bunch of workers were running towards Mrs. Crandell's lakeside home.

"Wow, there's black smoke everywhere." Allie, who was a summer student working at the Marina, stared at the flames shooting out of the windows, her eyes widening in alarm.

They ran towards the growing number of people who were helping douse the flames.

Red and orange flames continued to shoot out of four windows on one side of the cottage.

Widow Crandell stood staring at the cruelty of the flames that were destroying her home. Tears ran unheeded down her cheeks. Her daughter's arms were around her, offering comfort.

"We're here to help, Mrs. Crandell." Zach spoke with

concern as he hurried to help the others.

"Zach Stevenson, I'm so glad you're here." The older lady was beside herself with worry and fear.

"Don't worry. We'll do everything we can to put the fire out. The Fire department will be arriving soon."

"I'm grateful for everybody's help. It's just that I'm terribly worried about Scruffles and Bentley." Olivia Crandell's tormented voice rang through the darkening sky. She pressed her hand over her face convulsively and sobbed.

Zach lifted an eyebrow, a question in his eyes as he looked over at Emily. "Who?"

"Mom's worried that her cat and dog won't make it out of the house in time." Emily pulled her mom close bringing comfort to the frightened woman.

"I'll see what I can do." Zach nodded and hurried away to where a crowd of people stood arguing about what to do next.

The disorganized chaos of people who had come to help wasn't going to get anything done. He needed to take charge.

"Folks, it's good that you're all here to help." Soon everyone turned in Zach's direction. "We can be more efficient if we work together. We want to put this fire out as quickly as possible, right?"

Folks nodded in agreement.

"My suggestion is that we form a line from the lake to the house and keep a continuous flow of water buckets coming, pouring much needed water onto those parts of the house where the fire is the worst."

"Good idea." Drummond Grumwald, another worker

from the Marina spoke up.

"I'll fill buckets with water." Ollie offered and hurried to find as many buckets as he could, carrying them to the lake.

A line of people formed quickly and soon they were like a production line in a factory. Buckets filled with lake water were handed from one person to the next until the last person poured the bucket of water over the fiercest part of the house fire.

Seeing everyone working together as a team, Zach got busy connecting the large water hose to the outside tap on the house. He began to spray water on the flames nearest him.

He noticed Doc White hurrying across the grass. The same charming young woman that captured his attention earlier was by his side.

The more times he saw her, the more interested he became. He decided he would need to do something about that.

Doc was a fixture in Paradise Lake and everyone who knew him loved him. Over the years, he had helped a whole lot of patients in their small town. He was semi-retired from his practice now, but still continued to help people with their health whenever he could.

Zach was glad Doc was here today. Mrs. Crandell needed a doctor to look at her shoulder, which had been hurt as she escaped her house after the fire started.

He glanced once again at the assistant by Doc's side, curious about who she was. Soon, Jeb Wheezly arrived and seeing Zach, hurried towards him.

"How can I help?"

Zach smiled and quickly handed him the water hose. "Jeb, perfect timing as always. Here you go."

Jeb nodded. "Thanks." Jeb worked as an office clerk at Walker's Cove Marina and was an older, kind man who was always eager to help.

"While you add more water to the house, I'll be going inside. I have a cat and dog to rescue."

"What? Wait, you can't go in there…" Jeb called out after him.

But, Zach was hurrying to the side of the house where there were no signs of fire.

With eyes smarting from the smoke and finding it difficult to breathe, Zach made his way through the hallways, looking in each room and closet trying to find Widow Crandell's cat and dog.

He called out their names in a friendly voice a few times, before he heard a dog's bark.

Following the sound, Zach opened double doors to a hall closet where he saw a beautiful brown and white Collie dog. The dog was crouched down and curled up next to him was a white longhaired cat.

Zach sat down on his haunches and reached out to pet the two of them, to calm them. "You two must be the missing Scruffles and Bentley. Mrs. Crandell will be so happy to see you two. Up you come." He lifted both of them gently into his arms.

Suddenly, a loud crack pierced the air and a long length of wood fell from above him. He raised his arm up to protect the animals and the burning length of wood landed on his arm.

Wincing in pain, Zach pulled the pets closer to his

chest, doing his best to calm them as he hurried back through the house and finally out the side door into the fresh air.

As Zach reached the outside air, he heard the fire trucks come onto the yard.

He expelled a sigh of relief as the firefighters quickly retrieved their fire hoses and began dowsing water on the flames.

Zach hurried forward, coughing and sputtering. He forced himself to slow down and breathe trying to rid his lungs of the smoke he had inhaled.

Scruffles and Bentley squirmed in his arms trying to escape. Zach made a beeline through the folks gathered round trying to get the pets to their owner.

"Oh Zach, thank you. You saved my precious ones! I don't know how I can ever thank you." Mrs. Crandell reached for her cat and her daughter took the dog in her arms.

"I'm glad I could help. Anyone would have done the same." Zach smiled at the pretty picture the older lady made as her face lit up the moment she hugged her cat close to her heart.

"Not just anyone would have ran into a burning building to save these pets, Zach. You have a heart of gold. Thank you." Emily's large eyes misted and she looked up at him.

"You're welcome." Zach felt uncomfortable with all the praise. He nodded and looked over at Widow Crandell who snuggled her fluffy cat. The wide smile he saw on her face, was thanks enough.

He winced from the pain in his arm and looked down.

The skin was red and he was sure it would blister. It stung a lot, but he hid the pain behind a smile. "Well, I should get going. Stay safe ladies."

Zach nodded to both women and quickly turned.

Without warning, he bumped into a soft body.

Automatically, he reached out to steady her. As he looked down, he was struck by vivid violet blue eyes that stared wide-eyed up at him.

Large, nondescript glasses perched on her slender nose, as if trying to hide those beautiful eyes.

She was the same woman he'd seen walking by Doc White's side earlier.

At first glance, she looked frumpy in her baggy, colorless clothing.

Now that he saw her up close, Zach was strangely drawn to her.

Her flawless oval shaped face was framed by wavy black hair, which was wrapped in a thick braid that hung carelessly over a slender shoulder.

As her gaze connected with his, she colored fiercely and hurriedly stepped away from him.

A mixture of fear and frustration flitted across her face.

Zach dropped his hands from her shoulders and let them hang loose by his side. "Sorry, I wasn't watching where I was going. Are you okay?"

Violet eyes studied him for a moment and he noticed lines of tension on her face before she looked down. She nodded quickly and whispered. "Yes."

Hurriedly, she stepped back.

He hesitated, torn by conflicting emotions. She

jumped away from him fast enough, and yet he still wanted to know more about her. Zach rationalized that he was a stranger to her and most likely she was scared of him.

For some reason the realization made him a little sad.

Zach shook his head, as if he could erase the weird feeling. He was overthinking things about this woman he just met. He would need to take it slow.

Shoving down the mixture of emotions that sifted through him, Zach replied, his voice calm and casual.

"I'm glad you're okay." Zach turned to step away from her so she would be more comfortable, but suddenly she gasped and lightly touched his shoulder.

❧

"Oh, my goodness. You've got a bad burn on your arm." Cassie sucked in her breath, automatically stepping closer to him. Gently, she lifted his arm, peering closer at the wound.

"Have you cleaned the wound?" She questioned and looked up at him.

The stranger shook his head, offering a short reply. "It just happened a few minutes ago. I'll go dip my arm in lake water. That should take care of it."

"No, that water won't be clean. Just a second, let me ask my Uncle Gus how to best clean the wound." Cassie turned quickly and searched for Doctor White.

Gently, she removed her hand from his arm and gave him the hand signal to wait for her. She hurried toward Uncle Gus. He was standing near a crying child that was being held by her mom. He spoke in a calm voice as he added a soothing salve to the child's leg.

Cassie waited by his side until he finished bandaging the child's leg. She hoped her uncle would take care of the wound on the arm of the handsome stranger.

He was so disturbing to her for some reason. In fact when she'd first seen him yesterday, she'd been mesmerized by his rugged good looks.

The boldness of his gaze brought her untried senses to life. But, it had also brought back familiar fears. He was attractive and compelling and her own awareness of him scared her.

She wasn't about to get into a relationship with a man. Any man.

It wasn't going to happen.

Which was why she really wanted Uncle Gus to take care of him.

Doc White finally turned to her. "Cassie, I could use your help."

She quickly blurted out. "But Uncle Gus, I need *your* help." Turning, she looked back at the man who was looking in their direction.

She looked back at her uncle and explained. "There's a man over there who has a serious burn on his arm. He's the same man we saw yesterday at the boating event. Now, he's hurt and needs your help."

Uncle Gus's eyes followed hers as she nodded to the man wearing designer shorts and shirt.

"Ah, you're talking about Zach Stevenson. Well, I will tell you what to do and you can fix him up."

She shouldn't have been surprised that Uncle Gus

knew this man. Doc White seemed to know everyone in Paradise Lake.

She saw more people that came to stand near her uncle waiting for him.

"Please come with me, uncle Gus?"

"Cassie, I can't. Look at all the people who have come to me for medical help." Her uncle leaned closer and whispered. "You don't need me to come with you. You can do this. Explain to me what's wrong and I'll tell you what you need to do."

She sighed and explained what was wrong with the stranger's arm.

"I'll give you this antiseptic and gauze." Doc White searched through his medical bag and gave Cassie what she needed. Then he spoke again. "Oh, tell Zach I'll need to take a look at his arm soon."

Cassie took the ointment and gauze that her uncle handed to her and with a sigh, she turned to walk back to the man.

As she walked back, she peered at him from under long dark lashes. Since he was watching the firefighters who were still battling the final sparks of the dwindling fire, Cassie let her gaze rest on him.

He was a handsome man with his sandy colored hair that was tinged with auburn highlights. His face was finely sculpted with a straight nose, high cheekbones and full lips.

Broad shoulders with muscled arms on his tall form, only added to his appeal.

Cassie looked up, only to see Zach's big blue eyes peering at her intently.

Her heart took a perilous leap.

An unwelcome blush crept into her cheeks, when she realized that he'd caught her staring at him.

A rogue grin turned up the corners of his lips.

Cassie bit her lip and looked down at the medical supplies in her hands. She felt flustered at his scrutiny.

So, this man was Zach Stevenson.

She knew a little about the Stevenson family, since she came to live in this small town.

Her friend Razelle had married Luke Stevenson, but ever since Cassie had come to Paradise Lake she avoided large gatherings of people, so she had only met Luke a few times.

Most of what she knew about the Stevenson family was from her friend because she didn't get out very much.

She preferred to stay hidden. That way, there was less chance of being found by the two people who wanted to hurt her.

But, hiding away meant she didn't meet many new people, especially good looking men.

Zach was handsome enough to stop any woman's heart, but that didn't mean she would be falling for him.

In fact, she was determined that it wasn't going to happen.

Cassie reached Zach, and forced a determination she didn't feel. "My uncle asked me to clean the wound. Come with me."

He walked by her side as Cassie led him towards an old blue truck. Opening the door to her Uncle's truck, she took out a large medical bag and brought out clean water and some medical supplies.

"I'll be gentle, but this might sting a little." Cassie cleansed the wound and then added an antibiotic ointment before covering the burned area with a sterile dressing.

She had continued to learn helpful tips from her uncle about how to help people who had smaller wounds. But, she still preferred when the Doctor treated people himself instead of asking for her help.

Zach winced a little at the pain from his arm.

"So, Doc White is your uncle. That explains how you know so much about fixing the burn on my arm."

Cassie's fingers paused from cleaning his wound for a moment. "I am learning, but truthfully, I asked Uncle Gus how to properly treat your arm."

"Well, that's good. Since you are doing a fine job taking care of me, I should probably introduce myself. I'm Zach Stevenson."

"My uncle told me who you are." Her tone came out sharper than she intended. She avoided his gaze and continued to clean the wounded area.

"Well this is a small town, I suppose. Many people know our family because we've lived here for years. And yet, I'm surprised I don't know you."

"I haven't lived here very long and don't really get out much." She kept her eyes focused on his arm, but heat rose up from her neck and into her cheeks at her admission.

She was frustrated by her own vulnerability to him.

"Since you know my name, it seems only fair that I know yours." Zach persisted in asking questions.

Her hand paused its movement and peered up at him

for a moment. His blue eyes peered into hers intently, waiting for her answer.

She sighed, annoyed at his persistence.

"I'm Cassie." She spoke hurriedly as she finished covering his burn with a sterile dressing.

Before he could say anything else, she spoke again. "Your wound has been treated, but you'll need to check it everyday. My uncle told me to ask you to come visit him at his office soon, so he could check the wound."

Zach nodded. "I can do that. Is he home early in the morning?"

"Yes, but…"

Zach interrupted. "Good. I'll stop by tomorrow morning."

Heat filled her cheeks at his words and an expression of satisfaction showed in his eyes.

He leaned a little closer and whispered. "Thank you for your help today, Cassie. I'll see you in the morning."

Motionless, she stood and stared at him, her eyes widening. She was so surprised that no words came out of her mouth.

He grinned, looking quite pleased with himself before he nodded and walked away.

Cassie tried to throttle her unexplainable curiosity and attraction for a man she just met.

She would need to squash any other thoughts of Zach. She would need to try to get him out of her mind.

Except there was one problem with that: *Zach was planning to stop by the cottage to see Uncle Gus sometime the next morning.*

How would she be able to avoid seeing him?

CHAPTER TWO

Cassie

Cassie cut the dough for cinnamon buns into half inch pinwheels, placing them on the large baking pan.

Setting them on top of the warm oven, she covered them with a tea towel and hoped the sweet buns wouldn't take too long to rise.

Next she added several scoops of ground coffee to the large coffee maker and, filling up the water, turned it on.

Soon, the coffee was percolating merrily along.

The light clip-clap of dog paws tapped along the wood floor, and before long her dog rounded the corner.

"Hey there, Cocoa." She rubbed the chocolate brown fur behind her ears. As usual she leaned closer, enjoying the attention.

Cassie had found the dog one day on her daily walk, lying in the ditch with deep cuts on her stomach and legs, her fur covered in blood. She'd rescued the dog and brought her back to the cottage.

Somehow she had convinced Uncle Gus to let her keep Cocoa.

After Cocoa healed, they started to walk often along the beach. The dog had become a wonderful companion.

"Cocoa, do you want your food?"

A small bark emerged and her tail wagged rapidly.

Cassie smiled and poured fresh dog food into her bowl, setting it next to her water bowl.

Happy that her dog was fed, she walked back to the kitchen and looked at the time. It was almost time for everyone to meet at the breakfast table.

She could hear the water running from upstairs and realized that soon Uncle Gus and his six friends would be downstairs ready for their breakfast.

It had become her job to make all the meals. That was what uncle Gus had asked her to do when she arrived unexpectedly on his doorstep two years ago.

She agreed.

Her meals had been very simple at first. She made many mistakes along the way. However, with a lot of practice she'd become a much better cook.

Peeking into the lunch containers that she'd set on the kitchen countertop for each of her uncle's six friends, she noticed each one was missing an important item.

Quickly, she wiped her hands on her apron and sat down at the kitchen table to write a note.

Happy, you are a treasure and a very encouraging friend. I hope you have many moments that make you smile today. Your friend, Cassie.

She quickly wrote out five more short notes to her uncle's friends and then a last one to her uncle.

There were too many reasons to count to be grateful for Uncle Gus. He'd helped her out by giving her a place to live and a sense of purpose as she worked to help him by cooking their meals and making their lunches.

But, the little notes were just her simple way of showing gratitude to each of them for who they were and for their kindness to her.

She wanted the words they heard the loudest in their day to be something that gave them confidence in who they were and put smiles on their faces.

A memory of her stepmother's hurtful words flashed across the screen of her mind.

You are nothing but a nuisance. Now that your father is gone, you have become my biggest problem. I wish you would simply disappear, so I wouldn't have to see your face anymore.

In the end, her stepmother had gotten her wish. She had left the only home she'd ever known and journeyed to the small town of Paradise Lake.

Near the end of her time living in her childhood home, her stepmother had begun to make her feel afraid. Cassie could only hope that Larissa White wouldn't discover her location.

Shaking off the anxiety that always came with reminders of her stepmother, Cassie stood to her feet, quickly finishing her task.

Whistling could be heard down the hallway, and she hurried to place the handwritten notes in each lunch bag.

Just as she pulled the cinnamon buns out of the oven the men entered the kitchen and sat down at the dining table.

Holding the pan, she smiled and breathed in deeply, savoring the cinnamon and brown sugar scent that wafted in the air. These fluffy cinnamon buns were the best she had made yet.

Setting them on two large platters, she placed them at each end of the long wooden table.

"Cassie, those sure smell good. I don't know if I've ever been this eager to eat breakfast." Ollie Hapfield wore a big smile on his weathered face.

"That's so nice of you to say. Thanks, Happy." Cassie had given each of the men a nickname the first year she'd become part of their unusual family. Each nickname had been her way of gently teasing them and making each of them feel like they were one big family.

The men had fun with the nicknames, so they had stuck.

A tall thin man made his way to the end of the breakfast table and sat down before he sneezed. "Sorry about that."

Ollie piped up beside him. "Sneezy, I sure hope you aren't allergic to these cinnamon buns. But if you are, I'll gladly eat yours."

Jeb Wheezly sneezed once more and using a handkerchief wiped his nose before responding. "Happy, there's no way I'm giving up one of Cassie's homemade cinnamon buns."

Another shorter man stumbled into the room, yawning. He sat by his spot at the table and glanced back and forth between Cassie, Sneezy and Happy and mumbled something before he yawned again.

"Sleepy, I wasn't sure if you'd make it out of bed in time for Cassie's breakfast."

Eli Sylvester was a balding man who seemed to need more sleep than the rest of them. He yawned another time before he answered. "I know. I can't help it if I need more sleep than the rest of you."

Cassie poured a few mugs of coffee and brought a steaming mug over to Eli first. "Here you go, Sleepy. Perhaps this will help wake you up."

"Thanks Cassie." Eli slowly lifted the mug to his lips and took a long sip. "That's just what I needed."

"You're welcome." Cassie walked back to the kitchen and began pouring more coffee into mugs for the others.

A few stragglers finally made their way into the dining room. The last man had a thick head of red hair with slivers of green and broad shoulders.

He frowned, his gray eyes level under drawn brows as he shuffled his way to the chair at the far end of the table.

Cassie had noticed months ago that Drummond Grumwald was in the habit of waking up unhappy.

"Good morning, Drummond." Cassie volunteered with a smile.

He looked up with a quick nod. His Scottish accent was thicker whenever he was frustrated. "Aye, it might be a good mornin' for most but no' for meself. I hardly slept last night, 'cause someone was up coughing and sneezing and carryin' on."

He turned and looked pointedly at Sneezy.

Cassie grabbed one of the coffee mugs she recently filled and handed it to Drummond, hoping to stop a war of words between the two men.

"Maybe a hot cup of coffee will help cheer you up, Grumpy." She winked at him. "Most likely what you heard at night is simply someone getting over a cold. It'll pass."

Drummond grimaced, took a sip of his coffee and sighed heavily. "Aye, I sure hope so." He shook his head, his eyes downcast for a moment before he looked up at her. "Sorry for complaining, lassie. Thank you verra much for the coffee."

Cassie smiled warmly and squeezed his hand. "It's alright. I hope your day gets better."

"Aye." He murmured silently.

Her lips trembled with the need to smile as she walked back to the coffee pot and grabbed a couple more cups of coffee for the last men to sit at the table.

Memories filled her thoughts about the first time she arrived at her uncle's lakeside cottage.

She'd noticed within the first month that Drummond complained about something almost daily. It seemed like nothing was to his liking and everyday was a bad day.

In her mind, he had earned his nickname Grumpy. But, lately it seemed Drummond was making an effort to catch himself or apologize when he grumbled about something.

If this change continued, she would need to switch his nickname to one that fit him better. She would think about it.

At last, Doc White walked into the dining room. He

smiled brightly and thumbed the suspenders he liked to wear. Stepping closer to her, he whispered in her ear. "Sure smells good, my dear. I hope you have enough food for one more."

Cassie smoothed her hands down her apron. "Of course." She turned expecting to see a Doctor friend of Uncle Gus.

Instead she saw the far-too-handsome Zach Stevenson leaning against the doorway.

Her eyes widened and her heart hammered against her ribs at seeing him standing there.

His blue eyes roved and lazily appraised her. She didn't miss his obvious examination and approval.

The interest in his gaze surprised her.

There was a tingling in the pit of her stomach at the intense look in his eyes.

Heat travelled upward from her neck to her cheeks.

She wasn't used to this kind of attention, at least not since she moved here.

He would have to show up early, when she was dressed in her patched up brown skirt and casual short sleeved floral blouse. On top of that, her apron was splattered with flour.

Today, she definitely looked the part of a work-worn housekeeper.

But, why should that matter to her? She didn't want to attract a man — not Zach or any other man. At least that's what she continued to tell herself.

She swallowed and tried to regain her composure, to be polite. He was her uncle's guest after all.

"Hello, Zach." She waved her hand to the empty place

at the table, and her words toppled out hurriedly. "You're welcome to stay for breakfast. There's an extra chair beside Uncle Gus, if you want to join us."

"Don't mind if I do." Zach chose the chair at the table beside her uncle. His blue eyes roamed over the table laden with fresh cinnamon buns and coffee and real butter. "These cinnamon buns smell delicious."

Uncle Gus looked over at Cassie who carried more coffee to the table. "That's my niece. Makes some of the best meals I've ever tasted."

"Ah, Uncle Gus. You might be a little one-sided in your opinion." Cassie murmured as she handed the coffee mugs to her uncle and Zach.

"I'll admit my partiality for you niece, but all the same it's still the truth. You've outdone yourself, my dear." Uncle Gus pulled out the chair beside him. "Come and sit down Cassie, you've worked hard enough this morning."

Cassie sat down, murmuring a quiet thanks to her uncle. She looked around the table of men, finally until her gaze finally landed on Zach.

He was staring at her like she was a puzzle he couldn't figure out.

She could feel her cheeks heat up again and was sure her cheeks blossomed red.

Turning quickly, she looked to uncle Gus to begin. "I'll say thanks and then we'll enjoy Cassie's delicious breakfast."

Cassie was grateful for a reason to look downward for a minute. Seeing Zach here in Doc's cottage was making her very uncomfortable.

But, ever since she saw him yesterday she couldn't get him out of her thoughts.

She had only wanted to help clean his wound so he would heal quickly. But, from the way his blue eyes had studied her every movement, it seemed something about her had piqued his interest.

Cassie certainly hadn't meant to capture his attention at all. In fact, attracting a man was the very last thing she wanted to do.

It was the reason she dressed in plain and frumpy clothes. It was also the reason she was content to live and work in her uncle Gus's home ever since she moved to Paradise Lake two years ago.

A shiver shook her body as memories returned. Fear still haunted her days. Nightmares plagued her sleep as she remembered back to the years she'd lived with her stepmother.

Larissa had treated Cassie with a selfishness that hurt her. Despite Cassie's many attempts to do something nice for her stepmother, as a young girl, she had been shoved aside or told she was a bother.

If her father had been alive, he would have put a stop to Larissa's scheming. However, Edmund White III had passed away when just before Cassie was about to bloom into womanhood.

For so long, she'd wished that her father hadn't married Larissa. But, he had married her. It was no use crying over spilled milk.

Her dad had been lonely ever since her mother passed away. Her mother had died from complications during her birth and Cassie never got the chance to know her.

When Cassie was still a little girl, one day her father had simply told his daughter that he had asked someone to be his wife.

Only three months later, Larissa had married her father and become her stepmother. Cassie had been excited in the beginning to have a new mother in her life.

She longed to enjoy mother-daughter dates and to go shopping and bake cookies or a cake with her new stepmother.

However, Larissa hadn't been interested in doing any typical mom and daughter activities.

In fact, within a few months, it became very clear to Cassie that her stepmother didn't want her around at all.

By the time she was eleven years old, her stepmother had begun to talk to her father about sending her away to boarding school.

Her dad had told his wife that Cassie was too young at the time. But, as the weeks and months went by and Larissa continued to pressure him, he finally sent Cassie away to boarding school.

She had only had one more year with her Dad, until he was gone.

Cassie grabbed a tissue and hurriedly dabbed at her eyes as memories overwhelmed her.

She hated her own weakness as she thought of her Dad's death and the whole situation with her stepmother.

Sighing, a resolve settled inside her. It wouldn't do any good to dwell on what might have been. She was just grateful to be far away from her stepmother's prying eyes and hurtful words.

But, now she had the new problem of Zach Stevenson.

It seemed her uncle was determined to include Zach in their snug family.

"Amen." Her uncle ended the prayer of thanks and surprised Cassie out of woolgathering.

She started to pass the platter around and waited until everyone had helped themselves to the cinnamon buns.

Cassie passed the fresh butter around the table, and was happy to see smiles on the men's faces as they ate.

With one finger, she gently pushed the glasses up the bridge of her nose. She began to eat, hoping to avoid conversation with the handsome man at the end of the table.

"These are really delicious, Cassie." Zach murmured between bites.

"See, I was telling the truth." Doc White spoke and the corners of his mouth lifted in a proud smile.

Cassie blushed again and placed her hand on her uncle's arm and squeezed. "Thanks, Uncle Gus. I'm happy my cooking has gotten better over the last couple years."

"That it has." Uncle Gus winked.

Her first tries at baking that she offered the men had tasted like leather and was just as dry. She was happy she'd improved.

Breakfast passed by quickly with Uncle Gus asking Zach about his boat design business.

Cassie learned a little more about him by the time the meal was finished.

The men stood to their feet, ready to get to work.

As they filed out with their lunches in hand, each of them spoke a thank you.

Cassie nodded and smiled happily. "You're welcome."

Uncle Gus turned to her. "I'm going to take a look at Zach's arm. Thank you for another wonderful meal, my dear."

"You're welcome. I'm happy you liked it." Cassie kissed her uncle's cheek and he walked toward Zach.

Zach looked back at her and spoke. "That was delicious, thank you. I might have to come back for another meal sometime."

His gaze was bold and bore into her in silent expectation, waiting for an answer.

She felt an unwelcome surge of anticipation formed in her belly.

Cassie stood motionless for a moment as she tried to throttle the dizzying current racing through her.

Briefly she nodded and whispered. "Sure."

She found herself strangely flattered by his interest, especially since she had gone to so much trouble to make herself look drab and uninteresting.

She quickly pushed those feelings down.

Uncle Gus spoke in his usual confident way, his words warm and welcoming. "You'd be welcome anytime, son."

Cassie hoped Zach wouldn't take her uncle up on the offer. She would be just as happy to avoid any more chance meetings with Zach Stevenson.

He was far too disturbing for her peace of mind.

Was it too much to hope that after Doc checked on Zach's arm that he wouldn't come around anymore?

Somehow, Cassie didn't think she'd seen the last of him.

❧

A COUPLE OF HOURS LATER, Cassie enjoyed the sun in the morning room as her paintbrush flew over the canvas.

Cocoa's large furry body was stretched out on a sunny spot on the rug where she liked to nap.

Cassie was glad for the company. It was comforting to know that the chocolate brown golden retriever was beside her during the day. Sort of a protector and friend rolled into one furry package.

Her brush tapered the outline of the light shining through the trees in this new painting and it delighted her to see it coming to life.

Drawing and painting had always been a love of hers, ever since she was a little girl.

However, she kept this part of her life private. So far only uncle Gus, her late father, her aunt Lottie and her friend Lydia knew of her passion for capturing beautiful pictures on canvas.

The new painting she worked on now, was inspired by a picture she'd taken a week ago of Walker's Cove Marina. She'd been drawn to the quietness of the place.

The sandy beaches, the old fashioned buildings along with the boats moored along the pier was a picture of small town tranquility in her mind.

The other picture she'd snapped was from a secluded part of the shore near the Marina. It was a sheltered and sandy inlet on Paradise Lake that was a private haven.

Many times she would go and sit for hours on a rocky crag overlooking the lake to watch the white-capped waves.

Uncle Gus had taken her out on the lake one day in his

old fishing boat and they just drifted along, enjoying the morning sun.

Cassie had spotted the rocky crag and had captured many photos. They were beautiful with the warm golden hues from the morning sun fingering their way through the tall poplar trees.

Cassie decided to paint that one next. It captured the essence of what she craved -- place where she could forget all about her fears and discover a sense of belonging, acceptance, safety and peace.

A smile hovered over her lips as she remembered how her father encouraged her to paint. She hadn't been a very good artist as a ten year old, but her father had reassured her to keep working at it.

Her dad had been convinced someday her artwork would make a meaningful impact to those who truly saw it.

In fact, he had searched their state for a well known professional artist who would be willing to tutor her.

By the time she was sixteen, the artist who tutored her, had praised her paintings saying she was ready to show them to audiences.

But she didn't feel ready.

In fact, she didn't think she ever would be.

The artist's side of her life was private. She put so much of her true self into her paintings that she didn't want others to see too deeply.

She sighed with happiness, pleased with how the painting was beginning to form on the canvas.

Suddenly, her phone beeped with an incoming text message.

Hey you. How's your day going?

Cassie smiled. Her friend Lydia must be on her break. She worked as a cook at the busy seaside restaurant that was located near the Marina.

Good. Just having some fun this afternoon.

You're painting aren't you?

She smiled at how well her friend knew her. *Yes.*

I'm not surprised. That usually makes you happy. So, is there anything new with you?

Cassie sighed and responded quickly. *Helped some people who were hurt at Widow Crandell's house fire. One guy stopped by to see Uncle Gus today to get his arm checked and ended up staying for breakfast.*

Oh? Do tell. Is he single and handsome?

Yes to both. Cassie realized now that she told her friend about Zach that she was going to be asked twenty questions. That is not what she wanted. *Oy.*

So, spill. Are you attracted to him? And are you seeing him again?

Biting her lip, she replied to her friend honestly. *As much as I hate to admit it, I do find him attractive, but I don't plan on seeing him again anytime soon. You know I'm not interested in dating.*

Yeah, I remember. I just keep hoping the right man will come along and prove to you that there are still a few kind, gentle and protective men left in the world.

Well, sorry to disappoint you, but I don't think a man like that exists. Cassie replied back.

Cassie, one day you're going to be surprised. You will meet the perfect man for you and you'll come out of that protective shell. That man who will adore you when he gets to know the real you, will want to marry you as fast as possible.

Cassie grimaced, knowing a tall tale when she heard one. *Keep dreaming my friend. Not going to happen.* Hearing footsteps, Cassie quickly texted. *Need to go. Chat again soon.*

She set down her phone. Lydia was always trying to find a man for her and encourage her to start dating.

Cassie had already told her friend that she wasn't interested in getting into a relationship with any man. Still Lydia persisted in trying to introduce her to single men. Well, her friend would just have to understand that she wasn't interested.

She turned to see Uncle Gus walking slowly into the room.

Greeting him with a warm smile, she asked. "Hey, uncle. What's up?"

His normally rosy cheeks were pale and he had shadows under his eyes. "I'm just tired today." He sighed. "May I ask a favor of you, my dear?"

"Of course. What do you need?"

Uncle Gus ran a hand through his grey hair. "It seems Zach left his watch here at the house when he stopped by this morning. Could you bring it to him? I'm not feeling too well this morning."

"You're sick? What's wrong and what can I do to help?" Cassie had never heard her uncle complain about being sick before, other than the occasional headache.

"Not to worry, Cassie. I'll just have a little rest and feel right as rain in no time."

"Okay, if you're sure."

"I am sure." He handed her the watch. "Here it is. Don't wait too long, I have a feeling he'll be needing it today."

Cassie couldn't say no to a favor for her uncle. She took the watch and slipped it into the side pocket of her skirt.

If she didn't know him better, she would think he was matchmaking.

No, that couldn't be true. His pale face gave away the fact that he wasn't feeling well and that worried her.

"Alright." She stood to her feet and pulled off the painting smock she wore. Kissing his cheek lightly, she whispered. "You should rest while I'm gone."

Uncle Gus sat down in his favorite chair. "I'll just sit here and enjoy the sun."

"Okay then. I'll be back soon." Cassie looked back at him when she reached the door, only to see her uncle's head laid back, his eyes closed.

Cocoa had awakened and ran to follow her, not wanting to miss out on any fun.

"Alright you can come with me, but you have to be good." Cassie spoke to the dog and her ears perked up.

Hurrying to the kitchen she pulled two large batches of chocolate chip cookies from the counter and placed them into plastic containers with lids.

Then she made two pitchers of juice and added ice before she sealed the lid tightly.

She double checked her hair in the hallway mirror. Her dark hair had grown a lot in two years. Now it hung in thick waves to the middle of her back.

Cassie tied it back behind her neck with a silky brown and yellow scarf. She was surprised at how different she looked now that she had the longer hairstyle.

Perhaps it was time she started to wear more flattering clothes. Maybe it was time to come out of her shell like Lydia suggested.

Fear tightened like a knot in her belly at the thought.

No, she wouldn't do that. She was definitely not ready. Past experience had taught her that wearing flattering clothes and looking beautiful brought out the worst in people.

Pushing her glasses up on her slender nose, she grimaced. She was thankful for the added touch of glasses, which emphasized the dull and mousy look she'd created for herself.

Maybe Zach would see her today and realize she wasn't nearly as interesting as he originally thought.

Warding off men had been her goal from the start.

Her emotions surged in inner turmoil. She could sense her feelings towards Zach becoming confused. In fact, she experienced a gamut of perplexing emotions whenever she was near him.

Forcing her confusing emotions into order didn't work.

Her mind wanted to do the safe thing, but her heart had other ideas. Cassie found herself puzzled and more than a little nervous at the startling revelation.

The strange surge of attraction she felt towards Zach frightened her. Her breath caught in her throat and she felt her heart pounding. Somehow she had to do what she'd always done.

Trample down any sort of unwelcome emotions and keep her distance.

That's the only way she would be safe.

CHAPTER THREE

ach

"MAN, this fire really did some damage, Zach." Bud's voice called out from his position on top of the ladder.

Bud Granger was the Contractor he'd hired to fix the building that had seen the worst of the fire.

Bud and his crew had already gutted the area that was damaged by the fire, which ended up being about half of the building.

"I'm grateful for the workers that caught the fire in the nick of time. They immediately got the water hose and threw buckets of water onto it. It didn't take long before they had the fire out." Zach ran a hand through his hair as he peered at the ravaged building.

Zach's belly clenched like a fist. He'd almost lost the

building that was most important to him. To make matters worse, if the fire had spread he could've lost the entire Marina.

Fear knotted inside him.

He couldn't lose Grand's Marina. This place had been a big part of his life and his family's life for so many years that he couldn't imagine it being gone.

He wondered what happened. How did the fire start?

The police had looked over the building and surrounding area and said the fire had been an accident. If he were honest, there was a part of him that questioned that.

Grand's Marina had always been loved by most folks here in Paradise Lake, but there were some people who would like to see Walker's Cove Marina shrivel up and die.

Mayor Al Riggs and a few other town council members' faces came to mind. When Zach had brought up the idea of expanding the Marina into a peaceful resort for families, immediately he pointed out what was wrong with Zach's idea.

Zach recalled the Mayor's words from last month's town hall meeting.

Our small town needs to see more progressive ideas, not old fashioned ideas like a resort. We need a mall with hotels that would invite more tourists to Paradise Lake.

Zach had been unable to convince Mayor Riggs to see his point of view. But certainly the Mayor wouldn't stoop so low, as to start a fire to get what he wanted.

No, there had to be another explanation.

More than likely, the fire was started by some teenagers trying to have their own sort of fun or trying to stir up trouble.

But, it felt like a blow against what he loved and his dreams, just the same.

Once again, his gaze swept over the building and the damage that had been done.

This building had been the first one that his great grandfather Walker Stevenson had built when he first bought the land for the Marina.

That had been decades ago now. Still, the old buildings had held up over the years.

Since Grand's death, they had become a historical place for many of the guests that visited the fifteen acres of lakefront property.

It was also the one building that Zach remembered most, because he'd spent the most time there with Grand. It was the one place he felt he truly belonged.

Rubbing the back of his neck, it hit him much harder that somehow he needed to figure out a way to receive his inheritance.

He couldn't lose this Marina. Staring at the ruins of his favorite building on Grand's Marina had shown him that.

To get it, he must marry in less than three weeks.

Where would he find a woman who he liked well enough, who would agree to a fake marriage?

A picture of Cassie formed in his mind. In his mind's eye he could see her large violet eyes set in her oval face, hidden by those large-rimmed glasses.

He couldn't really tell much else about her form,

because she wore those drab looking clothes that hung on her frame like a much-too-large sack.

Yet, he had experienced her kindness to him as she cleaned and bandaged his arm. He'd also witnessed her kindness to her Uncle and his friends.

She had been a refreshing and surprising change from any women he'd been interested in before.

Zach hesitated, measuring the idea that suddenly sprouted.

After much thought, he decided he would make an effort to get to know Cassie better.

What could possibly go wrong?

※

CASSIE DROVE Uncle Gus's old blue pickup truck up the tree-lined road towards Walker's Cove Marina.

The front seat was stacked with the few baked goodies she had brought with her.

Cocoa's furry head was stuck outside the half open window on the passenger side. It was her dog's favorite place to sit whenever Cassie needed to drive somewhere.

Pulling the truck to a stop, she got out and Cocoa scurried after her ready to explore.

While her dog was walking around and sniffing the grassy area, she gathered the containers of cookies and the juice. She walked to a grassy knoll with a picnic table close to the lake and not far from where the workers were busy.

Seeing Ollie Hapsfield working outside on one of the boats, Cassie waved and began to walk towards him.

"Cassie, what brings you here today?" Ollie wiped his hands on a drying cloth he kept at his side.

She grinned. "Happy, it's good to see you. And to answer your question, I'm bringing chocolate chip cookies for the workers here."

Her hands hidden in her pockets, twisted nervously out of sight. "Also... Uncle Gus wanted me to bring Zach his watch. He forgot it at the house."

Ollie's eyes widened and he grinned. "You'll spoil us with all you do for us. And that includes the encouraging note you gave me this morning. Thank you, it made my day."

Cassie grinned and nodded. "You're welcome. I'm glad."

"Well, I'll go tell the others about the cookies." He started to leave, then turned suddenly. "If you're looking for Zach, he's over there helping to fix the fire damaged building over there." Ollie pointed to a building that had two walls gone.

She turned and saw half a dozen construction workers busy working, rebuilding from the ground up.

"Thanks, Happy. I'll find him." As Cassie turned and walked towards Zach, her hands fidgeted nervously.

He was busy helping one of the construction guys lift a large beam of wood as she approached.

She stood nearby. With one hand above her eyebrows she shielded her eyes from the sun as she watched them work.

As soon as they finished lifting the heavy beam, the construction worker noticed her and turned to Zach. "It looks like you've got company."

Zach turned and seeing her, a grin turned up the corners of his mouth. His pearly white teeth looked dazzling against his tanned skin.

"Cassie, this is a pleasant surprise." He pulled a clean cloth that was hanging by his belt and wiped his hands.

Their eyes locked for a moment and his blue eyes softened.

He looked up at the sun and down at her and then gently grabbed her hand. "Come with me. Let's get you out of the heat of the sun."

Cassie was too startled by his actions to offer any objection.

She followed him over to a tall oak tree with a very large trunk. The overhang of branches and leaves shielded them almost completely from the hot midday sun.

His thoughtfulness to protect her from the heat of the day surprised her. Zach's actions were beginning to destroy all her preconceived ideas and expectations from past experiences with men.

She had to resist a sudden desire to be closer to him.

Her hand tingled from the warmth of his touch. Hurriedly, she pulled her hand away from his much larger one.

Being near him aroused old fears and uncertainties. She looked up at him and gave him a hesitant smile. "Thank you."

"You're welcome." Zach put his hands in the pockets of his jeans and looked up lazily through half-closed lids. "So, what did you want to talk to me about?"

As Zach's blue eyes studied her, the smile lines deepened by his eyes.

Heat flew to her cheeks and she looked down quickly, embarrassed to have been caught staring at him.

For a moment her fingers fidgeted with her skirt, wiping off nonexistent lint before she looked over at him again.

All her nervousness slipped back in and gripped her. She hurriedly spoke. "Uncle Gus wanted me to bring your watch back. I think you accidentally left it at the cottage this morning."

Zach's eyes grew wide. "Ah, yes. I noticed it was missing a little while ago and figured I must have left it in Doc's office. I guess I was a little too distracted by Doc's tending to my arm."

"How is your arm feeling?" Without thinking, Cassie moved to touch the part of his muscled arm near the wound.

She looked up at him, waiting for his answer.

Something intense flared in his blue eyes as he watched her.

He sucked in a deep breath at her touch and gently placed his large hand over hers.

"Your uncle said it was healing well. It just needs a few more days. But, the wound still stings on and off throughout the day." Zach's voice sounded hoarse as he spoke. "I have you to thank for acting so quickly to clean and bandage it. Thank you, Cassie."

Warmth tingled through her as he said her name. The electricity of the touch of his hand on hers sent a shiver up her arm.

Clearing her throat, she pretended not to be affected and looked up at him. "I was happy to help."

He squeezed her hand and she was very aware of the strength and warmth of his flesh.

Blue eyes riveted on her own. An undeniable magnetism was building between them.

His gaze moved from her eyes down to her lips and back up to search her eyes.

Swallowing convulsively, she could no longer deny that she wanted him to find her attractive.

Without warning, loud sounds of laughter echoed over to where they were.

Cassie broke eye contact as if from a trance, and looked over to see the Marina workers enjoying the juice and cookies she'd brought.

She removed her hand from his arm and stepped back. Her words came out hesitant and disjointed.

Hurriedly, she reached into the pocket of her skirt and pulled out his silver watch and handed it to him. "Here you go."

Heat rushed to her cheeks and her heart thudded.

"Thanks." He slid it onto his wrist with ease.

Cassie looked over at the workers who were indulging in food. "We should hurry, if we want to have a hope of finding any leftover food."

He grinned and nodded. "Sounds good."

As they began to walk together towards the picnic table, Cassie's composure was a fragile shell around her. Being near Zach, muddled her emotions.

She was attracted to him and didn't want to be. How was she going fight these feelings?

Zach's heart seemed to rush to the spot that she touched. He wondered at his unexpected reaction to Cassie.

Even though she wore clothes that weren't very appealing, he was captivated by her smile, her kindness and her gentle touch.

He felt drawn to her like he'd never felt drawn to any other woman.

Which made her very dangerous to his heart.

He questioned how he could let his heart soften like this for a woman he'd just met?

Zach had to remind himself of his decision to not fall for a woman ever again.

But, right now it seemed like his mind wanted one thing, but his heart had other ideas.

Looking over at the picnic table he saw Jeb Wheezly, Ollie Hapfield and Drummond Grumwald all eating their snacks and grinning about something.

A couple of high school summer workers, Allie Hatfield and Joanne Murphy were also enjoying the snacks and giggling together.

"It was nice of you to bring some food today." Zach smiled. "The Marina workers are always happy to stop for a break with good food and juice."

Cassie grinned widely. "I enjoy baking and I love to see people happy. There is far too much unhappiness and worry in the world already. If one small dose of kindness everyday helps only one person, then it's worth it to me."

Zach shook his head. "You are a very special woman, Cassie. You have a generous heart."

Her cheeks stained red again like they so often did, but he thought it was adorable.

They joined the others at the table.

"Zach, have you tried Cassie's chocolate chip cookies? You won't be able to stop at one." Ollie grabbed another cookie from the almost empty container.

"I guess I'd better try one then." Zach reached for one and bit into it. "Man, these are delicious Cassie. You could go into business."

Cassie smiled as she poured a small cup of juice for herself and handed the other one to him. "I'm not interested in starting a business from my baking, but I'm glad you like them."

"Good. That way we can have more of your baking to ourselves."

Cassie chuckled and nodded.

"This Marina is sort of like that." She spoke suddenly as she looked around the area at the large Marina store, boat refuelling area and slipways.

He raised one eyebrow, curiosity filling him. "What do you mean?"

Her large violet eyes gazed up at him before turning to take in the panorama of the boats docked along the pier and the rocky crag that made up the waterfront area.

"Well, just like with my baking, I want to keep things simple and bake to make people happy. It seems similar to what happens here at Walker's Cove Marina." She waved her hand to encompass the pier, the beach as well as the rocky area.

"This Marina is a wonderful place where visitors come to enjoy a peaceful slice of heaven on Paradise Lake."

She sighed contentedly. "It's a quiet, serene and safe harbor for folks and it makes them happy. It's not big and splashy, but simple and safe. Sometimes that can be what more people are looking for."

Zach looked at her, amazed at her insight. "I couldn't have said it better myself."

"Really?"

"Yes. That's exactly what I see for my great grandfather's Marina. A quiet place that is fun, but also quiet and safe. To me it seems like a safe harbor for folks who need a place to come in the middle of life's storms."

She turned to him. "Was that your great grandfather's vision too?"

Zach nodded. "Yeah. He wanted a quiet spot along the lake where people could come and enjoy a place to rest from their troubles."

"Well then, it sounds like you're on the right track with what you see for this Marina."

"Yeah, I think so too." Zack sighed heavily. "The only problem is, there are other people in town who keep trying to force me to do things their way or who want to push me out permanently."

Cassie looked at him and spoke suddenly. "Well, my father used to say that when there are other folks suddenly very interested in your business, it's even more important for you to stick to your convictions. It means there's more at stake."

Her gaze met his. "Don't give up now. Dig your heels in deep and stand for what's best for this Marina."

Zach looked at her thoughtfully, wondering how she became so wise for her young age. "Thanks. I needed to hear that."

She nodded. "You're welcome."

Her dog came and lay down half under the picnic table where there was some shade.

The workers were finished with their short break. Just as they went back to work, Zach spotted Mayor Al Riggs, Damian Court and Heath Bollwood from the town council.

They emerged from out of a large black SUV, along with a stylish looking woman and man.

"Speaking of folks that cause potential problems, I need to talk to someone. See you a little later, Cassie. Thanks for the snack." Zach finished drinking his juice and raised his glass in a small salute.

"Of course. You're welcome." Cassie watched him walk away and missed his company as soon as he was gone.

She looked at the cookie containers and the pitchers of juice and noticed they were all empty.

Looking down at Cocoa she whispered. "Well, at least everyone got a little snack."

Humming she cleared the table and put everything into her uncle's truck. Her faithful dog trotted by her side with his tongue hanging out.

Closing the truck door she looked down at him. "You look like you're sweating, Cocoa. Let's go to the lake so you can cool off."

Her dog seemed to nod and groaned a little. Cocoa had already finished drinking the three full dishes of water that she had given to her earlier.

Cassie slipped the leash on her dog, and Cocoa stayed close to her side as they walked across the grass toward the lake.

While she walked near the edge of the lake, her dog bounced in the water until soon her furry body was submerged, with only her head poking out.

She kept an eye on Cocoa, but couldn't help but notice many people around her enjoying the sunny day at the lake.

Giggles of children and laughter of parents drifted to her ears. She looked over to see a family of six walking over to a small motorboat that docked at Walker's Cove Marina.

It reminded her of the few times in her childhood, when her dad took her for the day on his sailboat.

They got out onto the water, with only the ocean around them and it was just the two of them. Her dad taught her how to steer the boat and how to hoist the sails upwards and to pull them down.

As memories of time spent with her father rushed through her mind, her eyes moistened with unshed tears. How she wished to have family time like that again.

Looking back, she treasured those times spent with her father and had always deeply felt the loss of her mom. She never knew what it was like to have a close connection and bond between mother and daughter.

When Larissa had married her father, her stepmother had been too focused on her own status and how she looked to others, to bother with her stepdaughter.

The heart to heart connection and gentle love of a mom for her daughter — the one thing for which she truly longed — had been denied her.

She yearned for it and mourned its loss.

Water splashed up against her skirt and quickly brought Cassie out of her reverie.

She bent down and patted her dog's head. "Cocoa, does that feel better?"

Cocoa shook herself and sprayed Cassie in the process. She giggled and grabbed her dog's leash. "Okay, I'll take that as a yes. Let's go take a walk on the Pier. It has the best view of the lake."

She tugged on Cocoa's leash and together they walked toward the end of the Pier.

As she sat on the end of the Pier with her legs dangling over the end, her gaze was transfixed on the vastness of Paradise Lake. Cocoa sat by her side and the peace of this moment surrounded her. She released a happy sigh of contentment.

Far too soon, Cocoa began to get restless forcing Cassie to her feet. Looking at her watch, she realized it was time to get home to check on Uncle Gus and to start supper.

"Let's go home, Cocoa." Cassie grinned at how her dog ran ahead tugging gently on the leash. "I'm not running wearing this skirt, Cocoa. You'll need to slow down a little."

Cassie turned her gaze towards the large Marina store and the land that surrounded it.

She spotted Zach talking with the Mayor and some of the councilmen. The well dressed man and woman who Zach had seen earlier, stood with them.

Cassie was curious about what they were talking about. What did Zach mean when he said there were some people trying to stop him?

Just as she was pondering that thought, there was a sudden jerk on the leash.

Cassie squealed as her dog jumped off the Pier into the lake below.

With her hand wrapped around the leash, she immediately followed.

She sank down underwater and after a bit of difficulty, paddled her way up to the surface. Gasping for air she looked around and realized her glasses had fallen off her nose when she dived into the water.

It wasn't like she needed them, as glasses were only part of her disguise.

However, it was a disguise that had become a comfortable habit. Cassie wasn't ready to leave her protective covering behind.

She would simply need to find new glasses soon.

As she began to move her legs, she struggled to swim without her legs getting tangled in the bulky weight of her wet skirt.

Without warning, she was submerged under water again and came up gasping for air.

She had just started to get her bearings to swim forward, when she heard another splash nearby.

Suddenly, Zach's head popped up near her, his eyes filled with concern.

"Don't worry, I've got you." Zack's strong arm pulled her close to his chest.

Cassie breathed out, her voice hoarse. "Thank you."

His blue eyes peered at her intently, searching her eyes. "Are you okay?"

"Yeah. Just a little water-logged." Her giggle sounded strained even to her own ears.

"Good. I'm just glad you're okay." He held her tightly to his chest, and Cassie could feel his hand shaking on her back. She was surprised at the intensity of his emotions.

He cleared his throat. "Now, I want you to just relax and float beside me. I'll get you to safety." Zach held her close with one hand and she felt safe as he swam to shore.

It was a strange sensation to feel safe in the arms of a man. But with Zach, she felt like she could trust him.

Before long they neared the sandy beach and Zach stopped swimming as soon as his feet could touch the bottom. He pulled her further until she could reach the bottom of the shallow part of the lake.

"Can you stand okay?" Zach kept one arm around her waist and pulled her close to his side.

"I'm a little shaky, but maybe that's normal." Cassie looked up at him with gratefulness. "Thank you. I don't know if I could've made it back to shore without your help."

Zach was looking at her with an odd expression. "You lost your glasses when you fell into the water."

"Yeah, I did. It's okay. It's happened before." Her cheeks heated up as she looked at him. She was sure they were apple red.

His eyes searched hers and he moved his free hand to move a wet strand of hair away from her eyes. Then the back of his fingers gently touched her cheek.

She was entranced by the silent sadness of his face and wondered what caused it.

Cassie stood there motionless, her emotions confused

by his nearness. Her feelings for him were intensifying and she realized that her mind was at war with her heart once more.

Without warning a voice spoke from the nearby shoreline.

"Well, well, well. Look who I found."

Cassie recognized that strident nasal sounding voice at once. She turned her head and the blood drained from her face.

Pale and shaking, she stared at Larissa White.

Her stepmother stood on the shore, wearing white and gold designer pants and blouse. Her dark brown hair was cut in a short chic style that her stepmother insisted made her look younger. Her large dark eyes narrowed as she peered at Cassie.

"Hello, stepmother." Cassie's voice shook as she spoke. "What are you doing here?"

"Well, we visiting and looking to buy real estate in this area. But now that I see you here I might just change my mind." Larissa's voice took on a menacing quality.

Cassie suddenly recognized her stepmother was the same woman who had stepped out of the SUV to talk with the men from the town council earlier. From her conversation with Zach, it seemed like he might have Larissa before.

The strident voice sounded louder this time.

"It's time to drag you home where you belong. You shouldn't have run away, Cassie."

She drew a deep breath and forbade herself to tremble.

"I'm afraid I won't be able to come to your home, Stepmother." A determination rose up inside Cassie even as her voice shook.

"You must know I'm twenty-one now and can decide for myself where I want to live. And I choose to live with Uncle Gus." It felt good to stand up for herself to her controlling stepmother.

"You father's eccentric brother? Gus White is a nobody, living in this tiny, dead-end town. You'll be better off living at home. Come on, let's go." Larissa started to insist.

Zach interrupted, his voice curt. "I believe Cassie has already spoken for herself. She doesn't want to accompany you, Larissa."

Her stepmother put her hands on her hips. "Since when do you have any say in Cassie's decisions? When did you become her protector?"

Cassie looked up at Zach and suddenly saw a determination in his eyes she'd never seen before.

"Since she became my fiancé."

Cassie released a small gasp at his words. What was he saying? What was he doing?

"Cassie is under my protection now, so you won't be forcing her anywhere." Zach's voice sounded like a steel edge.

Larissa stiffened at his words. "Well. I don't think you realize what you're doing to yourself by choosing Cassie for your wife, Zach."

"I have a pretty good idea. She's compassionate, beautiful and courageous. She can decide for herself what she wants. So, I'll kindly ask you to leave." Zach's voice was firm, final.

Larissa nodded abruptly and walked away, anger in her every step.

Still in shock, Cassie walked with Zach until they were finally on dry ground again.

Workers from the Marina soon showed up asking questions.

Cassie looked over at Zach. "I've got to go. We'll talk later." She stared at him wordlessly, as he walked away.

CHAPTER FOUR

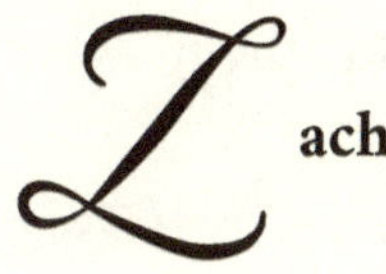

ZACH STOOD at the helm of his sailboat staring out at the surrounding lake, his thoughts on Cassie.

He had invited his four brothers to go for a morning sail. Today, he needed their combined years of wisdom.

"So, spill Zach." Gabe turned to him from where he leaned against the railing of the boat. "You invited us to join you today for a more important reason than simply spending the morning together."

Adam nodded. "I agree. So, is this about a woman?"

Zach grimaced and nodded slightly.

"I knew it." Gabe chuckled and whistled into the wind.

Luke and Jack chuckled somewhere behind him.

"Who is she?"

"Alright. I'll tell you." Zach slowed the boat until they were barely drifting along. "Her name is Cassie White."

"I saw her first at the event at Stevenson Sea Adventures, but I didn't meet until later that day when we were both helping with Mrs. Crandell's house fire. Cassie is Doc White's niece. She helped clean my wounded arm after the fire."

"You don't say." Jack crossed his arms over his chest, a big grin on his face.

Zach could feel heat burning his cheeks.

"So tell us more about this new friend of yours, Zach."

He grimaced at their teasing, but was aware it was all in good fun. Turning to them, he told them what happened at the lake.

"So, I heard a loud squeal and turned to see Cassie jumping into the water. I panicked and ran into the lake and swam to where she was and pulled her back to safety."

"Gallant of you. There's nothing like a rescue mission to win the heart of the woman you love." Jack grinned.

Zach remembered when Jack had rescued his own wife from the clutches of a human trafficking sting. Rescuing people was something his brother knew well.

Still, Zach could feel heat rising from his neck to his cheeks. "Yeah well, that's not what I was thinking at the time. I panicked when I saw Cassie fall in the water. I couldn't let her drown."

"No you couldn't Zach. Ever since you were a teenager, you've felt compelled to save anyone who was in trouble. I admire that." Gabe spoke up.

Zach knew his brother Gabe's meaning encompassed far more than he was saying, especially considering his personal development expertise. However, Zach didn't want to bog down in that quicksand at the moment.

"Thanks, Gabe." Zach nodded thoughtfully.

Luke spoke up. "Come on, let's hear what happened next."

Zach grinned, knowing Luke's impatient nature. "Alright. What happened next was I helped her to get to safety. We hadn't got to shore yet, before Larissa White showed up. She is Cassie's stepmother, and her words sounded a little threatening, to be honest."

"Basically she told Cassie to come back home, or else." Zach remembered. "That's when I informed Larissa that Cassie was my fiancé and that I would protect her. I told Larissa to leave her stepdaughter alone."

"Ha! Sounds like something I would've done. Good job, Zach." Jack slapped him on the shoulder.

Adam cleared his throat. "What did Cassie say to you about your unexpected announcement?"

Zach rubbed the back of his neck. "I haven't had a chance to talk to her about that yet. I'm a little concerned about her response, to be honest. I plan to talk to her this afternoon."

"Do you want to marry her?" In his usual calm voice, Adam asked the obvious question.

Zach experienced a gamut of perplexing emotions at the question. "I do want to marry her — if she'll agree to a marriage in name only. Cassie is kind and compassionate and a better choice for my fake wife than any woman I've met yet."

Adam simply nodded and grinned. "But you are hesitating."

He nodded. "I always told myself I wouldn't marry a woman who was beautiful. So far, all the beautiful women I've met have been shallow and only interested in my money."

Zach's expression stilled and grew serious. "I thought Cassie was perfect because she wore colorless and frumpy clothes and really large ugly glasses. But, when I helped her out of the water yesterday, I realized she was… well, beautiful on the inside as well as on the outside."

Zach ran a hand through his hair and grimaced at how odd his confession sounded to his own ears.

Luke grinned.

"And you're afraid that if you marry her, your heart will be on the line." Jack spoke up.

Zach shrugged. "Yeah, that about sums it up." His gaze swept over each one of his brothers. Each one's face featured unique amused expressions.

"So, what do I do?" Zach was frustrated at his brothers. He wanted some straight answers.

Adam sighed and smiled. "You talk to Cassie. Explain that you offered marriage as a way to protect her from her stepmother."

"Then you ask her to marry you — and convince her that a marriage of convenience will benefit both of you." Jack smiled.

Zach swallowed nervously. "I can do that, I think."

Jack laughed. "Yes, you can. Each of us did it and you can too, Zach."

Zach nodded. After a moment, he looked over at his brothers with a new determination. "Alright, I'll do it. I'm going to ask Cassie if she'll be my fake wife."

As he spoke those words out loud, his belly clenched like a fist. What had he just committed himself to?

&

"So, Zach just blurted out that you were his fiancé?" Lydia sat across from her at the picnic table just outside the employee's entrance at the Lakeside restaurant.

Cassie nodded and whispered. "Yeah, he did. It was right after Larissa demanded I come back home. It all seems so strange."

She had hardly slept last night thinking about it. And it was the reason she had stopped by this morning to talk to her friend.

"You know what I think? I think he was trying to protect you from your stepmother. And I also think Zach is attracted to you." Lydia sipped her cool fruit drink, giving her a knowing glance.

Cassie shook her head. "He might have been trying to protect me, but I don't think he's attracted to me. Considering the colorless and frumpy clothes I've worn, I wouldn't attract any man."

She was puzzled about yesterday's encounter with Zach.

"I wouldn't be so sure, Cassie. You could wear a flour sack and still be beautiful my friend." Lydia winked at her. "However, I do think you need to talk to him. Ask Zach about what happened yesterday."

Cassie nodded. "I think you're right. I do need to get this cleared up so I can have peace of mind again."

Lydia looked at her watch and stood to her feet. "I have

to get back to work, but I want to encourage you to talk to Zach today Cassie. Don't wait, otherwise it might be too easy to chicken out."

Cassie stood to her feet and gave her friend a quick hug. She sighed heavily. "I will, although I have to say I'm not looking forward to it. You know I've not wanted to date any man and marriage hasn't even crossed my mind."

"I know, but things can change." Lydia winked, and Cassie frowning at her friend's teasing.

"I don't plan on changing that part of my life. And I won't marry Zach."

Lydia started dancing away from her, with a big grin. "We'll see. I look forward to hearing all about it, later."

Cassie simply shook her head as her friend waved and disappeared behind the employee kitchen door of the restaurant.

She picked up her purse and began to walk toward the beach, thinking of their conversation.

Lydia seemed to think Zach was just waiting to marry her, which was so far from the truth it was laughable.

Cassie smiled and shook her head.

However, she did need to find Zach so they could talk. She hurried down the beach, spotting Walker's Cove Marina in the distance.

As she glimpsed her stepmother's large yacht — *The Violet Diamond* — a wave of apprehension swept through her.

She switched direction and turned to walk up a back alley where she knew she could follow a trail, which was a different way to reach the Marina.

The reminder that her stepmother and her boyfriend

had shown up in Paradise Lake caused her whole body to tighten with tension. Her father's favorite yacht — which he'd named after her mom — was now in the possession of her selfish stepmother.

It didn't seem fair. Nor did it seem right.

The sad thing was that there was nothing she could do about it, at least not at the moment.

As she reached the Marina, she looked around the area as she walked, searching for Zach.

Finally, she spotted him down by the pier where the rental boats were kept.

He was standing beside a teenage boy and they were looking inside the panel of instruments at the front of the boat.

Cassie stopped as she neared and waited. "Always double check the instrument panel when you do the safety checks each morning."

Zach pointed to the instrument panel. "It's very important to see if there might be any problems with each boat. That way we can fix them before any guests take the boats out on the water. We want to keep everyone safe."

"I understand, sir."

Zach put one hand on his shoulder. "I know you do, Daniel. You're getting the hang of this. Is your foster mom okay with you working some late nights this summer?"

"Yeah. She knows I'm working to save up money to go to college or something. I only have two years left until I'm done high school."

"That's good. Is everything okay at the Gundersons?"

"Yeah. My foster mom is always on me to study and do well in school. And my foster dad seems glad I'm working at the marina. It's better living with the Gunderson's than any of the other families I lived with before, so I can't really complain."

"Good. I'm glad to hear it. What will you study in college?"

Daniel shrugged his slender shoulders. "I was thinking I might like to study boat design and building like you, Mr. Stevenson."

Zach nodded. "It's a great career. I've always loved it." He rubbed his chin, thoughtfully. "Tell you what, if you continue to work hard and go to college and finish, you'll always have a job with me. Count on it."

Daniel's bright smile transformed his face. "Thank you Mr. Stevenson."

Zach patted him on the shoulder. "You're welcome. Now, it's your turn to check for problems on the next boat."

As Cassie overheard the exchange between Zach and the teenager, she found herself questioning some of her preconceived opinions she'd had about him.

She was impressed with the fact that he was compassionate and willing to help troubled teens.

Perhaps she had misjudged him.

At that moment Daniel saw Cassie out of the corner of his eye and spoke to Zach. "You've got company."

Zach turned and grinned. "Hello Cassie."

She nodded and murmured. "Hi."

"Daniel, why don't you begin checking out the details of the next boat on our list? I'll join you a little later."

"Sure thing, Mr. Stevenson." Daniel walked to another rental boat nearby.

Zach turned and walked towards her.

Cassie wiped the palms of her hands on her skirt and spoke hurriedly. "I was hoping to talk to you, Zach."

"And I wanted to talk to you." Zach looked around and nodded toward the trail that led to the solitude of the rocky cove. "Let's walk to some place where we can have a little bit of privacy."

"Sure." Cassie fell into step with him unsure of where to begin.

Zach turned to her and spoke in a calm voice. "You're probably here to talk about what happened yesterday."

Awkwardly, she cleared her throat. "Yeah."

"I thought so." His voice was thick and unsteady. "After I rescued you from the water and we heard your step-mother challenge you or maybe I should say threaten you, I felt I needed to say something. I wanted to protect you, so I told her you were my fiancé."

Zach's eyes clung to hers, as if analyzing her reaction.

She sucked in a breath and nodded quickly. It was as she suspected. He had announced their engagement, simply because he was being protective.

They reached the rocky crag and everything was quiet around them except for the lapping of water against the rocks below.

"Maybe I'm mistaken, but Larissa White sounded like she was trying to control or force you into going home. I've seen her in action in business when she wants something, and she's like a bull in a china shop." He grimaced and peered over at her.

"Sounds like my stepmother alright." Cassie nodded and she shivered.

Looking over at Zach, she saw his eyes narrow and his jaw set with determination.

"Maybe you do need protection from her."

Cassie sighed heavily. "Well, I was safe enough, until she found out I was living with Uncle Gus in Paradise Lake."

She shrugged. "But, it's okay. I've avoided her for this long, I will do it again."

Cassie hurriedly spoke. "I wanted to let you know that while I appreciate your offer to protect me by pretending to be my fiancé, you don't need to do that. And just so you're not worried, I won't hold you to your offer of marriage, as I have no intention of marrying."

Zach's eyes widened slightly and he stared at her with a puzzled look on his face.

Cassie was about to explain more, when suddenly the ringing of her cell phone interrupted them.

"Sorry, I just need to get this quick." Cassie looked down and answered the phone.

Ollie was calling and the news wasn't good.

After she hung up the phone, she whispered to Zach in a wobbly voice. "That was Ollie. Uncle Gus is in the Hospital. He's had a heart attack."

She felt the blood drain from her face and she swallowed.

Her uncle had been the one faithful father figure in her life since her father passed away and now he was hanging onto life by a thread.

Uncle Gus couldn't die. She needed him to live.

A small sob escaped. "I've got to go."

She turned to leave, but Zach grabbed her hand. "Come on, I'll take you to the Hospital."

At her simple nod, they hurried back to the Marina where they came from, running towards Zach's pickup truck.

His grip tightened on the steering wheel as he sped along the streets that led to Paradise Lake's Hospital.

As they stopped, Zach ran to her side and opened the door as they hurried through the Hospital doors. Through it all, he held her hand.

His presence beside her really helped to give her strength needed to face seeing Uncle Gus.

Soon, the nurse was leading them to the second floor where her uncle had been placed in intensive care.

The grey haired buxom nurse turned to them, her voice calm. "I want you to be prepared when you see your uncle.

He is very pale and has been sedated, although just now he has begun to awaken. It's important that when you see him, you stay calm and avoid saying or doing anything that would make him agitated."

"I understand." Cassie nodded.

"Alright then. You can go inside and see him now for a short time." The nurse opened the door to the room.

"I'll wait for you here." Zach's voice was calm, his gaze steady.

Cassie nodded and whispered. "Thank you."

She knew the Hospital policy was to allow only family members into patient rooms.

Slowly she stepped into the hospital room. As her gaze swept the room, she saw Uncle Gus lying so still on the bed. She walked over to him and pulling a chair close, sat beside him holding his hand.

"Cassie my dear, I'm glad to see you." Her uncle's eyes opened a little and his voice whispered. "Was that Zach I saw in the hallway?"

"Yes."

"Good. I want to speak to him after I've had a chance to talk to you."

"Of course." Cassie nodded quickly, her gaze wandering over her uncle's motionless body.

Her normally big strong uncle looked so frail and weak.

A new anguish seared her heart at the possibility of losing another person she loved in her life.

Swallowing back emotion she forced herself to speak in a calm voice. "I'm here now, Uncle Gus and I'm so glad to see you."

Cassie was determined to stay strong for her uncle. But, in spite of her best intentions, her voice wavered with emotion. "You gave me a little scare today."

Uncle Gus offered a weak smile. "Yeah well, you know I'm a tough guy. I'll be fine Cassie."

He didn't look fine, he looked worse than she'd ever seen him. But, she remembered the nurse's words to do what she could to keep him calm. "I know you are, uncle. And right now getting better is the most important thing to focus on."

His grey eyes caught hers and a furrow formed between his brows. "I hope to get completely well my dear, but the truth is this heart attack has made me aware of some things I've left undone. And the most important is seeing to it that you are taken care of after I'm gone, dear niece."

Her brows creased in worry and Cassie squeezed his hand. "Don't talk like that, Uncle Gus. You're going to be fine. You just need time to rest and heal."

She desperately wanted to believe that was true. She refused to believe that her beloved uncle wouldn't get better.

"And I will heal. However, I am serious about this. I want to see you settled." His grey eyes searched hers and she could hear a new determination in his voice.

"What do you mean?"

"I mean, I would like to see you married to a good man. A kind and thoughtful man who will see to it that you are loved and taken care of."

Cassie simply smiled at her uncle's old fashioned ideas. She remembered he was from a bygone era where it was expected that men would take care of women they loved.

In today's day and age it certainly didn't seem to be part of the deal from most of her friends who married.

For a moment a wistful feeling came over her. What would it feel like to be truly loved by a man so much that he wanted to see to it she was taken care of?

She sighed. Well, that was something she would never know. She was used to taking care of herself. And on top of that, from past experience she didn't really have a reason to trust most men.

"Cassie, did you hear me?" Uncle Gus whispered and squeezed her hand.

"Sorry, uncle. I was thinking about what you said."

"Good. I mean to take care of you, Cassie. It's what

your father would've wanted." Uncle Gus's voice was firm, final.

"But, you don't have to worry about me..."

Uncle Gus whispered. "I know I don't." He smiled, a mysterious light in his eyes. "My dear, I'm beginning to tire out, so would you ask Zach to come in here? I want to speak with him."

"Alright, Uncle Gus." Cassie kissed her uncle on the cheek and walked to the door. Opening it, she waved for Zach to come into the room.

"Uncle wants to talk to you." Zach hurried into the hospital room, looking at her and then at her uncle a mysterious expression on his face.

"Uncle Gus, Zach's here to see you."

A big smile broke out on her uncle's face. "Good. Now give your uncle a kiss and then you can wait in the hallway for Zach."

Cassie was too surprised to do anything except as he asked. She kissed her uncle's cheek and raised her eyes to find Zach watching her with a spark of some indefinable emotion in his eyes.

Expelling a breath she nodded to the two of them. "I'll be in the waiting room if you need me."

She turned and walked out into the hallway, puzzled at why Uncle Gus had insisted on talking with Zach.

For a moment, she felt a little miffed that her beloved uncle had felt the need to talk privately with Zach Stevenson.

What in the world did Uncle Gus need to say to that man anyway?

ZACH LEFT Doc White's Hospital room and walked towards the waiting room.

His gaze immediately found Cassie sitting there, thumbing her way through a magazine.

With his mind whirling from his conversation with Doc White, he walked towards her.

He had agreed to do what he could to help. But, he was a little nervous about the conversation he needed to have with her.

As if sensing his approach, Cassie looked up, staring at him through a new pair of unsightly looking black-rimmed glasses.

"Is Uncle Gus alright?" Setting the magazine down, she asked in a halting voice, her eyes big and round with apprehension.

A fresh wave of compassion washed over him, at the tension he saw in her features.

"Yes. He was dozing off into a peaceful sleep just as I left." Zach was pleased when he saw her smile.

"I'm glad." Her shoulders sagged with relief, matching her tone of voice. "I don't know what I'd do if I lost him."

"Well, it looks like you won't need to find that out for a long time." Zach held out his hand. "Could we talk?"

He sensed her hesitation. "Don't worry we won't leave the Hospital grounds. You'll be able to stay within walking distance to your Uncle."

Cassie nodded and said softly. "I suppose that would be okay." She put her hand in his and he helped her to her feet. Just as quickly she pulled her hand away. He missed the touch of her small soft hand in his.

She pulled the cardigan to wrap around herself. He led her to the downstairs area and through the French doors that led into the flower garden behind the Hospital.

"So, what did you want to talk to me about?" She stopped near the edge of the garden next to a few well manicured trees and peered at him. "Is this about what Uncle Gus talked to you about?"

Zach nodded. "In part, yes." He went on to explain. "I've known your uncle for quite a few years and I've never seen him more determined to see something through as he was today."

"To see what through, exactly?"

His gaze came to rest on her questioning eyes. "Your uncle wants to see to it that you're safe."

Cassie nodded and sighed heavily, her fingers fighting with the material on her skirt. "I know he does. When I first came to live with Uncle Gus a couple of years ago, I told him why I ran away from my stepmother's home. He took me into his home and cared for me. He kept me safe."

Zach watched as tears misted her violet eyes and he sensed there was more to the story than she was telling him.

But he wouldn't pressure her to share. He hoped to earn her trust. He wanted to be her friend, but right now she didn't know him well enough to trust him. He would need to change that.

"Your uncle is a good man and he just wants to protect you."

Cassie looked over at him. "But, I'm safe enough living with Uncle Gus, he should know that."

"But, your uncle doesn't feel that's enough." He turned to her and saw her gaze looked off in the distance. She began pacing with her head down, a worried expression on her face.

"I know. And I admit to worrying about what my step-mother or her boyfriend will do next. What does uncle want me to do? I don't want him to continue to worry about me."

Zach began to share his thoughts. "I've been thinking about your situation. And I've come up with a solution that will help both of us."

"You don't need to be concerned about me." She crossed her arms over her chest and a crease formed between her brows.

He didn't relent, but instead pressed on. "I know you can take care of yourself, however your uncle worries about you. Doc won't rest until he sees a solution that satisfies him."

"As much as I hate to admit it, you have a point." She stopped pacing suddenly and smiled in exasperation. "Okay, I'm listening."

His mouth curved into an unconscious smile at her willingness to hear him out.

Zach shared the details of his great grandfather's will. "So, now I have only two weeks to marry, if I want my inheritance."

He hesitated a moment before he continued. "What I'm offering is a marriage of convenience for one year. I would give you one million dollars and see to it that you are protected at all times. And as a bonus, your uncle will hopefully be less worried about you."

"Hmm. I suppose that's true." The tensing of her jaw betrayed her deep frustration. She eyed him warily. "And this would be a marriage in name only for one year?"

He nodded. "Yes. Partly because I need my grandparents and mom to believe we married for love. If mom got wind of this idea, we would never hear the end of it."

Cassie nodded and a small smile lifted the corners of her mouth. There was a sad, faraway look in her eyes for a moment. "I'm sure Uncle Gus would want to believe we married for love instead of a fake marriage. But, this probably would stop him from worrying."

She turned to look at him and stood motionless for a moment deep in thought.

Zach sent her a disarming smile, trying to set her at ease. "Think on the idea and we'll talk in a few days okay?"

She nodded. "Okay."

After driving her home, he waited until she waved to him at the door of Doc White's cottage.

As he drove home, he worried at the paleness of her cheeks and the way she had withdrawn into herself.

He wanted to make her smile. He wanted to hear her laugh. He wanted to make her happy.

Zach smiled to himself at the depth of his emotions. He hoped she wouldn't make him wait too long to let him know if she would marry him.

He was filled with a strange inner excitement at the prospect of Cassie as his wife — even if he had to settle for her being his fake wife.

CHAPTER FIVE

Cassie

CASSIE ADJUSTED the train of her wedding dress and looked at her friend Lydia through the reflection in the floor length mirror.

Zach's grandmother had given her grandson his great grandmother's wedding dress for his bride to wear.

It was a silk creation overlaid with intricate lace that hugged her bodice and hips and flowed outwards down to the floor, which trailed behind her when she walked.

The wedding dress was styled in a nineteen hundred and twenty fashion that Hannah Stevenson wore when she married Zach's great grandfather.

"You're a beautiful bride."

Cassie put one hand on her stomach, hoping to calm the nervous fluttering there.

Looking at Lydia in the mirror, she whispered. "I'm a fake bride."

Cassie still felt guilty that she was wearing the wedding dress of Zach's great grandmother — especially when this was to be a fake marriage.

She felt like an imposter, even though Zach had assured her that this was best for both of them.

Right now, all she wanted was to get through the wedding ceremony in one piece.

Lydia pursed her lips and smoothed out the white satin gown. "Despite your doubts, I still say marrying Zach Stevenson is a good idea. I've never seen your uncle look so happy and content."

Cassie nodded. "Well that's good, because I'm doing this mostly for Uncle Gus."

She recalled stopping by the Marina to see Zach, after a talk with Lydia. Her friend had convinced her that by marrying Zach, it would take care of several problems at once.

The biggest one was that her uncle was constantly worrying about her safety. It would keep her uncle calm and happy which would hopefully stop another relapse with his heart.

On the other hand, maybe there was nothing to worry about. After all, she hadn't heard from her stepmother since she had confronted her at the lake a couple of weeks ago.

Perhaps Larissa and her boyfriend were too busy to cause problems for her anymore. She hoped that was the case, but had her doubts.

As she adjusted the white flowers that were tied

together with small pearls forming a crown on top of her head. She felt very regal in this wedding dress.

But, Cassie felt like she didn't really deserve to wear this beautiful wedding dress that had been worn by a much beloved Matriarch of the Stevenson family.

Walker and Hannah Stevenson's marriage had lasted more than half a century and her fake marriage to Zach wasn't meant to last longer than a year.

She felt like the worst kind of fraud.

Even though she didn't know her groom very well, the few times she had seen or talked with him, he had surprised her.

Her thoughts swirled with memories even of the past two weeks. He had saved Mrs. Crandell's pet from the house fire, he was committed to helping a foster boy, and he had seen her fall in the water and dove in to save her from drowning in the lake.

All of these acts of selflessness and compassion messed with the preconceived ideas she had assumed about rich men.

Was it possible Zach was different? She was beginning to change her mind about who she assumed he was.

Maybe, it was time to stop being so tough on him.

"Are you ready?" Lydia asked, a smile on her lips.

Cassie nervously ran her hands down the silk gown. "As ready as I'll ever be."

Following her friend down the stairs of Uncle Gus's cottage, they walked outside the front door.

Waiting for her on the front lawn, was Uncle Gus in his wheelchair with his six friends by his side.

Tears moistened her eyes at their thoughtfulness. She

hurried over and gave her uncle a kiss on the cheek and slipped her arms around him. "Thank you."

"Ah, my dear girl, where else would I be but right here to bring you to your waiting groom?" Uncle Gus chuckled and his friends joined in.

They all assumed Zach and her had fallen in love very quickly and that they couldn't wait to be married.

Cassie didn't want to tell them the truth, so she just went along with it. "I wouldn't want to be on anyone else's arm, Uncle Gus."

"I'm the luckiest bride anywhere. I have seven men at my side." She smiled as each of their cheeks stained pink. Walking over she kissed each of them on the cheek.

"Thank you to all of you." They walked the short distance from Uncle Gus's cottage to the beach area where the small group of wedding guests waited.

Ollie pushed Uncle Gus in the wheelchair. The doctor had said it was too soon for her uncle to be on his feet for too long.

Cassie walked beside her uncle and held his hand, happy that he was content.

It was a quiet evening on Paradise Lake and the sun was just beginning to set. A mixture of the orange and red glow shone across the lake, reaching the sandy beach.

Cassie sighed. It was a perfect evening for a wedding.

A large wood dance floor was set up for dancing. Tiny lights shimmered from the wooden pillars that surrounded the dance floor, spreading out toward the tables where the guests would mingle and eat later.

Nearby, the string quartet was playing some of her favorite love songs.

She looked up and smiled nervously at Zach. He stood under the archway at the end of the rows of chairs that were filled with wedding guests. Standing beside him, the minister waited to begin the ceremony.

Suddenly the music changed and the string quartet began playing the country song, *My Wish* by Rascal Flatts.

Cassie's eyes widened and she blinked back tears as she remembered the words to the song.

It meant so much to her that Zach wished for her dreams to be big, her worries small and that her life became all she wanted it to be.

A smile formed on Zach's mouth and a glimmer of satisfaction shone in his blue eyes. When she finally reached him, he held out his hand and Uncle Gus placed her small hand in Zach's.

Her heart jolted at the action. It was a meaningful gesture that meant she was now going to be living with her husband instead of living in the home of her kind uncle.

A knot formed in her belly at the thought.

She forced a smile and dutifully kissed her uncle's cheek. Zach squeezed her hand as she walked with him towards the waiting minister.

She missed most of the words the minister spoke, as a wave of apprehension swept through her.

Wide-eyed she stared at Zach. He took both her hands in his and leaned over to whisper. "You are beautiful, Cassie. I'm the luckiest man alive to be marrying you."

The sound of his soft whisper in her ear affected her deeply and soothed her fears.

She looked into his eyes and saw sincerity in his blue eyes. A new awareness of him flooded her senses.

The invisible web of attraction that had been slowly building between them since they first met was now stronger than ever.

Cassie looked into his eyes as the minister asked them to speak their vows to each other.

All the words seemed to meld together in her mind, until she heard the minister speak again. "You may kiss the bride."

Cassie felt her pulse beat in her throat, as Zach's large hand took her face and held it gently placing his other hand at her waist.

Gathering her into his arms, he held her snugly against him and leaned his head downwards to hers.

She put her arms around his neck. The warmth of his arms around her was so male, so bracing.

Softly his breath fanned her face and his warm lips touched her own. He pressed her lips to his, caressing her mouth in a kiss that was as tender and light as a summer breeze.

She quivered at the sweetness of his kiss.

Her knees weakened and she melted into his embrace. She felt transported on a soft wispy cloud and shivers of delight followed his gentle touch.

A sense of wonder flooded her and she felt safe in his arms.

Someone cleared their throat and suddenly Cassie was brought back down to earth.

She pulled away from Zach, only to see a satisfied grin on his face. Heat rose from her neck to her cheeks.

The minister pronounced the final blessing and introduced them. "Introducing the newlyweds, Zach and Cassie Stevenson."

As the wedding guests clapped, Zach slipped an arm around her waist and pulled her close to his side.

They walked side by side between the rows of guests until they reached a clearing in the grass at the far end.

Cassie was about to say something to Zach, but all too soon they were surrounded by well wishers.

Zach's mom, Eliza Stevenson walked up to Cassie. She looked elegant in a teal colored cocktail length dress.

Her blond hair had streaks of grey and near her eyes were smile lines that only added to the graceful features of the lady she was.

"Welcome to our family, Cassie." Eliza's gentle voice resonated with a missing piece in heart. It was the gentle mother's heart of love that she had never had a chance to know for herself.

Her eyes welled with unshed tears at the memory.

"Thank you, Mrs. Stevenson." Cassie smiled nervously, unsure what to say to her new mother-in-law.

Eliza grabbed her hands and held them. "Oh darling girl, you're my daughter now. You must call me, Mom." She looked at her son with a big smile. "Convince her, Zach."

Zach simply nodded once, a warm smile lighting his face.

She smiled at Eliza's insistence. "Okay, I will. I'm happy to be part of your family, Mom."

"Ah, that name sounds sweet coming from my newest daughter." Eliza pulled her into a gentle embrace. Cassie blinked back tears as she felt the warmth of a mother's love in her mother-in-law's embrace.

She was still tingling from all that love even after Zach's mom stepped away to talk with her son.

Immediately, she was pulled into another hug. This time it was Zach's grandfather, William Stevenson.

She remembered meeting her new husband's grandparents, his mom and the rest of the Stevenson family earlier in the week, when Zach brought her to his mom's house for a light lunch.

The family had welcomed her as Zach's soon-to-be wife and she had seen for herself what a loving and kind family they were.

The large Stevenson family that shared such a close bond and looked out for each other, sort of intimidated her. Her memories of her own family were simple.

She had a loving father and later on she got to know her Uncle Gus, but she had no memories of her mother, or grandparents.

Loneliness had overwhelmed her after her father died. Her stepmother had treated her like an unwanted stepdaughter. The deep pain inside had been almost unbearable.

Cassie desperately wanted to be loved again. Which was why she was so devoted to her Uncle Gus, for helping her and for loving her when she needed it most.

A big loving family was something she had always longed for, but had basically given up on that dream. It was wonderful to be part of Zach's large family even though she knew it would only last for a short time.

"Welcome to the Stevenson family, granddaughter."

William Stevenson kissed her cheek and stepped back to stand beside his wife. "We'll need to have a party to welcome you into the family properly."

Catherine Stevenson nudged her husband, offering Cassie a warm smile. "That party will have to wait, my love. Cassie and Zach will be away on their honeymoon. They need some time to themselves. We'll plan a party for you two in a couple of months. What do you think of that idea, Cassie?"

"That sounds lovely." Cassie felt a warm glow flow through her at all the love she was receiving from Zach's family.

"Good. We'll plan for that. Welcome to our family, dear." Zach's grandmother embraced her gently and kissed her cheek.

Soon they were talking with their grandson and Cassie was surrounded by Zach's brothers and their wives.

Elle and Adam each held the hands of their energetic toddlers. Elle spoke to Cassie. "It's so good to have one more daughter in the family. Now that you're here, us girls will have an even chance at winning in our family discussions." Elle winked at her.

Cassie grinned. "I'm happy to do what I can to help."

Jack and Bella were right behind them with their two children. Jack held his adorable little girl. She had Bella's large brown eyes and was pretty as a picture.

Jack kissed Cassie's cheek. "Welcome to the family, lil' sis. Tell that workaholic brother of mine that he needs to take you on a long vacation and he's not to think about work until he gets back home."

Cassie smiled and could hear her husband chuckle

beside her. Zach replied. "This from a man who works harder than anyone I know."

"But, I've become a changed man since marrying my beauty." He pulled Bella to his side and kissed the top of her head. "I have started to slow down and make more time for my family."

Zach nodded. "Point taken. I guess this will be a true vacation then." He winked at Cassie and her cheeks blossomed pink at his reference to their honeymoon.

She reminded herself that this wasn't a real honeymoon. It was only a vacation for the two of them to make their fake marriage seem real.

Next, Gabe and Rory hugged Cassie and welcomed her into the family, as did Luke and Razelle. Her friend Razelle hugged her and whispered in her ear. "I'm so happy you married Zach. Now, we are truly sisters."

"I'm glad too, Raz. We'll always be sisters of the heart." Cassie embraced her friend, grateful for the unexpected surprise of being a part of the same family as her friend.

Ollie pushed Uncle Gus's wheelchair until he was next to her. "Cassandra, you are a beautiful bride and today you look just like your dear mama did on her wedding day years ago, God rest her soul."

Tears pricked the back of her eyes. "That means a lot to me, to hear you say that. Thanks, Uncle Gus."

She couldn't help but wish her mother could have lived to see her grow up and to be here on her wedding day.

Her uncle shook his head and grimaced. "I wish your Mama could have seen you today, my dear."

Blinking back tears, she reached over and embraced her uncle. "I know. I wish that too. But, you're here today to support me Uncle Gus, and that means the world to me."

Drummond Grumwald cleared his throat as he stood nearby with the other five of her uncle's friends.

"Lassie, don't forget about the rest of us. We're here for you too." Grumpy's voice wavered.

Cassie grinned. "Yes, you are. Thank you." She looked at all of her uncle's friends who had been very good to her. "You've all been wonderful to me and I appreciate each one of you."

The men's features turned a slight shade of red as she hugged each of them.

Each of the men moved toward the food tables, following all the other wedding guests who were seated at the tables.

The caterers were standing by a couple of large tables covered with large platters of food and containers of drink.

"I think they're waiting on us to serve the food. Shall we?" She nodded and Zach slipped an arm around her waist pulling her close to his side.

A delightful shiver ran through her at Zach's hand on her waist. She looked over at him, stirred by his gentle smile. His intense gaze held a possessiveness that seemed reserved just for her.

Her heart thumped uncomfortably in her chest. Her instinctive response to Zach was so powerful that she worried.

This was supposed to be a fake marriage for only one year and then they would go their separate ways.

She wasn't supposed to fall in love with her fake husband. But, already she was beginning to care for him far more deeply than was wise.

Cassie would need to really guard her emotions, if she was to make it through to the end of this fake marriage with her heart intact.

ZACH TIGHTENED his hand around his bride's slender waist as they swayed to the country song.

As was tradition, the bride and groom were expected to lead the way when the dancing began.

If he was honest, he had anticipated dancing with his new wife ever since he'd first glimpsed her walking down the aisle towards him.

In fact, after she walked down the aisle to the song *My Wish* by Rascal Flatts, he'd asked the band to play this song again for their first dance together.

"I remember this song." Cassie whispered, peering over at him with wide violet eyes.

Zach pulled her closer. "It's one of my favorite country songs. I thought the words were especially suitable for our wedding day."

"Do you mean them?"

Zach smiled and leaned over and kissed her forehead. "I do. I wish only good things for you, Cassie. I wish that your life will become all you want it to be and that you'll never forget the ones you left behind who love you just as you are."

A single tear escaped her eyes and she hurried to wipe it away. Swallowing, she clamped her lips tightly for a moment before she spoke, her voice hoarse with raw emotion. "Thank you Zach."

Another tear escaped and trailed a path down her cheek. Zach reached over and caught it with his thumb, gently removing it.

"Hey, why all the tears?"

Cassie's bleak smile tore at his insides. He still had a lot to learn about his new bride.

She dropped her eyes quickly to hide the hurt for a moment.

With gentle fingers he lifted her chin and looked into her eyes. Violet eyes that glistened with tears and darkened with emotion, met his own.

"Tell me." Zach encouraged.

Her hoarse whisper broke the silence. "It's just your words mean a lot to me. I don't think I've had anyone other than my father and Uncle Gus, who truly accepted me for who I really was."

"I'm sorry, Cassie." Zach pulled her close, kissing the top of her head as he held her in his arms.

Her words made him wonder at her childhood and her family life growing up. He would make it his mission to discover more about her and the hurts and scars she carried.

"Well, now you have me too. And I happen to think the real you is beautiful on the inside as well as the outside." Zach leaned back to study her face.

His new bride's violet eyes widened at his words. "You do?"

"You seem surprised, Cassie." Zach whispered in her ear. ""Would that have anything to do with the fact that you've done everything possible to hide your beauty by wearing colorless, frumpy clothes and large ugly glasses? Sometime soon we'll need to talk about that."

Zach looked at her face and could see her blossoming cheeks even in the dim lights of the canopied dance floor.

"But for now, I think we'll simply enjoy each other's company." Zach pulled her close.

She quivered in his arms and hesitantly put her arms around his neck. Cassie whispered. "We're so close."

"Not close enough." Zach leaned down and kissed the tip of her nose. "I think maybe we need to convince my family and your uncle that we've married for love."

"Oh." As his new wife looked up at him, he could no longer resist tasting those strawberry lips.

Lowering his head Zach pressed her lips to his, caressing her mouth more than kissing it. She tasted like strawberries just as he imagined she would.

Holding Cassie in his arms and kissing her felt like coming home. It scared him.

Zach feared what being vulnerable would cost him.

If he fell in love with her, would his new wife try to use him or lie to him like Felicity Kingston had done? He was through with women who wanted to use him for their own gain.

Memories as far back as High School flitted across his mind and haunted him. He wasn't about to let that happen to him again.

He slowly ended the kiss, savoring each second until he lifted his head to look into her eyes.

Cassie's eyes widened and she stepped away from him.

Disappointment filled his senses as Zach no longer held his new bride in his arms. He could admit that holding his lovely wife in his arms gave him pleasure.

However, a new awareness had been building on the inside of his feelings for Cassie, and this new knowledge had shaken him to the core.

As Zach studied his bride's face, he could see she looked strained and pale.

"Thank you for the dance, Zach. I think we've convinced them." Her gentle voice was shaky and it sent waves of concern like fiery darts directly to his heart.

"I do too." He leaned over and whispered in her ear, hoping to put a smile on her face. "Dancing with you in my arms was entirely my pleasure."

He was about to ask her if everything was alright, when Doc White tapped his shoulder.

"May I have this dance with my niece?" Zach smiled. "Of course."

"Uncle Gus you're standing. Shouldn't you be in your wheelchair?" Cassie looked wide-eyed at her uncle. Concern flooded her features as she grabbed his arm.

Doc patted Cassie's hand on his arm, lovingly.

"My lovely niece, one dance isn't going to hurt me. And since your father isn't here, I thought maybe you could dance with your dear old uncle on this special day." Doc's voice shook and there was moisture in his eyes as he spoke.

Cassie's smile widened and joy bubbled over in a

gentle laugh. "Uncle Gus, I would love to dance with you more than anything."

As Doc began to lead her away, Zach spoke. "Don't be gone too long, my love." He kissed her free hand and pink stained her cheeks. Zach was pleased with her uninhibited response to his words.

Doc White looked over at him and chuckled. "Cassandra, I believe your father — my brother — would have been thrilled to see you married to a man who is eager to keep you by his side."

Zach was momentarily speechless, surprised at Doc's words. He nodded and smiled, encouraged to receive a stamp of approval from the man whom his bride loved as a father.

As he went in search of his Mom for their turn to dance, Zach couldn't help but think about his lovely new bride.

She was beautiful inside and out, but he sensed there were secrets hidden deep inside. Somewhere along the way, she had been hurt badly by people she trusted.

A wave of protectiveness welled up inside him along with a fierce anger at those people who had caused his wife pain and heartache.

He intended to do whatever it took to care for her and to gain her trust. Doc's words were spot on: he *was* eager to keep Cassie by his side.

At that thought, his stomach churned half in anticipation, half in fear.

He was scared of falling in love with his new bride, but at the same time he was anxious to spend time with her.

Expelling a breath, Zach calmed his churning emotions.

At this moment, he was looking forward to the surprise trip he had planned for the two of them.

Would Cassie be excited to be with him? Would this journey be a fresh beginning for them?

He hoped so, because more than anything Zach realized he was eager to please his new bride.

CHAPTER SIX

assie

STARING at her reflection in the wide full length mirror, Cassie ran her hands down the silk crepe material of the pink sleeveless top and the navy colored Bermuda shorts that hugged her slender body.

The glow from the morning sun shone through her large bedroom window, one of eight bedrooms in the Stevenson family's large ocean side home.

They had arrived in Honolulu Hawaii yesterday after a half a day's flight in Zach's private jet. After a light lunch, Zach had insisted on taking her shopping.

Her new husband had bought her designer brand shirts, blouses, pants, shorts, swimming suit and a couple of evening dresses. And of course, Zach insisted on the accessories to go with every purchase.

Looking down at her new leather sandals, she appreciated the softness of the leather and how the shoes complimented her outfit.

As Cassie looked at herself in the mirror, her eyes widened at how different she looked now.

Gone were the frumpy and colorless skirts and blouses that she had worn for the last couple of years.

Wearing these designer clothes like the Gucci and Alexander McQueen brands she wore today, made her realize how much her life had changed now that she was married to Zach Stevenson.

Now, she needed to look the part of a billionaire's wife. At least until their fake marriage arrangement was over.

An odd twinge of disappointment ripped through her. Why did the thought of ending her fake marriage with Zach weigh her down?

It had been less than forty-eight hours since they had been married, surely, she hadn't formed a deep attachment to him in that short amount of time.

Perhaps this feeling was from the realization that the ending of her marriage to Zach would bring deep disappointment to Uncle Gus. That must be it, she reasoned.

She placed her large glasses on her nose and then touched up her full lips with pink lipstick.

Suddenly she stopped. Wiggling the lipstick in her fingers, she remembered this was the same lipstick she'd worn on her wedding day.

As she recalled that memorable day, all she could think about were Zach's toe curling kisses.

Thinking about it sent the pit of her stomach into a

wild swirl again, just like it did less than forty-eight hours ago.

Her lips tingled as memories of her new husband's intoxicating kisses flooded her senses once more.

This marriage of convenience was beginning to be far more difficult than she first imagined.

She could feel herself falling a little more for him, each time they spent time together. The thoughtful things he did for her had forced her to rethink her original ideas of him as a selfish and wealthy playboy.

No, her husband might be wealthy, but he was consistently generous and kind with those around him.

She ran a hand down the flattering designer blouse and shorts, remembering Zach's insistence that she buy more clothes. She'd finally told him she had more than enough clothes to wear for this vacation.

To which Zach replied that he would take her shopping again when they returned to Seattle.

A small smile lifted the corners of her lips as she remembered.

Even with the new wardrobe, she couldn't shake the urge to hide herself again in the comfortable and safe frumpy clothes.

But that had changed now that she married Zach.

Well, she might be wearing flattering clothes at this moment, but at least she still had her large rimmed glasses. Wearing these glasses made her feel like a part of herself was safe from judgmental and prying eyes.

Running the brush through her shoulder length dark hair once more, she set the brush down.

Expelling a breath, she released some of the nervousness that she always felt when spending time with Zach.

She straightened her shoulders, giving herself a pep talk and left her room and hurried down the hallway.

Zach had asked her last night to meet him for breakfast.

The Stevenson family's home on the beach had eight bedrooms, each with their own ensuite. Then there was a media room, a large family room, a great room and a large kitchen and eating area. The kitchen and breakfast area were somewhere near the back of the house, but at the moment she couldn't remember.

As Cassie walked down the hallway, she finally reached an open space and could hear the sounds of pots and pans.

Hurriedly, she walked to the kitchen and saw the dark haired native Hawaiian woman she'd met briefly last night. She was Zach's cook, Luilani. The air smelled heavenly as she pulled blueberry muffins out of the oven.

Hearing Cassie's footsteps, Luilani turned toward her with a bright smile on her beautiful olive skin.

She slipped the oven mitts off her hands and walked towards Cassie and grabbed her hands.

"Missus Cassie, you are awake. Good. Mister Zach is having coffee on the deck outside. You want?" Luilani's smile was so warm and motherly that Cassie's heart melted. She already liked Zach's cook and she had just met her.

"Yes I would love some coffee and one of those delicious smelling muffins you made. Thank you, Luilani."

Cassie turned toward the large archway that led to the breakfast nook."

Just through there you will see the patio doors. Mister Zach is outside." Luilani directed her.

Before long, Cassie found the patio doors. Opening them, she spotted Zach sitting at a table for two on the sprawling deck that overlooked the sandy beach.

Her husband turned to her and took off his sunglasses, his blue eyes widened as she approached.

"Good morning. You look amazing." Zach kissed her cheek and pulled out a chair at the table for her to sit down.

Heat rose up her neck to her cheeks, and she was sure a red stain clung to her cheeks. Why did she always blush at his compliments?

"Good morning to you too." She spoke softly and managed a small smile.

Zach studied her intensely for a moment. "You really do look beautiful, Cassie."

"Thank you Zach. It must be the clothes you bought me. That was really nice of you, thank you." She looked over at Zach, only to see him frowning at her.

"I get the feeling that when someone compliments you on how great you look, it makes you uncomfortable." Her new husband commented. She stirred uneasily in the chair with the awareness that her husband didn't miss much.

However, she wasn't ready to answer his probing questions.

She blushed to the root of her hair and whispered. "Maybe."

Just then, Zach's cook walked out onto the deck carrying coffee and food.

A soft sigh of relief escaped her lips happy she wouldn't need to answer his probing questions.

"Well, this week we have time to get to know each other better. I'll need to discover more of your secrets." Zach grinned.

Cassie laughed softly as Luilani set the tray of breakfast food on the table. The heavenly scent of the plate of muffins and two steaming mugs of coffee caused Cassie's stomach to stir in hunger.

She looked out towards the ocean in awe at the scenery, happy for an excuse to change the subject. "Zach, your family's home here in Hawaii is simply beautiful. You have white sandy beaches nearby and you also get to enjoy whale watching right out your back door."

Cassie sighed as she watched a dolphin's head emerge above the water for a moment before it dove back under the surface of the ocean.

"Yeah. It is pretty amazing. Our family doesn't come here to enjoy the beauty often enough." Zach's words seemed to reach deep inside, running all the way down to her toes.

"Why?"

"All of us are so busy with different projects, charities and our businesses that time just seems to fly by." Zach ran a hand through his hair.

"Well, maybe we could change that by scheduling in your calendar a few vacation times throughout the year." Cassie spoke quickly without thinking.

By nature she had always been good at organizing things, but perhaps her new husband wouldn't appreciate her speaking her mind. "Sorry, I spoke without thinking."

"No, don't apologize. I think you might have the right idea. Each year, I somehow do everything on my schedule, so it makes sense that if vacations were on the schedule, it would happen."

Cassie nodded. "That's what my dad used to say. What gets scheduled in your life gets done."

"Smart man." Zach looked over at her and reaching a hand over he ran his hand lightly over hers. "You must still miss him."

"Yes, I do. Very much." Cassie tensed, going silent for a moment. "Since living with Uncle Gus, I've been able to relive some of the favorite things I appreciated about my dad, because my uncle is so similar."

"Simple things, like the way he would ask me about my day and have a coffee with me in the morning or the way he would encourage me to pursue my passions."

Cassie went on. "But, my Dad would have loved your place here on the Island. Every summer until I was ten years old, we visited my Dad's sister Lottie in Hawaii. I remember those visits fondly."

Zach looked over at her, a curious light in his blue eyes. "Your aunt lives here?"

Cassie nodded. "Uncle Gus asked if we would visit her while we're here. I told him, 'I wasn't sure what your schedule was for this week, but that I would try.'"

"Of course we can visit your Aunt Lottie." Zach took a sip of his coffee, as a thoughtful look returned to his face.

"All I really had planned was to explore one or two of the Marina's here on the big island this week. I thought maybe you might like to see the Art Museum and some of the other historical sites. But, we'll make time to visit family."

"Thanks, Zach. That means a lot to me." Cassie was grateful for his thoughtfulness.

Zach was quiet for a moment and Cassie spoke. "Is your plan to be inspired by ideas you find here and from that to redesign your great grandfather's Marina?"

"Yeah, that's the idea."

Cassie looked at him. "I'd love to hear about what you have planned."

Zach's blue gaze brightened as he spoke. "Well, originally I had an idea to add a resort to the Marina. So guests could not only come for the day, but they could spend a week with their families enjoying the lake and our small town."

"That's a great idea." Cassie smiled at the animated look on his face. She could tell, Zach carried a lot of passion for this project.

"Yeah, it's a great idea, but there's just one problem. I need to double the size of acres of land for the Marina in order to have a decent size for a resort."

"Maybe, you need to buy out some of the neighboring properties."

"Yes, that was my thought too. However, Mayor Riggs told me that there is another buyer who is interested in those properties. He says this other buyer has the right idea of wanting to replace those old houses with a trendy looking mall and some condos alongside that area of the lake."

"Maybe that's what the Mayor would like to see, but that doesn't mean that will happen. Don't the folks in Paradise Lake have the final say on those types of zoning issues?"

"Yes. But, maybe they will side with Mayor Riggs, I don't know." Zach sighed.

"Well, I hope not."

"Thanks for the vote of confidence, Cassie." Zach sighed. "But, perhaps we'll save all those problems for another day. Let's think of the fun we'll have today, instead."

Cassie nodded. They could talk about his ideas for the Marina later. Surprisingly, she really wanted Zach to be able to develop the resort and to do all that was in his heart to complete the vision that his great grandfather had begun when he founded the Marina years ago.

But, this issue wouldn't be solved in one day. And she found herself really wanting to spend some fun days together with Zach.

"Sure. That sounds good. I am looking forward to spending time with you, doing those things you love. I want to enjoy the world through your eyes today, Zach." Cassie smiled warmly at him, a little nervous at the intensity of his blue eyes on hers.

"You know, I'm really looking forward to spending the day with you, Cassie." Zach stood to his feet, and reached for her hand and kissed the back of it.

"I'll do my best to make this a memorable week for both of us."

❧

"Today, we will be watching some of the very best in sailboat racing." The grey haired announcer looked out towards the ocean to where the sailboats were waiting to begin the race.

"The Waikiki sailboat races are a favorite of many sailors across North America."

"As usual the sailboats will race from Waikiki out to Diamond Head and back. It's great weather for sailing today. We want to wish each one sailing today the best of luck." The announcer finished speaking and the race began.

Zach looked at Cassie and pointed to one of the sailboats waiting for the race to begin. "That white sailboat with the royal blue design on the outer hull was one of the first sailboats I designed and built. Tom Ledbetter is a friend of mine and owns the ship."

"How exciting that one of the sailboats you built will be racing today, Zach." Cassie turned her head to see where he pointed. "You must be proud to have one of your boats in today's race."

He nodded. "I am. It always feels good to see other boat enthusiasts enjoying them."

Cassie nodded, a big smile on her face as she watched the sailboats begin the race. "I'm glad that they thought to have a drone follow the sailboat race, so that we can watch the race on the big screen."

Zach nodded as he watched the close-up of the race on the screen in the corner of the lounge that looked out toward the waterfront.

Just at that moment, a movement caught his eye near the lounge's bar. A grey-haired man wearing a light colored Panama hat and casual green floral Hawaiian shirt stood by the bar ordering a drink.

Zach instantly recognized his dead friend's father, Makoa Lightfoot. Swallowing, memories came back along with the usual heavy dose of guilt that followed.

He remembered that Koda's father had moved back to Hawaii, shortly after his son's death years ago.

Suddenly, Mr. Lightfoot spotted him and waved.

Zach smiled and waved back. Leaning down, he whispered in Cassie's ear. "I see a friend at the bar I haven't seen in a long time. I thought I'd go chat with him. Would you like to meet him?"

"Yes. I'd love to meet a friend of yours Zach." Cassie's grin flashed briefly, dazzling him once again with her beautiful smile. He couldn't help but feel proud to have Cassie by his side as he met an old friend.

"Alright." He grabbed her hand, and they made their way through the crowd, towards the bar.

"Hello again, Mr. Lightfoot." Zach's voice sounded strained, as a terrible tenseness filled his body at seeing his dead friend's Dad again.

"Zach Stevenson, it's so good to see you." Mr. Lightfoot's hand enveloped his in a strong grip.

"It's good to see you too. It's been a long time." Zach rubbed the back of his neck, thinking of all the years that had passed.

"It has. And time has changed things for both of us." Mr. Lightfoot looked meaningfully at the woman by his side. "Who is this lovely lady by your side, Zach?"

Zach put a hand on the small of her back as he introduced her. "This is my wife, Cassie."

"You are a beautiful bride." Cassie's face flushed at the compliment.

"Thank you. It's nice to meet you, Mr. Lightfoot."

The older man grinned and pushed back his hat, scratching his grey head. "Both of you don't need to call me mister. I'd feel more comfortable if you would simply call me by my first name, Makoa."

Cassie smiled and nodded. "Of course. Makoa, it's nice to meet a friend of Zach's. How do you know each other?"

Her question was innocent enough, but it aroused old regrets and uncertainties in Zach.

"Well, my son and Zach were the best of friends during their teenage years. We lived in Paradise Lake until my son passed away." Koda's Dad's eyes misted a little as he talked about his son. "It wasn't long after, that I moved back to my home state of Hawaii."

Cassie touched his arm gently. "I'm sorry, I didn't mean to bring up something so painful. I am sorry for the loss of your son."

Zach swallowed as emotion clogged his throat. As he saw the tears form in Makoa Lightfoot's brown eyes, he remembered his best friend.

"It's okay. I've had eleven years to grieve and in many ways I've healed from the loss of my son." Mr. Lightfoot smiled warmly.

A friend walked over and whispered in Makoa's ear and he nodded. "Looks like I need to get going. However, I would really like to talk some more with you both. Would the two of you have the time to come to lunch at my home tomorrow?"

Zach nodded. "Yes. We'd be happy to join you for lunch."

"Good. Here's my card with my home address and phone number. I'll see you then." With a wave Makoa Lightfoot was gone to meet up with his friend.

A jumble of conflicting emotions welled up inside him after the conversation with his best friend's father. He felt the incredible loss of his best friend and was confused to hear Koda's father tell them he was healed from what happened years ago.

"It will be okay, Zach." Cassie reached over and squeezed his hand. Her large violet eyes filled with compassion and she spoke softly.

"Maybe when we meet with Mr. Lightfoot for lunch tomorrow, you'll have a good conversation that will help both of you heal from your loss."

He nodded, although deep inside he didn't really believe it would do any good.

Somehow, he was convinced the regret of the past would always stay with him like a dead weight he needed to carry day after day.

THE WAVES CRASHED against the beach as she walked beside Zach along the sandy beach.

The red and orange glow of the beautiful sunset glistened on top of the ocean waves that rolled onto the shoreline.

Cassie sighed contentedly as she stared into the distant horizon, amazed as perfectly clear turquoise water mingled with a breathtaking sunset.

This day had been one of those rare perfect days as she spent time with her new husband.

He looked over at her and smiling, he slipped his large hand in hers and squeezed. She was enjoying Zach's closeness as he checked his long stride to match her own.

She felt blood surge from her fingertips to her toes at his touch.

"Thanks for a wonderful day, Zach." Cassie spoke softly.

Zach smiled. "I'm glad you enjoyed it. The sailboat racing wasn't too boring for you?"

Cassie shook her head. "No, not boring at all. In fact, watching those people as they navigated their sailboats brought back fond memories of sailing with my Dad."

Zach raised one eyebrow, surprise flooding his features. "I didn't know that about you. So, you're a born sailor then."

"Well, I don't know about that. But, I think I did start going out on the water with my Dad from the age of six until I was ten years old. We stopped going on our weekly sailing adventures when he married my stepmother."

"He told me Larissa didn't like to sail, so he thought they should do things where my stepmother would feel included." Cassie sighed. "I was very sad when my time spent sailing with my Dad was over."

"I bet." A furrow formed between Zach's brows and it seemed like he was pondering something. "That seems odd that your Dad would tell you that your stepmother didn't like to sail."

"It seems like that must have changed, since Larissa seems to be quite comfortable sailing your father's yacht now that he has passed away."

"I know. Weird isn't it?" Cassie gave a choked, desperate laugh. "But, I learned when I was a teenager that it didn't do me any good to try to point out any inconsistencies I saw in my stepmother. Doing that only got me in trouble."

Zach stopped and turned her towards him. His hands were gentle on her shoulders, and his blue eyes intense as he studied her. "What sort of trouble?"

Her eyes darkened with pain as she remembered. "Before my father passed away, my stepmother wasn't as cruel towards me."

"At that time she did her best to convince my dad to send me off to boarding school, which he agreed to do. However, it was after my Dad died that things changed for the worse."

Her throat ached with despair and defeat as memories washed over her.

"There were a few memorable times after my father died when my stepmother ruined a big day for me. On my coming of age birthday party, I had a lot of friends who planned to come over to our house and we were going to sit by the pool and just have fun."

"But, that morning before the party was to begin, I dressed in my favorite pink matching skirt and knit top that my father had given as a gift to me. I came downstairs ready for my friends to show up in an hour."

"My stepmother was staring at herself fixing her makeup in the hallway mirror and turned to look at me — and gave me such a hostile glare that I stopped in my tracks."

"Larissa turned and pointed at me, stabbing at my chest with her red lipstick, ruining my shirt. She told me: You look like a whore in those clothes. If you think I'll let you make me look like I'm the stepmother of a tramp to all your friends, you have another thing coming."

Cassie shuddered as she thought back to Larissa's words. "You aren't having a birthday party today. You will stay in your room for the rest of the day and think about how you plan to dress in clothes that are humble looking and extremely modest from now on."

A tear slipped out of the corner of her eye. "Needless to say I had to apologize to some very upset and disappointed friends when I finally went back to school."

Zach shook his head and his jaw tightened in anger. "It makes me angry just knowing that Larissa would say so many deliberately hateful things to you."

A swift shadow swept across her face. "Yeah. It was very painful."

"Was that the reason you started wearing clothes that were not as stylish and clothes that were buttoned up to the neck?"

Heat rose to her cheeks. So, he had noticed the way she disguised herself in those frumpy and lackluster clothes.

She nodded, remembering her birthday being the turning point for her. "Yes. That's when I started dressing in the most unflattering clothes I could find."

"But, it was the benefit gala that I attended with my stepmother when I was twenty years of age that really scared me."

"What happened?"

Swallowing the fear in her throat, Cassie explained. "We went to the benefit gala for a children's hospital. Both of us wore designer gowns, I had on a violet evening gown that night. One person commented and both of us overheard her: *Well, it looks like Larissa White's days in the spotlight are over. Her stepdaughter Cassie has officially taken first place in both influence and beauty.*"

"After that comment, I turned to my stepmother. Her face was pale and I could see her hands were shaking. She was angry. When we got home she didn't even speak to me. The next morning, I was supposed to go back to my college dorm."

"Larissa's bodyguard Jackson was supposed to drive me back to college, but he turned toward where my father's boats were docked. He brought me on board one of my dad's boats, *The Emerald Adventure.*"

"Emery Jakes was on the boat. There were also many young people from different ethnic backgrounds working and a large drunken party was going on. Jackson was about to turn me over to Emery Jakes, when I heard him mutter: *I can't do this. Let's get out of here, Cassie.*"

"As we drove away, Jackson told me that I needed to get on the bus and get as far away as possible from my stepmother. To go somewhere where she couldn't find me."

"He gave me a large fistful of cash as he dropped me

off at the bus stop and told me I should go visit my father's brother Gus. That I would be safe there." Cassie shuddered visibly as she remembered how scared she'd been. Her stepmother's actions still haunted her to this day.

Zach shook his head and a crease formed between his brows. "Well, that's good that your stepmother's bodyguard protected you. It kind of makes a person question what your stepmother had planned for you."

Cassie shuddered. "Something terrible that would've ruined my life, I'm sure."

Zach squeezed her hand as he stared at her intensely. "And that's how you ended up living in Paradise Lake."

"Yes. That's why I am so thankful for my Uncle Gus. I owe him so much. He's given me a safe and loving home to come to when I needed it most. I would do anything for him." Tears slipped unheeded down her cheeks.

Zach placed one hand gently on her waist, while his other hand rested on the back of her head.

She leaned against his chest and wrapping her arms around his waist, she yielded to the tears that flowed down her cheeks.

"Shh. It will be okay. I'll do whatever it takes to protect you from now on, sweetheart." Zach's whispered words against her hair, was like a soothing balm to her wounded heart.

Cassie's heart softened and warmth filled her. Clamping her lips together to stop the flow of more tears.

Finally, she took a step back from Zach and released a shaky sigh. "Thank you, Zach. I feel better knowing that

I'm safe with you. I'll try not to be too much of a burden to you."

Zach stepped close to her once again. "The last thing you are is a burden, Cassie. If anything, you are more like an inspiration."

Her heart fluttered wildly in her breast and a familiar shiver of awareness rippled through her as he gathered her into his arms.

She sighed as his lips slowly descended to meet hers. Shivers of pleasure surged through her veins at the tenderness of his kiss. It was a kiss for her tired and wounded soul to melt into.

After a series of slow shivery kisses, he lifted his head.

Blue eyes darkened with intensity as his gaze captured hers.

Her knees weakened and her emotions whirled and skidded as she was lost in his gaze.

Another large wave hit the shoreline and suddenly, she was aware of her husband in a whole new way.

She was falling a little more in love with him each day she spent with him.

Her feelings shouldn't have come as any big surprise. She'd known there was something special about Zach from the very beginning.

Only, today was different somehow.

His compassion, protection and care for her at a time when she needed an anchor to hold onto the most, put Zach at a new level than any other guy she'd dated in the past.

It softened her heart towards him even more and that made her afraid.

Her vow not to let her feelings get in the way of her fake marriage to Zach was crumbling like dust at her feet.

Cassie didn't know how to deal with the need for love and her own vulnerabilities and insecurities that he aroused inside her heart.

At that moment all she knew was her emotions were in a mess, and all because of Zach Stevenson.

CHAPTER SEVEN

ach

ZACH TOOK the cool drink Makoa offered, trying to focus on what the older man was saying.

Ever since he'd kissed Cassie last night, all that had been on his mind was his beautiful wife.

Fake wife.

He'd do well to remember that fact.

However, he could admit that she had his emotions all tied up in knots. It wasn't part of his plan to fall for his marriage-in-name-only wife.

He peered over at her sitting beside him, all dressed up in another new designer outfit with a yellow top and dark green capri pants that hugged her slender frame. For a moment, he could wish she was back to wearing the frumpy clothes she used to wear.

No, he truly didn't wish that, even though her new attractive look was driving him a little crazy each day.

His wife looked stunning in the new clothes she wore today. Even more important, since being here in Hawaii, Cassie had a more peaceful look on her face. The worry lines that had formed between her brows had been erased.

Makoa sat down on a chair across from them and lifting his glass towards them he spoke. "Here's to friendship."

Zach lifted his glass in salute echoing the sentiment. He had been surprised and grateful that Koda's father had welcomed him again, especially after what Zach felt was his responsibility in son's death.

Looking at the flowers that surrounded his backyard and the large swimming pool in the center, he appreciated the view.

"You have a beautiful place here, Makoa."

The older man nodded. "I agree. When my mother passed away five years ago, she gave me the house. Many Hawaiians pass down their homes from one generation to the next, as homes are a premium price here on the Island. So, I am thankful for the many wonderful memories in our family home."

"That's a beautiful sentiment, Makoa." Cassie smiled warmly. "Was your son born here?"

Makoa nodded. "Yes, my son was born here in Hawaii. My wife and I didn't move to the mainland until Koda was thirteen. My job required that I move to Paradise Lake. The change was hard on us as a family, but most difficult for my wife. She passed away only two years after we moved."

Zach swallowed back emotion. He remembered when Koda's mom had died. His best friend had been desolate and inconsolable for months after that.

That was when Koda started to busy himself with his boats on the lake. Doing that had brought a little bit of joy back to him.

"That must have been very difficult." Cassie's compassionate tones seemed to resonate with Makoa, proven by the moisture in his eyes.

"Yes. It was very difficult. It was especially difficult for my son, but Zach's friendship with Koda really helped bring a little happiness to his life."

"He was the best of friends." Zach's grip tightened on the glass in his hand as once again he remembered his friend.

Makoa leaned forward in his chair. "Zach, you were the best thing that happened to Koda when we lived on the mainland. He even learned to wear his baseball cap backwards because of your influence."

Mr. Lightfoot grinned and chuckled as memories rose to the surface. A sudden memory of Koda in Science class with their strict teacher came to mind.

He grinned. "Maybe not such a good influence. I still remember Koda coming to Science class with his baseball cap backwards on his head and Mrs. McCarthy yanking it off. She told him in no uncertain terms: *I don't want to see you wearing that cap in my classroom again.*"

Makoa grinned and shook his head. "My son told me about that. Well, maybe that Science teacher couldn't appreciate good sports gear when she saw it."

"I guess not." Zach shook his head as he remembered some of the good times he'd had with Koda.

All of a sudden, Cassie spoke up. "You two share a lot of good memories, Makoa. I wonder, do you have some photos of him that you wouldn't mind sharing with us? I would love to see them."

"I don't mind at all. Come with me inside the house, I have many photos for you to see in the family room." Makoa stood to his feet and waved his arm for them to follow.

Zach took Cassie's hand as they followed Makoa into the house. He shared pictures of Koda when he was six years old and he'd caught a fish with his dad.

There was a picture of Koda with his dad and mom. Makoa handed a framed picture of his son with Zach on Koda's old motorboat. "This is one of my favorite pictures of Zach and my son."

Zach could feel the blood rushing out of his lungs as he stared at the picture.

Memories haunted him once more of the day when Koda and him had raced on Paradise Lake to the rocky crag and back. Except, they didn't make it all the way back. His best friend's boat exploded just before they reached the rocky point.

He stumbled as memories hit him, and he sat down on the nearest sofa, placing his head in his hands.

Cassie sat beside him, touching his hand with her gentle touch. "Zach, is everything all right?"

He swallowed back the emotion. "I'll be alright in a little while. It's hard to remember Koda, that's all."

Makoa sat on the sofa across from Zach and spoke

softly. "I remember how that feels. Years ago, it was very difficult for me to think of my son's death too. In fact, I avoided going to any place where Koda had been when he was alive for years."

Zach listened quietly, not saying a word.

Cassie said. "That's understandable."

Makoa nodded. "I thought so too, until one day when I needed to go into Koda's old room to clean out his stuff, I found an old tattered book."

Moisture filled Makoa's eyes. "Opening it, I realized my son had written thoughts about his life in a journal. I was mesmerized and read it from start to finish in just a few hours."

Zach had never heard Koda mention anything about keeping a journal. It surprised him to say the least.

"Are you saying you found something your son put in his journal that helped you heal from his unexpected passing?" Even as Cassie questioned Makoa, she squeezed Zach's hand.

He knew she was being kind and compassionate, but his new wife didn't realize that nothing could help take away the stain on his life that he was at fault for his best friend's unexpected death.

Makoa nodded. "Yes, reading about my son's life written in his own hand, made me realize he had a unique way of looking at himself and his family and friends. His words brought healing to my heavy heart."

Zach looked into Koda's father's brown eyes, absorbing his words. He could see the lightness in Makoa's eyes. He could see that he was no longer haunted by his son's death.

He couldn't say the same. Regret still clung to every waking hour, like a bad odor that just wouldn't go away.

Zach's throat ached with defeat. As he looked at Koda's father, he longed for some sort of absolution from his constant guilt and regret that surrounded him, but none came.

"Zach, the look in your eyes reminds me of the grief I felt for years after my son's death. Those feelings didn't simply go away, but I experienced more of a gradual healing." As Makoa spoke he stood to his feet.

Searching in the bookshelf behind him, he pulled out a well used book with tattered edges.

Koda's father spoke in a gentle voice. "Before you leave today, I want you to take this book home with you, Zach. It's my son's journal, written in his own words. After I read it, I began to heal."

"My hope is that you will have a similar experience. Read it. I'll plan on grabbing the journal from you when I come for the annual Fourth of July motorboat races in Paradise Lake." Makoa reached over and placed the journal in Zach's hands, a gentle smile on his face.

Zach's eyes widened, shocked. "You're planning to come to the motorboat races, after what happened to your son?"

His hands shook as he held the journal, surprised that Makoa would want to be at the event that only a few years earlier had killed his son.

Makoa nodded. "I'm okay now. I have visited all the places that my son enjoyed over the last five years. Watching the motorboat race is the last place I need to go

— and the hardest. But, my gut tells me I need to do this, so I will."

"Man, you're brave." Zach could feel his throat closing up as he stared at the journal. He stood to his feet, his voice sounded raw and raspy as he spoke to Koda's father. "I don't know if I can do this… read my friend's journal I mean."

Makoa placed one strong hand on his shoulder. "Yes, you can. You must read his journal. Do it for Koda, Zach. Read it, simply because he would want you to know him better."

Zach nodded, swallowing back emotion that threatened to clog his throat. "Alright. I will read it for Koda. I will do this for him."

"Thank you, son." Makoa patted his shoulder and walked with him and Cassie to the front door.

Makoa hugged Zach and Cassie before he spoke. "Aloha, to you both. Have a safe journey home and I'll see you soon."

"Aloha, Makoa. See you soon." Cassie spoke and grabbed his hand as they walked to their waiting car.

Zach held the tattered journal in one hand. For some reason, he couldn't shake the feeling that he'd just been offered a second chance.

He swallowed and his hands shook slightly, wondering what he'd find between the pages.

❦

THE OLD JEEP shook and rattled as it skittered over yet another pothole on the dirt road.

"How much farther?" Cassie asked the Hawaiian driver.

His brown weathered face crinkled merrily as he turned to her. "Just a mile or so."

Her Aunt Lottie owned five acres of land farther off the highway in Northern Maui, Hawaii. Her land was alongside a river with a roomy six bedroom house.

It had always been so much fun when her and her dad had come to visit years ago.

As the house came into view, Cassie smiled over at Zach. "There it is."

Ever since they had gone back to the Stevenson family beach house last night, Zach had avoided talking about their visit to Makoa's house.

Last night and again this morning, she had done her best to keep things lighthearted and to try to make him smile.

Cassie really hoped this visit to her Aunt's home would put a smile on his face.

Finally the driver stopped the Jeep, just outside the house.

Zach sent her a half-smile. "Happy we came to visit?"

"Yes. Thank you Zach for putting up with the long drive and hazardous roads to get us here." Cassie laughed as she jumped out of the vehicle.

Zach grabbed their bags and they turned to see Aunt Lottie standing on the wooden deck with a large smile on her face.

Warmth filled Cassie at the sight. She ran up the wooden stairs and threw her arms around Aunt Lottie.

"Oh my darling girl. I'm so happy you're here." Aunt Lottie whispered and kissed her cheek.

When she finally pulled back, she grabbed Cassie's shoulders as her gaze swept over her. "Let me get a good look at you, Cassandra. Beautiful as always."

Warmth flooded Cassie at her words. Her Aunt Lottie was the only person who had truly been like a mother to her. She had always loved her unconditionally throughout her life.

"It's so good to see you, Aunt Lottie. I didn't realize how much I missed you, until now." Tears welled up in her eyes and she quickly blinked them away.

"I'm glad." Aunt Lottie looked over Cassie's shoulders and smiled wide. "And this must be your new husband, Zach."

Zach grinned. "Nice to meet you, ma'am."

"Now, none of that ma'am nonsense. Call me Aunt Lottie, just like Cassie does. We're family now." Saying that she grabbed his hands and kissed him on the cheek.

"Now follow me and I'll show you to your bedroom suite where you can put your things." Aunt Lottie led them to the largest room on the second floor that overlooked the river.

"When I was a little girl, I always longed to stay in this room." Cassie looked around the room appreciating the large king size bed on one end of the room and the two sofas located in front of the fireplace at the other end.

"Well, now you'll finally have your chance." Smiling, she walked to the door. Turning she said. "As soon as you're refreshed from your journey, we'll enjoy some cool drinks on the deck downstairs."

"Sounds wonderful. Thanks, Aunt Lottie." Cassie called after her as she closed the door.

Zach turned to her with a grimace on his handsome face. "Your Aunt sure is a bundle of energy, isn't she?"

"Yep." Cassie giggled. "She's always been that way. That's how I remember her. Maybe it's why she was able to take over Uncle Henry's business interests when he passed away years ago. She's always been a whirlwind."

"Well this short visit will be fun then." Zach set down their small suitcases near the table in the middle of the room.

"It will be good. We'll just have to make the most of the two days we have here." Cassie glanced over at the bed on the other side of the room, nerves getting the better of her. "Um, my Aunt doesn't know that our marriage is fake. She assumes that… our marriage is real."

Zach tossed her his rogue grin, his blue eyes capturing her own. "Don't worry, I'll do my part to convince Aunt Lottie that our marriage is real."

Rose blossomed on her cheeks and she looked away from the sparkle she saw in his eyes.

She couldn't help the quiver in her voice as she spoke. "Well then, if you're ready to head down into the lioness's den, then I am too."

"I'm ready. But, just a second. There's just one thing we forgot to do, before we go downstairs." Zach walked over and he stood so close she could feel the heat of his body.

His compelling eyes riveted her to the spot and her heartbeat throbbed in her ears in response.

"What did we forget to do?" She cleared her throat, pretending not to be affected.

"This." He swung her into the circle of his arms and holding her snugly against his chest, he pressed his mouth to hers.

For a moment, her eyes widened in surprise and gasped in delight. Her knees went weak and a brief shiver rippled through her as his lips moved over hers.

She raised herself to meet his kiss, when suddenly it was over. He kissed her nose and put gentle hands on her shoulders and whispered. "Now that you've been properly kissed, we should have no problem convincing your Aunt Lottie our marriage is real."

He reached his hand for hers and turned toward the door and whispered. "Your cheeks are a lovely shade of pink."

Cassie blushed all the way down the stairs, sure that her cheeks were still glowing as they joined Aunt Lottie on the deck.

Aunt Lottie smiled as she saw them. "Perfect. Come join me." She pointed to the two chairs beside her under the large umbrella table. "Can I pour you each a glass of iced tea?"

"Please. Thank you Aunt." Cassie took the glasses and handed Zach his. They relaxed under the shade of the umbrella for a while talking about their trip and the things they had seen so far.

Suddenly, Aunt Lottie asked. "So, how is my brother Gus really doing?" She held up her hand as she looked at Cassie. "And don't try to make things sound better than they are, dear niece. I want to know the truth."

Cassie nodded. "The truth is, the doctor said his heart has been weakened by this heart attack. However, the surgery went well and the doctor is hopeful that Uncle Gus will make a full recovery."

"That must be difficult for Gus. He never could stand to have anything hold him back. Well, perhaps I need to plan to visit him soon then." Aunt Lottie swirled the straw in her tall glass as she stared out at the river below.

"Uncle Gus would love to see you."

Aunt Lottie turned to her, moisture in her green eyes. "And I would love to see him. The one thing I had in common with your father was we would see each other every summer. But, I haven't been as diligent to see my brother Gus. It's time for me to change that."

"I have fond memories of all those warm summer days spent here with my dad and you, Aunt Lottie." Cassie reached over and squeezed her Aunt's hand.

Her Aunt patted the top of her hand. "Me too. I still remember you sketching and painting down by the river. In fact, I still have those early paintings of yours."

"You do?" Cassie blushed and looked at Zach. "I wasn't any good, but it was fun."

"What do you mean you weren't any good? I took your passion for painting seriously. And I saw improvement in your work every summer. Also according to what I've heard from my brother Gus, you've continued to paint beautiful pictures."

"Uncle Gus shouldn't be telling tales about me." Cassie colored fiercely and was helpless to halt her embarrass-ment. She hadn't wanted Zach to know all her secrets, but it seemed it was too late now.

"Cassie, you're an artist?" Zach peered at her intently, a new light in his blue eyes.

She nodded quickly. "I am an artist, but I'm not very good yet." She didn't want him to think she was going to win any awards for her paintings or anything.

"Well, that remains to be seen. I would love to see your work."

Cassie flushed miserably. She knew Zach meant well, but for some reason she couldn't explain, she was shy to share her work with him.

Her paintings were the one thing she put her whole self into. All her feelings, thoughts and emotions were there for the world to see with each brush stroke she placed on the canvas.

"Maybe someday you will." Cassie spoke softly, giving him an answer that was vague and without any specific time frame.

Aunt Lottie smiled and stood to her feet. "Just a minute, I will be right back."

Cassie wondered where her Aunt was going in such a hurry, but decided not to worry about it.

Instead she needed to change the subject off her and onto her husband.

She turned to Zach and asked. "What would you like to do while we're here?"

Zach looked at her lazily over the top of his glass of iced tea. "Explore this place with you as my tour guide."

She observed him with a musing look for a moment. "Alright. I can do that."

Cassie was about to speak again, when Aunt Lottie's steps sounded behind them.

"Cassie, I found the painting you sent me last year for Christmas." Cassie's eyes widened and she groaned when she saw her Aunt pull out the large framed canvas from behind her back.

There it was in bold colors.

It was a picture of her dad with Aunt Lottie and Uncle Gus fishing down by the river on her Aunt's acreage. A little dark haired girl sat on a large rock with a chocolate colored dog by her side. The colors were brilliant with green blue water and trees that were green and beautiful.

"Cassie, your painting is beautiful." Zach expelled a breath as his gaze swept over the canvas.

A wave of warmth filled her at Zach's words. But, perhaps he was simply being encouraging.

Aunt Lottie spoke up. "To me, Cassie's art looks like Norman Rockwell paintings. I am curious, why have you placed yourself so far away from your dad and your uncle and I, my dear?"

"In the painting it feels almost like you're an observer or like an outsider looking in. I'm not sure what it is, but anyway I do love it."

Cassie expelled a breath. "Like you said, it's not important. And I'm happy you like the painting, Aunt Lottie. It's a picture of a happy family."

"That's right. You even titled the painting, *Happy Family Fishing.* How appropriate. I will treasure it always, dear niece." She squeezed Cassie's hand.

As her Aunt talked some more to Zach about the details of the painting, Cassie continued to think about why she had painted herself far away from the rest of their little family.

Her Aunt had hit the nail on the head with her comment.

Somewhere deep inside she did feel like an outsider, looking in. Somewhere along the way during her childhood — especially after her father died — she lost who she really was.

In her longing to stay safe, she hid who she really was and in doing so, abandoned her truest self.

There was a yearning deep inside herself to uncover what she'd lost in the middle of all the heartache and pain.

She wanted to find herself again.

Yet, it didn't escape her notice, that here she sat — still in hiding. Living a lie with a fake husband and not being completely honest with him or with those she loved.

How was she going to get rid of those deep-rooted seeds of fear and doubt to discover her true self once again?

CHAPTER EIGHT

ach

"It was fun exploring Aunt Lottie's acreage together. Thank you for being patient with me as I talked about my childhood memories from visits to the Island." Cassie turned to him, smiling.

She quickly let go of his hand as he opened the door to their bedroom suite.

Cool air wrapped around his hand as she let go. Zach quickly realized he missed the warmth of her touch.

They had a wonderful afternoon walking along the river, even hiking a little ways up the mountain to see the waterfalls nearby.

"Every moment with you today was a pleasure, Cassie." He admitted as much to her as to himself.

That in itself was a surprise as he couldn't remember

ever enjoying himself with any other woman as much as he loved spending time with Cassie.

He grinned as her cheeks turned the color of a pink rose. It was adorable how his new wife became suddenly shy whenever he complimented her. Yet, the way she seemed to ward off any praise, puzzled him.

Thinking back, he remembered his mother telling him that women were like onions and that you had to peel back the layers one at a time.

Well, maybe it was time he started to peel back the mystery that surrounded his wife.

"Thanks, Zach. That's kind of you to say." Cassie walked across the room and grabbed her small suitcase.

"Just saying the truth as I see it." Zach noticed she was taking out toiletries and preparing to go to bed.

She set her glasses down on the side table by the window. "Do you feel like relaxing by the fireplace and talking a while?"

She turned back to face him and with her hand, covered a yawn. "Maybe not tonight, Zach. I'm feeling so tired. It was a busy day."

He glanced around the room that held only one king size bed in the room, besides the sofa near the fireplace.

Cassie followed his gaze and shifted her feet nervously. She stammered. "Do you want to sleep on the bed? I can sleep on the sofa."

Her eyes widened, looking at him with uncertainty.

He gave her a small smile as he tilted his head. "Now, what kind of gentleman would I be if I let you sleep on the sofa while I took the bed?"

Cassie smiled slightly. "That's considerate of you Zach. Thank you."

He nodded. "Welcome."

She hurried into the washroom with her toiletries and came out only ten minutes later wearing a loose cotton t-shirt and shorts.

"It's all yours." Cassie spoke softly as she hurried to the bed and climbed under the covers, pulling them to her chin.

Zach was only in the washroom for a couple of minutes, but when he came back out, Cassie's lamp was turned off.

He settled onto the sofa, with his feet hanging over the one side. It was so short and the sofa was lumpy that he kept tossing and turning. He continued to shift his long body on the sofa, trying to find a comfortable spot.

"Zach." Cassie's voice whispered across the darkened bedroom and he stopped. "I'm sure you aren't comfortable on that sofa. If you want you can come sleep on the bed. We'll roll up one of those old throw blankets and set it between us."

"Are you sure?" Zach held his breath waiting for her response.

"Yes. My conscience will bother me too much if I don't rescue you out of your misery." Zach grinned at the sound of Cassie's deadpan voice in the darkened room.

"You don't have to ask me twice." Zach got up and rolled up the throw blanket that he was using on the sofa, he set it in the middle of the large bed.

Crawling under the covers on his side, he settled in

and then whispered. "Thanks, Cassie. This feels so much better. Maybe now I'll be able to sleep after all."

"I'm glad. And I hope you do sleep well. Goodnight, Zach." Cassie whispered and then shifted on the bed.

"Sweet dreams, Cassie." He whispered into the night. His thoughts swirled back to their day together. He loved being close to her. She had even grabbed his hand as they walked up the mountain to view the waterfalls.

If her actions were any indication, perhaps his fake wife was beginning to trust him the more time they spent together. He rolled onto his side, hoping to fall asleep, but no such luck. His thoughts wouldn't stop thinking about Cassie.

"Zach, are you having trouble sleeping?" Just hearing her soft voice brought pleasure to him.

"Yeah. My mind's too busy."

He could hear her shifting on the bed, until she must have turned in his direction because her voice was clearer.

"Want to talk about what's keeping you up?"

Zach sighed. He wouldn't tell her all the romantic thoughts about his sweet wife that were going around and round in his head. However, there were one or two things he'd wanted to talk to his wife about… maybe this was his opportunity.

"Since you asked, I was thinking about the painting you did titled, *Happy Family Fishing*. It's really good, Cassie. You are very talented." Zach whispered, as he recaptured the painting in his mind's eye.

"Thank you. I'm glad you liked it. I don't usually share my art with too many people." Her whispered words held a hint of pain and heartache.

"Why?"

Cassie expelled a long breath and didn't speak for a long while. "I haven't always felt safe by some people in my life. So, with my art I chose to keep it close to my chest because when I paint, it comes from my heart and so much of what I feel shows up on the canvas."

He could hear the vulnerability in her voice. Reaching over, he grabbed her hand. Gently, he squeezed and rubbed his thumb along the top of her soft skin.

"I can see that in your artwork."

"I find that when I'm painting, it's the only time I begin to uncover more of the missing pieces of my identity."

"So, when your Aunt commented on the fact that you painted yourself farther away from the rest of the family in the painting because you feel like an outsider, was she right?" Zach needed to know his wife better.

He was beginning to see the connection between his wife's need to disguise herself with frumpy clothes and the fact that she only allowed herself to show her truest self in her paintings.

From what he observed, it seemed like painting was the only place she could express who she really was and still continue to feel safe.

"Pretty much, yeah."

Zach's heart ached at the strained tone he heard in her voice. He shifted and without thinking pulled her close to his heart.

"I'm sorry for all the pain you've gone through and that you haven't felt safe, Cassie. I want you to know you'll always be safe with me." His wife's body trembled in his arms and he could hear her soft sobs.

He kissed the top of her hair and rubbed her back, letting her cry it out.

When she was spent and only had soft hiccups left, Cassie pulled away. "I'm sorry I cried all over you, Zach. I don't know what's wrong with me. Normally, I'm not such a watering pot."

He kissed her forehead. "It's okay, it really is. I understand." He kissed her wet eyelids and the tip of nose, before he touched her lips with his own.

Zach had just begun to enjoy her sweet kisses, when the blanket between them jabbed into his belly.

He pulled away and whispered. "That rolled up blanket is my reminder to say goodnight. And it couldn't have come at a better time. Sweet dreams, Cassie."

He heard her muffled laughter as she shifted to her other side. "Goodnight, Zach."

This time he lay there with a smile on his face, thinking about his sweet wife.

He was already making plans about how he was going to surprise her and put a smile on her face tomorrow.

It might just be the best day of their trip.

ZACH'S large hand gently touched the small of her back as they walked out of the restaurant.

They had just returned to Honolulu, Hawaii this morning from their visit with Aunt Lottie.

For lunch, he had taken her to one of the nicest restaurants she'd ever been to. It was an elegant restaurant with a French name she couldn't pronounce and there were no prices to be found on the menu.

"Now, I want to show you a place I think you'll love." Zach turned to her as they walked down the sidewalk.

"Zach, it's already been a wonderful day. Thank you. You really shouldn't do anything else for me, you'll spoil me." Cassie was pleased by how he had treated her so generously with his money and time.

He opened the door to another place of business and turned to her, his mouth curved into a smile.

"Maybe it's time you were spoiled. Especially by your husband." He leaned down to whisper in her ear.

Cassie shivered in response and the sounds of the many people hurrying past them, faded away until all she heard was the accelerated beats of her own heart.

She inclined her head with a small smile of pleasure at his thoughtfulness. "Well, if you put it that way, then I gratefully accept your generosity, kind sir."

He grinned and waved and reached his hand inside the door, indicating she should step inside.

As soon as Cassie stepped inside her eyes widened as she looked at the walls. There were many different genres of famous artists.

She breathed out, excited at what she was seeing. "This is an Art Gallery."

Zach reached for her hand. "Yeah. Since I learned of your love of art, I have been searching for art galleries to visit. I thought we'd start with this one today."

She turned to him. "This is very thoughtful, Zach. I love it."

He squeezed her hand. "Well, let's look around. Maybe you'll find some paintings you can't resist."

She expelled a breath. "I have no doubt I will."

They walked around the large gallery and Cassie stopped to look at many beautiful paintings that hung on the walls.

Reaching the second floor of the gallery, it was here that many incredible artworks were displayed by artists like Picasso, Rembrandt, Van Gogh and many more.

One piece in particular caught her eye and she stepped closer. It was a painting by Leonardo DaVinci titled *La Scapigliata.*

It was the face of a woman, portrayed in natural color. There was a mysterious demeanor on the beautiful woman's face.

Her head was tilted to one side with a thoughtful expression. It was almost as if the woman — a Madonna like lady — was deep in thought about her life and who she really was.

As Cassie's gaze swept over the detailed masterpiece, she recalled Aunt Lottie's comment that in her own painting, she portrayed herself as an outsider looking in.

If she were honest, that's exactly how she felt about her life. All her life she had done everything she could to please others and make them happy. But, since that hadn't worked with her stepmother, she had disguised who she was to protect herself.

But, as memories took her back to all those years of hurt and pain, she realized that she truly had lost who she really was along the way.

She swallowed back emotion as she studied the woman in the painting.

An intense longing filled her, to find the girl inside her who was lost all those years ago and to step into the person she was meant to be all along.

"You've been standing here, looking at this painting for a long time. What fascinates you about this one?" Zach's gentle voice whispered in her ear.

She shivered at his nearness as she thought about how to answer his question.

"The woman in the painting reminds me of myself. Lost and alone and trying to find who she really is." Cassie whispered; her words filled with yearning.

Zach placed his arm around her shoulders pulling her close. "Well, you're not alone anymore. You have me. Don't worry about your feelings of being lost and unsure of who you are, we'll figure that out together, honey."

She couldn't help but notice the tingle of excitement inside her at his touch and his words of endearment.

"Thank you, Zach. It means so much to me to hear you say that." She looked over at him, and a longing so fierce gripped her heart.

She desperately wanted his words to be true. She didn't want to be alone anymore.

She wanted to be by his side. She wanted his encouragement as she figured out who she really was. She wanted… well she wanted so many things.

Her gaze met her husband's with all the yearning she held in her heart.

Cassie looked up into Zach's intense blue gaze and her

heart lurched madly as she realized she truly had fallen in love with her husband.

This wasn't part of the plan. She wasn't supposed to fall in love with her fake husband. Together they had agreed that this marriage of convenience was only supposed to last for one year.

Her mind spoke rationally about all the reasons why falling for her husband was a terrible idea, but her heart refused to listen.

It seemed her heart had decided to love him anyway.

She could tell Zach was attracted to her, but was there any hope that he might fall in love with her too?

A few hours later, Cassie stood on the beach looking out towards the ocean, her thoughts still focused on her feelings for Zach.

They had driven back to Zach's family beach house. Since this was their last evening here in Hawaii, they agreed to enjoy an evening of sun and sand before they flew back to Paradise Lake.

She waited for Zach who said he'd meet her on the beach.

Cassie's thoughts drifted back to the painting once more.

Watching the waves come in, she imagined her life and discovering who she truly was reflected in the waves.

Cassie hoped that it would be like that. She yearned for fresh waves of awareness and discovery of who she was would flow over her gently, without worry or fear.

The woman Da Vinci portrayed in the painting, revealed her true colors to the world. Maybe she could do the same.

Footsteps sounded behind her and she turned to see Zach walking towards her in the sand. He was dressed in comfortable shorts and t-shirt, walking barefoot in the sand.

He inspired her. She slipped the sandals off her feet, and let her toes squish in the cool sand.

"I was wondering when you were going to take off your sandals." Zach grinned as he neared her.

She smiled and sighed. "It feels heavenly. I don't know why it took me so long."

He reached up and toyed with a length of hair that had fallen out of the make shift bun she'd piled her hair into on top of her head.

"Maybe seeing that painting today inspired you to let yourself go and be more of your true self." He whispered as he leaned closer, placing one arm around her waist.

"I think you're right." Cassie nodded. "I guess we both learned new things about ourselves. I learned to embrace a little more of my truest self and you?"

Zach chuckled and shrugged. "I think I learned that I have a lot of work to do to fix up the Marina."

Cassie shakes her head. "I'm not talking about that, silly man."

"What then?"

"What about the lunch we had together with Makoa Lightfoot? Are you going to do what he asked and read through your best friend's journal?" Cassie urged.

She really wanted him to be free of the guilt that plagued him about his friend's death years ago.

"I don't know." Zach said nervously.

Cassie hugged his arm as they walked along the shoreline. "I think you should give it a chance. You never know what will jump out at you as you read his journal."

"I suppose." Zach looked out towards the ocean and she wondered what he was thinking.

Suddenly, he turned to look at her, his blue eyes dark with intensity. "Did you enjoy the time we spent here, Cassie?"

Somehow she knew her answer was important to him. "Yes. I enjoyed seeing new places, but I especially enjoyed the time I spent with you, Zach."

His arms encircled her, and he slipped up her arms, bringing her closer.

"I'm glad. I enjoyed every moment with you too, Cassie." His lips pressed against hers, then gently covered her mouth.

His kiss sent the pit of her stomach into a wild swirl. Standing on tiptoe she touched her lips to his savoring his slow drugging kisses.

She felt transported on a soft and wispy cloud at Zach's tender kisses.

When he finally lifted his head, she could only sigh with pleasure.

Zach looked at her, and she could feel the trembling in his arms. She could tell he was as shaken as she was by their kiss.

"You are beautiful in every way, Cassie. Your emotions and everything you feel shows on your face, and if I'm honest, it scares me a little."

"Why?"

"Because it's beginning to chip away at all the protective barriers I've placed around my heart. And I don't know if I like that." Zach pulled her close and kissed her forehead.

"Perhaps, I'll grow on you and soon you won't mind if all those barriers are removed completely." Cassie whispered.

"Maybe that's what I'm afraid of." Zach held her close, and they could feel the beat of each other's hearts.

Cassie didn't know what to say, so she just held him tighter letting her actions speak for her.

Would Zach be able to fully let go of all the barriers he'd placed around his heart, and let himself love her completely?

With all her heart, she longed for that to be true.

CHAPTER NINE

Cassie

"I think I'm in serious trouble." Cassie peered across the table at her friend Lydia.

She was relieved when her best friend had agreed to meet her for a morning coffee.

Cassie needed someone she trusted. She needed someone to whom she could bare her heart.

Five days ago, they had flown back from their week-long vacation in Hawaii, and so far Zach had spent long days and evenings working late.

Zach had explained that he needed to check on a new boat design as well as oversee the restoration projects he was working on at the Marina he had just inherited from his great grandfather.

Cassie peered out the large window of Walker's Cove

Marina cafe. This beautiful historical cafe on the Marina had just been restored from the fire that had ravaged it only a few weeks ago.

But she missed him. She missed the closeness that had come from the time they'd spent together.

"Why do you say that?" Lydia stirred the cream into her coffee, a puzzled look on her face.

Cassie grimaced and set down her coffee cup with a slightly shaky hand. "Because I've done what I wasn't supposed to do. I've fallen in love with my husband."

Lydia's eyes twinkled and a light chuckle escaped her lips. "So, you spent a week with Zach and you've returned home in love. Doesn't sound so terrible to me."

Cassie shot her friend a penetrating look, her annoyance showing. "You don't understand, Lydia. Falling in love wasn't part of the agreement I made with Zach."

Lydia reached across the table and squeezed her hand. "Cassie, since when does falling in love go according to any plan? It just happens, unexpectedly."

Cassie closed her eyes for a moment, letting her emotions settle. With one hand she tucked some loose tendrils of hair behind her ear. "I suppose you're right. I just didn't expect it to happen to me."

"I mean, for years I've been a woman that's been so strongly opposed to any sort of relationship with a guy." She fluttered her left hand with its large ring in front of her friend's eyes. "Now I have this ring and all these confusing emotions that go with it."

Her best friend grabbed her hand and ran her finger across the shimmering wedding rings. Then Lydia lifted her head to look at her, eyes glowing with enjoyment. "His kisses must have been incredible to have made you change your mind."

A flush crept up her neck to her cheeks as memories of Zach's kisses invaded her senses. "He does kiss amazingly well."

Cassie shook her head, a sudden awareness of what she was saying and added forcefully. "But, that's not the only thing that has affected me."

"Zach has protected me; he's treated me so generously and he's been very kind and compassionate towards me. He went out of his way to take me to visit my Aunt Lottie and he took time to really listen to me."

She splayed her hands in an outward motion. "Spending time getting to know Zach has made me change my mind about him. The truth is, I really think I might be falling a little more in love with him every day, and that really scares me."

Cassie closed her eyes, feeling utterly miserable about the whole situation.

Lydia grabbed both her hands and squeezed. "Look at me."

Cassie looked into her friend's brown eyes, seeing the fire in them she listened. "I understand that you are scared and worried. I'm sure I would be terrified right about now if I were experiencing the same thing."

"But, from what you've told me Zach has been really good to you. He's listened to you, he's been honest with you and he is obviously attracted to you. Instead of running away, why don't you simply enjoy all the attention he's giving you?" Lydia's tone was persuasive.

"But, when I agreed to Zach's proposed marriage of

convenience, we agreed that our marriage was only so each of us could get what we want and then we'd get an annulment. This… *this whole falling in love bit,* wasn't part of the plan." Cassie muttered uneasily.

"Well, my dearest friend, the thing about relationships is they don't usually abide by our plans." Lydia's eyes sparkled and she grinned.

"Besides, what if your fake husband has decided that he not only wants his great grandfather's Marina, but that what he wants most is to make you his real wife?" Lydia leaned closer, her gaze steady and piercing.

Cassie's eyes widened and sighed in disbelief. "Well, I really doubt that. Besides, ever since we arrived back home, Zach has arranged his work schedule so we've hardly seen each other. That doesn't sound like he really wants this relationship."

"Have you thought that maybe Zach is scared, same as you?" Lydia tilted her head to one side, staring at her thoughtfully.

Cassie sighed heavily as her fingers twiddled with the edge of her coffee cup. "I suppose it's possible."

She grimaced. Perhaps, her irritation and frustration with Zach had caused her to overlook the fact that he might be experiencing similar fears of being vulnerable with her.

Lydia finished the last of her coffee. "Listen, I need to get back to work, but I really feel like you just need to give him a little grace and find the time to talk to him."

Lydia stood to her feet and Cassie followed.

Cassie nodded as she slipped the leather purse strap around her shoulder. "You're probably right."

Her friend grabbed her in a hug, holding her close for a moment before stepping back. "I am right, watch and see."

Cassie laughed softly. "You've always been a little too confident."

"I prefer to say that I happen to be right… a lot." Lydia giggled.

She simply shook her head, chuckling softly as they walked out of the Marina coffee shop.

Cassie looked across the large patch of green grass towards the pier where many boats floated in their places.

Noticing her father's old yacht, *The Violet Diamond,* anchored at the North end of the Marina, at the largest available spot for boats, she was reminded of her stepmother.

Her belly tightened knowing that Larissa and her boyfriend Emery Jakes were still here at Walker's Cove Marina.

She had really hoped the two of them would have left Paradise Lake by now.

Biting her lip, she was about to turn back to talk to Lydia, when she saw her stepmother step out off the bridge of the yacht followed by her boyfriend and two others.

She thought she recognized the two teenagers. The one with sandy blond hair was Addy and the other shorter girl with the brown hair was Olivia.

A couple of years back, the two of them had endured their own trouble with a human trafficking gang at a rough and tumble camp outside of Paradise Lake.

Perhaps that was the reason the nagging in the back of her mind refused to be stilled.

She nudged Lydia her gaze transfixed in their direction. "Isn't that Addy and Olivia talking with my stepmother and her boyfriend?"

Lydia followed her gaze and stopped in her tracks. "Looks that way."

Cassie turned to her friend and a furrow formed between her brows. "I thought Addy and Olivia were working at the restaurant with you?"

"Well, it turns out they both quit their jobs at the restaurant two days ago. Each of the girls told me they found a better paying job." Lydia turned to her with a worried crease forming between her brows. "Do you think they were talking about working for your stepmother?"

Cassie nodded and bit her lip from worry. "I think that's likely. I mean Larissa and Emery really adore having their yacht parties, so maybe they have been looking to hire workers to help serve."

Lydia swallowed and shook her head. "I didn't think the girls would choose work for your stepmother. Well, perhaps they were offered a big pay increase."

"That's probably true." Her misgivings grew as she thought of Addy and Olivia working at night on the yacht. "I'm going to do what I can to keep an eye on those girls. I sort of feel responsible to see their well-being."

Lydia nodded and expelled a heavy sigh. "That's probably a good idea." Her friend turned to her. "Well, I do have to get going or I'm going to be late for work."

Standing on the pathway that led to the restaurant,

Cassie turned. "Will I see you tonight at the community center for the discussion about the Marina and the related zoning issues?"

"Normally, I don't go to these things, but since I know the topic concerns you and Zach, I will be there to support both of you." Lydia bumped her shoulder and grinned. "You know I'd do anything for you, Cassie."

"I know. Likewise my friend." Cassie waved to Lydia as she hurried down the trail that led back to the restaurant where she worked.

As Cassie drove away, her thoughts raced back to their conversation about Zach.

Maybe it was like Lydia said, and he was scared of being vulnerable with her too.

He'd always seemed so strong, like he had everything in his life figured out. But perhaps he also was struggling with his feelings much like she was.

It seemed they would need to have that talk.

All she needed to do now was to see him long enough for them to have a serious conversation.

❧

ZACH HELD the door to the Community Center open and smiled at Cassie as she walked ahead of him.

As usual she looked gorgeous in another pair of designer shorts and blouse set they had bought on their trip. Leaning down he whispered. "You look beautiful tonight."

His wife peered over at him, and hesitated a moment before she spoke. "Thank you."

The soulful expression on her face nearly undid him.

Guilt gnawed at his conscience at the way he had avoided her for the past five days.

In truth, he did have a lot of work that had piled up, but he could admit that staying busy had been his way of running away from his ever-growing feelings for his wife.

Soon they would need to talk, but not now.

First, he needed to get through tonight's community discussion and decisions for zoning issues on his bid for more land to expand the Marina.

Zach pressed his lips together firmly, gearing himself up for the meeting ahead.

Placing his hand on the small of her back, they walked into a large auditorium where many folks from their small town were talking together.

He girded himself with resolve as he spotted Mayor Riggs and a few members of the town council standing at a distance, talking.

Seeing his two brothers he whispered to Cassie. "I'm going to talk with Adam and Jack. You're welcome to join me, or if you see someone you'd like to talk to, go ahead."

Cassie nodded. "I'll go chat with Lydia and a couple other friends. You go ahead and I'll talk with you later."

"Alright." He nodded and watched his beautiful wife join her friends.

A large hand clamped down on his shoulder. "It doesn't get any easier to let our wives go, you know."

Zach turned his head to see his brother Adam and grinned. Jack walked towards them both.

He greeted each one and slapped them both on the back. "Thanks for coming, both of you. It's always helpful to feel the support of family. I wish Gabe and Luke could've been here tonight too."

"Well, I'm sure Luke doesn't miss us at all as he's off on another beach vacation with his wife." Jack chuckled. "And lately Gabe's been a wanted man with all kinds of speaking engagements."

Zach nodded. "I forgot about that, good for them. Well, I'm grateful you two could be here."

"We're happy to be here for you, Zach." Adam smiled. "How are you feeling about tonight's discussion?"

"I'm a little nervous, to be honest. Maybe it's because I really want the people to vote in my favor." Zach ran a hand through his hair.

Jack nodded. "I understand all about that. Remember, I had to convince the Mayor and the town council about the zoning issues for my Adventure Park. But, in the end it all fell into place. It will for you too Zach, you'll see."

"I really hope so." Zach muttered uneasily as he looked across the large community center room where more and more people were filing in.

His brother continued. "Don't worry. The biggest thing to remember is to share your passion. Why do you want to expand Walker's Cove Marina into a resort?"

"Share your vision and dreams and watch how people's opinions sway in your favor. You are a Stevenson. If somehow I was able to convince them, you can too, Zach." Jack's words ignited a spark in him and he was reminded again of his roots.

"You're right, Jack. I can do this and I'm going to give it my best shot tonight."

Jack squeezed his shoulder. "I see you've got the fire back in your eyes. Now, you're ready."

"It's passion." Zach grinned.

"Good Zach." Adam looked across the room. "And speaking of your passions, how are things going with your beautiful wife?"

Zach sighed. "She has me so tied up in knots — I can hardly sleep. Because of that, I've chosen to work a lot more hours lately."

"Avoiding her Zach?" Adam shook his head. "Well, it definitely sounds like you're a man in love."

Jack nodded, chuckling. "So true. And we are definitely speaking from experience."

Zach didn't know what to say to that. "I'm not sure that it's love. I think maybe I'm just afraid of getting too close to her."

Jack shook his head. "Translated, that means you're fearful of what your feelings are for her. Welcome to the club of men who are crazy in love with their wives, Zach."

Zach could feel heat rising from his neck to his cheeks. He really didn't know what to do with all these unexpected feelings. Were his brothers right and he was falling in love with Cassie?

Just then the town council chairperson announced the meeting was beginning. Looked like he would have a short reprieve from thinking too deeply about his feelings for his new wife.

"Looks like that's our cue to join the others." Zach led the way to some empty chairs near the front.

Cassie came to sit beside him, her friend Lydia next to her. A warmth filled Zach to have his wife by his side.

She reached over and squeezed his hand and whispered. "You'll do great."

Her belief in him affected him deeply.

His eyes locked with hers and he whispered. "Thanks. I needed to hear that."

Mrs. Anderson, who was the designated chairperson of the meeting, finished welcoming everyone to the meeting.

"As you all know, tonight we are discussing zoning issues regarding waterfront property in Paradise Lake." Mrs. Anderson looked around the room until her gaze fell on Mayor Riggs.

"To start with I would like to introduce our first speaker, Mayor Al Riggs."

Mayor Riggs went to the podium and looked over the crowded room for a moment before he began. "We are happy so many of the good folks of our small town showed up for this very important discussion on the type of properties we want to encourage on the waterfront around Paradise Lake."

The Mayor paused before going on. "In the past few years, Paradise Lake has become increasingly well known as a place folks want to live and visit. We are grateful for the many unique ways that the good folks of our small town have made this community a better place through the years."

He stopped for a moment looking over the crowd. "However, we don't want to stay where we are, we want to keep improving. In my mind, that means keeping up with progress."

"That's why I'm happy to have these different ideas

from people like Larissa White and a couple of our own town councilors. We will also hear from Zach Stevenson so be ready with your questions, critiques and comments."

It didn't escape Zach's notice that the Mayor added his name as an afterthought. Maybe he should have expected that.

It was true that he didn't see eye to eye with Mayor Riggs on many issues — the most important one was about which direction to take the waterfront property in their small town.

He stopped his musings as Mrs. Anderson stood to speak.

"Thank you Mayor Riggs. As you know, each person who wants to speak on this topic has fifteen minutes before they need to hand the microphone to give someone else a chance to share their thoughts. Larissa White, if you would like to begin?"

Cassie shifted a little closer to his side and her cheeks went pale as she looked over at her stepmother.

When Zach noticed her reaction, he slipped an arm around her shoulders as a sense of protectiveness over-took him. There was no way he was going to let his wife's stepmother hurt her anymore.

He tuned into what Larissa was saying, if only to get a clear picture as to what her plans were.

"So when my boyfriend Emery and I anchored our Yacht at Walker's Cove Marina, immediately we knew this was the perfect place for us to stay." Her dark eyes flick-ered over the crowd and she swept her hair back with shiny red fingernails.

"That being said, we have decided to make our stay

permanent. So, we have added our name in competition to the others looking for approval for a waterfront property business." Larissa beamed, her eyes scanning the crowd.

"In fact, just the other day, Emery and I purchased a residential property that we'd like to rebuild into condos that would accommodate a variety of tourists that come through Paradise Lake."

"It's not too far from the Marina and would bring a whole lot of new life to your beautiful small town. Besides the Yacht Charter services we offer, we will build Condos that would attract tourists and bring more revenue to this town." Larissa's face glowed with a satisfied smile.

She was confident of swaying the people of Paradise Lake to her way of thinking.

As Larissa White sat down, Mrs. Anderson stepped up to the microphone.

"Heath Bollwood, a member of our town council, would like to speak to some concerns he has about zoning issues surrounding the waterfront properties."

A man in his late thirties stood at the front of the room.

Zach remembered him from his older brother Jack's meetings with the town council. Zach seemed to remember that Heath had caused all sorts of headaches for his older brother.

The town councilor began to speak. "As I've taken the time to study the properties that now exist along Paradise Lake's waterfront, the data shows that there has only been minimal growth there. I think it would be in our community's best interests to bring some growth to the waterfront area, which is why condos and even one or two strip malls in that area would be ideal."

"Instead of building a resort with cabins, I vote that we should build condos. It would bring in more tourists to enjoy our beautiful lake and small town and of course that would bring more revenue into Paradise Lake. As far as I see it, that's a win-win for everyone." Heath finished speaking and sat down next to the Mayor.

A spark of anger ignited inside Zach at the town councilman's words.

He shouldn't have been surprised that Mayor Riggs and the town councilman he had in his pocket would try to sway the townsfolk against his plans and towards the idea of Condos along the waterfront. That would be a big mistake as the town would never be the same again.

Besides, he was convinced there was something going on that was underhanded, but he didn't know what. Somehow he would get to the bottom of it.

"Next to speak is Zach Stevenson, who is the great-grandson of Paradise Lake's founding father Walker Stevenson." Mrs. Anderson nodded at him and he walked to the microphone.

A flicker of nerves coursed through Zach as he looked out at all the townsfolk who had shown up for this meeting. Seeing their faces, he felt an increased sense of duty to do his best to explain his vision for the Marina and Resort.

"I was quite nervous to stand here and talk to you all today. Quite possibly, it's because most of you have known me all my life and you've already witnessed my many blunders." Zach grinned and the crowd chuckled.

"But, in spite of mistakes and in spite of the obstacles I've faced lately at the Marina, my beautiful wife Cassie encouraged me to share my vision tonight."

He nodded at Cassie, whose gentle smile bolstered his courage.

"My great-grandfather Walker Stevenson had a vision for this town, when he first founded it over seventy years ago. The day he and my great-grandmother drove the wagon out of Seattle and over the hill and saw the blue water and the orange-red hues of the horizon line, it reminded him of what Paradise would look like and that's how they came to name this town."

Zach paused for a moment. "Grand told us boys that he never imagined after he bought this land that twenty-four families would move to Paradise Lake in that first year to make this small town their home. It pleased him to no end that this small town would be a place for families."

Memories swept over him as he remembered walking along the beach edge hand in hand with Grand.

"As a young boy, Grand would tell me his dream was to create a safe place along the waterfront where families could come and relax in the quiet and beautiful surroundings to have a rest from all their troubles."

"He wanted it to be a place where folks could find happiness again." Zach paused for a moment and looked out over the crowd where folks were listening closely to his story.

"So when people ask me what do I see for my great grandfather's Marina and the waterfront property? My dream is to expand Walker's Cove Marina. We are in the process of expanding and developing land so we can build cabins and greater rental facilities so visitors can enjoy vacations here."

Zach smiled. "I see a quiet place that is fun, but also safe. In my mind's eye, I see a safe harbor for folks who need a place to come in the middle of life's storms. That's my vision for our beautiful town and the waterfront properties that run alongside Paradise Lake."

The crowd clapped as Zach sat down. Cassie turned to him and whispered. "You gave an inspiring speech. I'm proud of you and love your vision for the waterfront property."

"Thank you, Cassie." Zach smiled and glanced towards the row of chairs on the other side of the room. Mayor Riggs and Heath Bollwood as well as Larissa White and Emery Jakes were all glowering in his direction. "Not everyone has the same viewpoint as you do."

Cassie turned to look at his competitors and she looked back at him. "Well, you simply have greater vision than they do." She smiled.

He chuckled. "If you're not careful, all your encouraging words will go straight to my head."

Cassie giggled.

Mrs. Anderson got up to the microphone. "Looks like we have one more person who would like to speak."

Old Widow Crandell walked up to the microphone, her grey head barely visible over the podium. "I have something to say."

She looked at the townsfolk, scanning their familiar faces. "I've known most of you all of my life. I know you all help your neighbors and love the small town and quiet life we have here."

Releasing an unsteady breath, she continued. "In fact, with my recent house fire I got a real glimpse into the heart and soul of our town. You all helped me and you helped each other. We are a close-knit community."

Folks clapped and she continued. "I love the quiet and peaceful atmosphere we have here. If we add condos and have a bunch of tall buildings and a strip mall along the waterfront, soon we'll be a big, loud city just like all those other beach towns. Do you really want that?"

"I love the sense of family we have in our small town. Since my beachfront property is next door to the Marina, I've decided to sell it to Zach Stevenson. That way he can expand Walkers Cove Marina into that Resort he was talking about. I love the idea that Paradise Lake would be a wonderful place for families to come to and find a little peace and happiness from their troubles."

Zach couldn't help but feel a warm glow at Mrs. Crandell's heartfelt words. He knew there were quite a few people who were against his plan to expand the Marina into a Resort, but hearing the older woman's words gave the shot of courage he needed to keep going.

"Well, as much as I respect the wisdom of the older generation, I have to disagree with Mrs. Crandell." Autumn Sommers, a famous TV star who had only recently moved to Paradise Lake, hurried to the podium and spoke closely into the microphone.

"As someone who has experienced the many benefits of progress first-hand, I have to agree with Larissa White. Condos are definitely what you all need in this small town. I mean, without progress, Paradise Lake will end up being a ghost town in a couple of years." She flipped her blond hair back and turned to Zach.

"And despite Mr. Stevenson's little family story that had us all floating in the clouds, we need to come back down to reality. It's time we all realized what the waterfront properties in this town really need: progress to attract more visitors and bring much needed finances into this community."

As Miss Sommers hurried back to her seat, Zach was surprised by the TV star's fervent support of condos, especially from someone who was new to Paradise Lake.

It seemed like he would make one step forward and then something would hit him and he would get knocked two steps back.

He did his best to temper the frustration rising inside him and was grateful when Mrs. Anderson got up to the microphone to bring the meeting to a close.

"Well, we've heard from everyone who wanted to speak on the waterfront zoning issue tonight. Watch the town's website for the next — and final — meeting in one week."

Mrs. Anderson closed the meeting. "After that, a decision will be made and announced at our annual Fourth of July celebration. Have a good evening everyone."

As everybody stood up to leave, Zach's thoughts were still racing dangerously.

Sometimes it was really tough to take a stand for what you believed to be the best decision to make.

Memories came back to him of what Cassie had told him the first time they talked about the Marina.

My father used to say that when there are other folks

suddenly very interested in your business, it means it's even more important for you to stick to your convictions. It means there's more at stake. Don't give up now. Dig your heels in deep and stand for what's best for this Marina.

Now, more than ever before he needed to dig in his heels.

It wouldn't be easy, but if he didn't Zach had a feeling he would regret it the rest of his life.

CHAPTER TEN

assie

CASSIE BRUSHED her dark hair back and quickly put it into a ponytail.

With one last glance at her appearance in the floor length mirror, she was ready to start the day.

As she stepped outside her second floor bedroom, she looked down the hallway and noticed Zach's bedroom door stood slightly open.

It was just as she expected. Her husband had already left for the day. Cassie expelled a breath. She saw Zach last night for only the evening and now it looked like he was gone again.

Sighing, she walked down the hallway towards the kitchen. She was still getting used to living in Zach's ten-bedroom home.

It was a beautiful lakefront property with incredible views of Paradise Lake, yet Cassie learned she could easily get lost in all the rooms and hallways.

Walking in the general direction of the kitchen, humming caught her ears. As she walked into the large cooking area, Cassie spotted her husband's cook and housekeeper.

"Good morning, Mrs. Beale." She smiled and spoke softly. "It's nice to hear you humming a happy song."

Mrs. Beale's cheeks blossomed pink. "Oh, Mrs. Stevenson, good morning. You caught me. I'm so embarrassed. I hum without thinking as I work."

"Don't be embarrassed. I love to listen to you." Cassie smiled and walked toward the coffee pot.

The cook stopped what she was doing and seeing where she was going Mrs. Beale reached for coffee mugs. "I will pour for you, Mrs. Stevenson. And I will pour a cup of coffee for Mr. Stevenson too. But maybe it's best if you bring it to him. He's in one of his dark moods."

The cook gave the sign of the cross and looked up as if to send a silent prayer to heaven for her boss.

So, Zach was home after all. He was plainly still upset after the meeting last night.

She sent a half-smile towards Mrs. Beale at her actions. Zach probably needed all the encouragement he could get right now.

As she thought of her husband's black mood, tension built in Cassie's shoulders. She caught herself glancing uneasily over her shoulder.

She expelled a breath and said. "I'll bring him some coffee. Maybe that will help cheer him up."

"Okay good." Mrs. Beale handed her the coffee mugs. Turning she walked down the hallway, trying to remember which room was Zach's office.

At the sound of papers fluttering, Cassie pushed on a door that was slightly ajar.

Stepping inside, she stopped when she saw Zach. He ran one hand through his hair making it more disheveled than it already was as he looked at the scattered papers on his desk.

At the squeak of the door, he sighed in exasperation. Turning his eyes widened when Zach saw her.

Cassie spoke quickly. "I've come with coffee. Maybe it will bring cheer to your morning."

He just stared at her as she walked towards him and handed him the coffee mug.

Taking it, he took a sip. "Thanks. As usual Mrs. Beale makes the best coffee." He set it on the countertop behind him, before he turned to her.

"I'm afraid I'm not very good company right now." Zach's tone was as cool as the blue eyes that appraised her.

"Yeah, your cook warned me about that. It's why she sent me to bring your coffee instead of coming herself." Cassie sent him a half-smile and studied him.

Zach's eyes glittered as he stared at her. "You're willing to brave the lion's den, are you?"

She chewed on her lower lip and stole a look at him. "Yes." After a moment's hesitation, she added. "I think your bark is worse than your bite."

He peered at her intently for a moment. She swallowed tightly as he moved to step close to her.

She couldn't tear her gaze from his handsome face. Even as she froze her senses leapt to life.

With one hand he touched the length of her ponytail before his features softened visibly. "You happen to be right. Mrs. Beale was correct in her guess that seeing my lovely wife would put me in a better mood."

Her heart thumped erratically and a rush of pink stained her cheeks at his words.

Suddenly he removed his hand and stepped back, turning towards the papers on his desk once more.

Forcing a casualness she wasn't feeling, Cassie stepped close to him and looked at the scattered papers. "So, what are you looking at so intently this morning?"

Zach gave her a sidelong glance of surprise. "You really want to know?"

"Of course."

He pointed at the large document in the middle of his desk. "This is the blueprint I had drawn up for the expansion of the Marina." He pointed at the connecting lines on the page. "This is where Walker's Cove Marina expands into a Resort."

Cassie followed his fingers as he explained the drawings. "It is so detailed. I can visualize it all coming together in my mind's eye. I'm excited for you. So all you need is to begin building right?"

She turned to see Zach shaking her head.

"I wish it were that easy." He ran a hand through his hair and his jaw tightened. "After last night's meeting, it looks like I might not get the approval needed for this project."

"I think you will."

"Well, you must be seeing the situation from a whole different viewpoint than what I do."

Aware of his frustration, Cassie tried to coax him into a better mood. "Well, I understand that there were a few folks who stood against your ideas, but Widow Crandell spoke passionately in favor of you and your plan to expand the Marina into a Resort. Not to mention, that you knocked it out of the park when you shared your own heartfelt stories."

"You think so?"

"Fishing for compliments, Mr. Stevenson?" Cassie teased as she peered at him with a merry twinkle in her eyes.

He shrugged, his blue eyes sparkling with mischief. "Maybe."

She enjoyed the gentle sparring between them as much as he did, but she sensed that some of his dark shadows still remained.

Determined to try to cheer him up, she spoke quickly. "I have an idea that will help inspire a change in perspective."

Zach lifted his eyebrow in challenge. "What's that?"

She broke into a wide smile. "Let's go sailing."

Suddenly, Cassie grabbed his hand tugging gently. "Let's spend some time enjoying the lake. It will be good for both of us."

His tight expression relaxed into a smile. "You might be onto something. Alright, let's do it."

Cassie rushed to her room to grab her sunhat, before hurrying across the lawn to the long pier where Zach was beginning to loosen the rope that tied the sailboat to the pier.

"Ready?" An easy smile played at the corners of his mouth as he reached out his hand.

"Yes." She nodded with a happy glow of contentment.

With one hand she held the hat on her head and with the other she slipped her hand into his.

There was a tingling in the pit of her stomach at his touch.

He was so disturbing to her in every way. But she couldn't help herself. She wanted to spend more time with her husband and get closer to him.

"The wind is perfect for sailing." Zach started the sailboat and unfurled the sails.

"Is this sailboat one of your own designs, Zach?" She watched how smoothly the sails were hoisted, impressed with how seamlessly the boat handled on the water.

"Yeah. I've continued to tweak it, but this is basically the original design." He looked at her with a seemingly hesitant smile. "Do you like it?"

Cassie grinned. "I love it. You are a very gifted boat designer and builder."

"Thanks. My dad inspired my interest in boat design and building." His gaze seemed far away somehow as he looked across the water.

Cassie knew his dad passed away when he was younger, but didn't know much more than that.

"How did your dad inspire you, Zach?" Cassie saw the unspoken pain glowing in his eyes and longed to know more.

Hesitantly he shared a little of himself. "When I was six

years old, my dad began teaching me how to make little wooden boats. Every year at the start of summer, we would have a little race between my brothers, my dad and I."

Something was flickering far back in his eyes as Zach remembered. "My dad was always so patient with me, even with all my mistakes as I built each boat. We did it year after year. Each boat I made got a little better."

"I remember when I was nine years old, that summer I figured out a new design and I built my boat so it went faster than it ever had. I raced my dad and my four brothers and I beat them all. I was excited and was really looking forward to the races we would have the following summer."

Zach's voice turned raw and hoarse. "But it wasn't to be, because my father died the next year, before we could race our boats together again."

Cassie swallowed hard and bit back tears as she listened to Zach's heart wrenching story.

Stepping closer to him, she tucked her hand in his arm leaning slightly against him, doing her best to offer him comfort.

"I'm so sorry you lost your dad at such a young age, Zach." Cassie whispered softly as she absorbed his pain.

He slipped his arm around her waist and pulled her close, kissing the top of her head. "Thanks. It was one of the most difficult things I've had to face in my life. But you know how it feels, because your father died when you were a young as well."

Cassie nodded. "Yeah. It was very painful. It felt like losing the one friend who loved me and stood by me no matter what." She paused remembering. "I went sailing with my Dad on Saturdays whenever the weather was good enough for us to go on the water."

"We have that in common. I loved to go on the sailboat with my dad. We had an old sailboat, but it worked and it was fun. He loved being on the water. Dad would take us boys on the motorboat too. He loved going fast. In fact, he insisted that we all join him to stay for the motorboat races every Fourth of July."

Zach stopped talking suddenly and she could feel a trembling in his arm as it encircled her waist.

She lifted her head so she could look at him. His blue eyes glistened with unshed tears.

"Oh Zach, I'm so sorry about what happened to Koda."

"It's okay. I'm fine, it was years ago."

She could sense Zach closing off his deepest feelings and she was determined to not let that happen.

"Zach, please talk to me. Your best friend died. It's not fine. I'm asking you to share what you're thinking. Share what you're feeling. Share what happened to your best friend. Please?" Cassie reached up and touched a hand to his cheek, needing him to look into her eyes.

He turned to look at her and swallowed, his blue eyes dark with pain.

"Talk to me." Cassie urged.

He reached up and covered her hand that lay against his cheek, and leaned his cheek into the palm of her hand for a moment before slowly nodding.

Clasping her hand tightly, he brought her close to his side. There was a faraway look in his eyes.

A brief shiver of awareness rippled through her at Zach's gesture, feeling closer to him than she ever had.

She squeezed his hand and her heart swelled with a great sense of devotion to this man who was her fake husband.

§

ZACH HESITATED A MOMENT.

So many raw emotions swept through him as the memories that had haunted him for years came back in full force.

Squaring his jaw in determination, he began. "I was friends with Koda Lightfoot since the day his family moved from Hawaii to our small town."

"When Koda and I began our middle school years, we became friends almost from day one. We both loved math and science classes and had fun working on science experiments together. We even had a couple of small explosions along the way, if I recall." He chuckled softly at the memory.

Cassie smiled softly. "I can picture the two of you having fun and causing trouble in middle school."

Zach nodded. "Yep, that was the two of us. Because we spent so much time together, it didn't take us long to discover we both loved boats and just being on the water."

"So, it wasn't that big of a surprise when Koda's dad gave him an old motorboat for his fourteenth birthday. It worked, but it just wasn't up to the same standards as some of the newer motorboats. My motorboat wasn't new either, but I had saved my money for two years so I could get a newer used motorboat."

He sighed. "But it was when we were both fourteen that each of us finally got our very own motorboats. It was a real highlight for both of us. We would spend as much time as we could out on the water, usually speeding back and forth between the two-mile distance from the Marina to Rocky Crag Point."

"By the time we were fifteen years old, we were serious about racing our motorboats. That summer we decided since we were too young to race in the adult Fourth of July races, we would create our own race for teenagers only. And we did. We even had four other teenagers who joined us that year."

"Sounds like fun."

Zach smiled. "We did have a lot of fun. However, things changed the summer we turned sixteen. When Koda first took his boat on the water that summer, I told him we should get the mechanic at the Marina to take a look at it because something wasn't working right."

"So, Koda asked Ben Mathers, the mechanic, to look at the engine. After inspecting the boat, Ben was convinced all it needed was a good cleaning. So that's what he did."

"After the boat's engine was cleaned, it sounded better, but I could tell something still wasn't quite right. In fact, I told Koda that we should just forget about racing that year because I didn't think his boat was in good enough shape." Zach sighed heavily.

"But Koda insisted. Once he got his heart set on something, it was almost impossible to change his mind. So, the Fourth of July arrived and Koda and I and two other friends got our boats all fuelled up and ready to go. We took our boats from the Marina to the starting place and when a guy brought the flag down for us to go, we each took off like a shot."

"It was exhilarating and fun, until we neared Rocky Crag Point and suddenly, I turned and saw the black smoke coming out of Koda's boat. The smoke looked like it was coming from where the engine was located. I waved at him to stop the boat, but he just shook his head and pointed to Rocky Crag's Point. It was his way of telling me, he would stop when he got there, but not before."

"I remember thinking, why doesn't he just stop and we can figure out what the problem is and fix it? We could always race another day."

Zach shuddered.

Horrible pictures flashed across his mind as he relived what happened years ago. "Next thing I knew, a loud explosion blasted through the air. I turned in shock to see flames surrounding Koda's boat."

"Just as I swung my boat around to try to rescue my friend, his boat exploded again and the fire got larger and larger, until the boat began to sink." Zach choked out the last few words. Regret and guilt flooded over him again as he remembered.

He looked down at Cassie and saw her violet eyes clouded with tears.

"I'm so sorry that you lost your best friend, Zach." Cassie looked up at him and her heart ached at the haunted expression on his face. "That wasn't easy to talk about. Thank you for telling me."

He pulled her close and kissed the top of her head.

"Since I first explained what happened to the police years ago, I've never shared that story with anyone else."

"Then I feel extra special that you shared it with me." Cassie leaned against Zach, hearing his accelerated heartbeat. "Did they investigate what happened to Koda's boat that day?"

"Yeah, but all the explanation they gave was that the boat was old. Those old motorboats, the fuel lines were often problems, which meant that explosions happened more frequently back then."

"With Koda's old motorboat the fuel line caught fire and the explosion happened so suddenly that he didn't have a chance." Zach ran a hand through his hair and he bit his lip, determined not to give in to his emotions. "But the fact remains, it's my fault that Koda died."

"No Zach, it's not your fault. Why would you even think that was true?"

His sorrow was a huge painful knot inside.

"Because if I would have insisted that we didn't race that day, Koda would still be alive now." His voice broke miserably and regret clung to him like an old wound that had never healed.

A crease formed between Cassie's brows as she digested his words. "If your friend was headstrong as you say, even if you had stopped him that day, most likely he would have found another way to race his motorboat."

Zach sighed heavily. "I take your meaning and yes, my logical mind tells me that Koda could have died another way. Yet, my heart is filled with guilt and regret at what actually happened that day years ago and my part in it."

Cassie squeezed his hand. "I understand." She ran

gentle fingers over his hand and he felt comforted by her presence.

After a moment's pause, she spoke again. "Now that I have a better understanding of what happened all those years ago, I can't help but remember what Koda's father asked you to do. Have you had a chance to read your friend's journal?"

Zach swallowed the lump that lingered in his throat. "No, I haven't read Koda's journal. It seems too difficult to revisit that painful time in my life."

He didn't want to tell her that Koda's journal sat on his night table ever since they returned from Hawaii. He saw it there, but was too afraid to open it for what he'd find there.

She squeezed his hand and her violet eyes shone with a gentle compassion as she whispered. "I can't imagine the deep pain and heartache you've gone through, Zach."

"But, I can't help but feel that there is something important waiting for you as you read your friend's journal. Makoa seemed confident that you would find a new understanding of his son between the pages of his journal."

Zach pondered his wife's words. She had a gentle way of speaking that had the ability to break down the barriers that had surrounded his heart for years.

He didn't like this chipping away at the walls he'd encased his heart in, but perhaps she was right.

It was time.

"You might be right. I'll begin reading it." Zach didn't know what he'd just agreed to, but hoped with all his heart that he wouldn't regret it.

His wife nodded. "I believe you'll be glad you did, Zach."

Zach doubted it, but didn't want to burst the bubble of confidence he saw in her upturned face.

He grimaced, desperate to change the subject. "Well, we should be getting home." He turned the sailboat so it was facing home. "I have a lot of work still to get done today. Are you ready for the benefit gala tomorrow night?"

"Sort of. Your mom called and invited me for lunch and shopping tomorrow. She told me to tell you, we would meet you at the charity event."

Zach grinned. "Good. Mom just wants to get to know you and will love the opportunity to spend my money."

"Oh, I don't…"

"Cassie, don't tell me you don't need a new dress. Shopping with my mom will be a great way for you to get to know each other better."

"Most likely grandmother will join you two as well. I'm happy for you to get to know the two women in my life who mean the world to me." Zach slowed the sailboat to a stop as they reached the pier.

"Then, I'll look forward to it even more." She whispered. "Thanks for today Zach. I'm glad we could spend time together."

Zach tied the rope from the sailboat to the pier, anchoring it firmly in place.

As he reached a hand to help Cassie from the boat, he thought about their day together and was astonished at the sense of fulfillment he felt at being together with his wife.

Pulling her close to him, he whispered. "Me too." He looked into her large violet colored eyes that peered up at him intently as if trying to learn him by heart.

He was captured by her innocence and felt powerless to resist her.

Leaning down, his lips pressed against hers and gently covered her mouth. His mouth moved over hers, devouring its softness, the sweetness of who she was.

Zach couldn't put it into words, but he knew his heart was opening more and more to this woman. She was gentle, compassionate and kind. She was everything he wanted in a wife.

Maybe their fake arrangement could become real. Just the thought of it, excited and scared him all at the same time.

He was falling in love with his wife.

For the first time he was with a woman he adored and he never wanted this to end.

CHAPTER ELEVEN

CASSIE WALKED ALONG THE BEACH, smiling as she thought about her time together sailing with Zach.

The way he'd pulled her into his arms and given her that toe-curling kiss after they stepped off the boat still brought a dreamy smile to her face.

Her lips still tingled at the memory.

Cocoa barked loudly and tugged on the leash interrupting the sweet memory.

A nearby sandpiper bird jerked its small body, scared at the sound, and instead of resuming its quick dance along the beach, flew away.

"Cocoa, be still." Cassie spoke firmly, grateful when her dog listened and sat on her haunches.

It had taken many hours of consistently training the

brown golden retriever rescue dog, but in the end it had paid off. Now her dog listened without hesitation.

With one hand, she gently ran a hand down the chocolate colored fur from Cocoa's head to her neck. Her dog sat still enjoying all the attention.

Cassie looked up and when she saw the coast was clear from birds and other distractions, she gently urged her dog forward, eager to get home.

She was just returning from seeing Uncle Gus. She stopped by the cottage to spend a little time with him this afternoon. Uncle Gus was feeling a little better everyday and she was so thankful.

Part of the reason her uncle was doing so well was because her thoughtful husband had paid for a live-in nurse to take care of him.

Cassie had so many reasons to be thankful for her husband. She truly was grateful for him, even though she was confused about where she stood with him.

When they returned from Hawaii, he had seemed to do all he could to keep his distance from her. But this morning when they went sailing, she sensed he wanted to develop a new closeness together.

It was the same yearning in her heart. She longed for theirs to become a real marriage, but wasn't sure if that would happen.

Cassie was so deep in thought, that she didn't notice the two girls until her dog barked.

"Hush, Cocoa." Looking up, she spotted Addy and Olivia walking towards her on the trail that led from the lakeside restaurant to the Walker's Cove Marina.

Both girls were dressed in royal blue dresses with

flared mini-skirts. Each dress had a white collar around the neck area, white cuffs on the short sleeves and a white apron with lace around the edges.

"Hi, Addy and Olivia. I see you two are wearing brightly colored matching dresses. Where are you off to?" Cassie had a fairly good idea of where they were going, but she wanted to hear it from them.

She noticed the girls glance at each other quickly, before Addy turned to look at Cassie with wide eyes.

"We got new jobs working evenings on *The Violet Diamond.*" Addy seemed to stumble over her words. "We like it well enough. It pays better than the restaurant."

Olivia shrugged. "It's a job."

Cassie couldn't help but notice the two girls didn't seem very excited about it. In fact, both of them looked a little skittish and nervous.

The smaller girl Olivia fidgeted with her dress and that's when she saw it. There was a purple bruise on her arm.

A wave of apprehension coursed through her. Before she could hold back, she stepped closer and slowly reached out a hand to look at her arm.

Olivia flinched.

"I'm sorry, Olivia. I just saw that your arm was bruised. Being Doc's niece, I can't seem to help myself from noticing when people are hurt." She smiled slightly, hoping to ease the girls' skittishness. "How did that happen?"

"I banged into something at our apartment." Olivia shrugged, her words stumbling and unsure.

"Yeah, she accidentally walked into the bathroom

door." Addy grabbed her friend's hand. "Sometimes she's clumsy that way."

Cassie had her doubts that they were telling her what really happened.

Both girls looked into the distance toward the yacht where they were supposed to work.

Addy swallowed and ran her hands down her waitress uniform nervously.

Cassie caught the gesture and turned to look in the distance, where she saw Emery Jakes, her stepmother's boyfriend, waiting at the entrance his arms crossed over his chest.

There was no smile on his features and she could see his unfriendly stare even at this distance. Memories returned of the way he used to ogle her when he came to the house after her father died, and she shuddered.

"We need to get going or we'll be late for work." Addy spoke hurriedly. "It was nice to see you Cassie — er, Mrs. Stevenson. See you later."

Cassie turned to look at the girls, still in a daze at seeing Emery Jakes watching them. "Yes of course. It was nice seeing you girls too. And be careful, okay?" They nodded and hurried away towards the yacht.

Her stomach churned in anxiety and frustration as she watched the girls walk away.

Turning, she thought of their conversation and a foreboding filled her. Those girls were jittery and nervous to talk to her. The bruise on Olivia's arm gave her more cause for concern. Were they telling her the truth, that it was an accident that happened at their apartment?

She wondered because both girls seemed scared when

they answered her questions. The more she thought about the teenagers, the more troubled she became.

As she walked the rest of the way home, she made a decision to talk to Zach about her concerns.

&

"CASSIE, you don't know how I've been waiting to get to know you better." Eliza Stevenson sat across the table from her.

Sitting on her right hand side was Catherine Stevenson. Cassie was nestled in on both sides of the table by Zach's mother and grandmother.

"I'm so pleased you invited me to lunch." Cassie replied with a warm smile to her mother-in-law. "I'm happy to get to know both of you better too."

"Well, it seems my grandson has been too busy since your wedding to bring you to us, so we could really get to know you, my dear. But you'll find that us Stevenson women have our ways of getting what we want anyway." Catherine winked at her.

Cassie giggled. The more she got to know them, the more she liked these two strong women in Zach's life.

"I'm glad." Cassie took a sip of her tea, thinking of the shopping spree they had been on together. "Thank you for helping me find a dress to wear to tonight's benefit gala."

"Oh my dear, we were happy that we could go shopping together. Zach is going to love that violet colored gown on you. It makes your eyes stand out and you look beautiful." Eliza smiled.

Her mother-in-law's smile lines beside her blue eyes

deepened, adding even more beauty to her face. Cassie could see Zach in her mother-in-law's matching blue eyes — the humor, generosity and kindness — these were all traits that Zach had inherited.

As the waiter came to take the lunch plates away, Eliza sipped her tea before she asked. "Tell us a little about yourself, Cassie. Zach mentioned that you love art."

"I do love art." Cassie smiled thinking of their recent visit to the Art Museum. "Zach gifted me a beautiful piece of art by DaVinci when we were in Hawaii. The woman in the painting speaks to me of the importance of under-standing who you are and becoming all you were meant to be."

Cassie smiled softly, picturing the large painting that hung on her bedroom wall. "It's something that I've really needed in my life."

"Well, I certainly understand that." Eliza wiped her lips with the napkin and gazed thoughtfully out the window beside their table before looking back at Cassie.

"I went through a time of not knowing who I was and not liking who I was. This was before I met Zach's father, Daniel Stevenson." Eliza sighed at the memory.

"It was the most difficult time in my life. My mother was ill and my stepfather was either on drugs or drunk much of the time. We were struggling to pay the bills and on top of that, I was personally confused about life."

"I'm sorry." She was surprised by Eliza's story and it had the strange effect of making her feel closer to her mother-in-law.

"It's okay. The love of family helped me heal." She looked over at Catherine with a warm smile. "And now I have a chance to help my daughter." Zach's mom reached over and squeezed her hand.

"I'm glad you're in the process of becoming who you were meant to be, Cassie. I'm also thrilled that my son gave you that painting. Sometimes we need reminders in our everyday lives of who we are and our purpose."

"Yes, that's true. Zach's generous gift has reminded me of that everyday."

Eliza nodded solemnly. "He's always been generous with a compassionate heart, especially to those he loves. Lately whenever I talk with Zach, he mentions little details about you and where you've been together and what you're up to. I can tell you are very important to him."

Cassie swallowed. Her mother-in-law didn't know of course that her son had no such feelings for her. She didn't know that theirs was a fake marriage. But, Eliza's words made Cassie long for her husband to love her, all the same.

Her longing for a family came back in full force, but she did her best push those feelings back down. It was no use to hope for something that would never happen.

Catherine set down her teacup and spoke softly. "There was a time in Zach's life when he lost his way and who he truly was."

Eliza nodded and sighed heavily. "Yes, that's true. When his friend Koda died in that tragic motorboat acci- dent, it was one of the hardest times in his life."

"But, Zach did discover a few years later his passion for designing and building motorboats with better safety. I believe that was inspired by the death of his friend. In fact, recently we were so proud when our son announced his newest line of motorboat design which Zach named after his friend Koda."

Cassie digested this bit of information. "We ran into Koda's father when we were in Hawaii. He said he was planning on coming to Paradise Lake's motor boat races on the Fourth of July."

"Wouldn't that be nice? But if Mr. Lightfoot is hoping to see Zach race again, he'll be disappointed. Zach hasn't entered any sort of boat race, ever since his best friend died in that accident all those years ago."

A furrow formed between her brows. It seemed there were deep wounds in Zach that hadn't healed.

"I'm sorry about that." Cassie sighed heavily.

Eliza's blue eyes clung to hers. "I am too. Ever since that tragic accident he's held everyone at arm's length. He's been scared to get too close, even to those he loves. Zach needs a woman who will be patient with him and love him through all the pain of his past."

Her mother-in-law's eyes shimmered with emotion. "However, I feel now that you've married my son, all your love for Zach will work miracles inside him. It will be like a healing balm to chase away the pain."

"I hope you're right." Cassie whispered offering a hopeful smile to her mother-in-law even though deep inside she had fears and doubts that anything would change in their relationship.

Cassie was still thinking about Eliza Stevenson's words a few hours later when she walked into the large ballroom at the Benefit Gala.

Looking around the large room that was filled almost

to capacity, Cassie suddenly grew nervous. As she continued to walk by people she looked for Zach, finally spotting him talking with his grandfather and brothers.

Adam whispered in Zach's ear, and her husband turned to her with a large grin.

Walking up to her, he placed his hand gently on her waist and kissed her cheek.

His warm breath tickled her ear as he whispered. "You are without a doubt the most beautiful woman here tonight. That deep violet colored evening dress makes your eyes shine like diamonds."

Heat rose up her neck to her cheeks at his compliment. She couldn't help but be pleased by his words of praise.

"Thank you, Zach. I'm happy you like it. As soon as your mom saw this dress she said, *"You must have this dress."* Cassie smiled brightly.

"It seems I will need to thank my mom for her impeccable taste." Zach slid his hand around her waist, pulling her close to his side. "I think I'm going to keep you close the whole evening, so no other man here tries to ask you for a dance."

Cassie blushed again, flattered by his possessiveness. She felt like she was seeing a whole new side of Zach she didn't know existed.

As the M.C. announced that dinner would be served soon, Zach led her to a large round table where the Stevenson family was gathered.

"Cassie, you look beautiful." Bella stood and pulled Cassie into a light hug.

"Yes, you do. I think I'm jealous that you can wear that color. Violet just doesn't go with my red hair." Razelle had her long auburn hair pulled onto her head and wore a deep green velvet colored gown that suited her warm toned skin well.

"My friend, you look gorgeous in green." Cassie hugged Razelle and then Elle and Rory.

Eliza and Catherine were already seated, their heads together in deep conversation.

Soon, Cassie was seated with Zach on one side and Eliza on the other.

"So, Zach it's less than two weeks until the Walker's Cove Marina's Fourth of July annual celebration. Are you ready for the big day?" William Stevenson eyed his grandson with a mischievous look in his eyes.

"Not hardly. Still planning the activities. There are always families and children that show up for the event. We want to make sure everyone feels included. Although, it's coming along. Will you be joining us, Granddad?"

"Your Grandmother and I wouldn't miss it for the world. The Marina's annual Fourth of July celebration is the highlight of the summer as far as I'm concerned." Granddad grinned and slid his arm around his wife's shoulders, pulling her close to his side.

Catherine Stevenson turned to her husband, and smiled warmly as his eyes caught and held hers.

Cassie watched the closeness of their relationship. They had been married fifty-four years and it looked like they were more in love now than ever.

She sighed.

Zach turned to her. "That sigh sounded like you were deep in thought. What are you thinking?"

Her cheeks warmed at Zach's penetrating look. "I was

just thinking how wonderful it is that your Granddad and Grandmom are so in love even after all these years."

"Yeah. It's a great example for each of us grandsons." Zach looked at his grandparents with a smile of satisfaction.

"It's rare nowadays to see marriages last that long, but it's inspiring for sure." Cassie blushed as he looked at her, with a smile that broadened in approval.

A part of her revelled in his open admiration of her, even though she continued to remind herself not to get too attached to her husband.

With his look she felt a bottomless sense of peace and contentment.

She felt a warm glow flow through her and decided she wasn't going to think of all of the things that could possibly go wrong. No, tonight she decided there would be no shadows across her heart.

They enjoyed dinner together as a family. After dessert the announcer said they would open the floor for dancing before they introduced the speakers for the evening.

Zach reached out a hand. "My lady, may I have this dance?"

"You may, kind sir." Cassie placed her hand in his large one and he steadied her as she stood to her feet.

Her husband pulled her close as the music to a waltz began. She looked up at him sure her heart was in her eyes.

"This is perfect." He whispered into her hair and his hands slipped her arms around his neck, pulling her closer.

Her head fit perfectly in the hollow between his

shoulder and neck and she relaxed, sinking into his cushioning embrace.

Warm tingles zigzagged from where his fingers touched her back, ricocheting all the way to her heart.

Their dance was almost over when the flash of a camera caught her off guard. She stumbled in Zach's arms.

"I think someone just took a picture of us." Cassie looked around and noticed a man with a camera weaving his way in and out of the crowded ballroom.

"As much as I dislike having my picture taken when I'm unaware, maybe this time we'll let it go. People take all sorts of photos at these types of charity events." Zach looked around the room.

Cassie gaze followed the man until he was out of sight. Turning, she looked at the people around them.

She inhaled a sudden breath. "I see my stepmother. What is she doing here?"

Zach turned to see Larissa White, before turning back to Cassie. He grabbed both of her shaky hands. "Someone who is on the invitation list to this charity gala must have invited her as their guest."

"As long as she doesn't cause trouble, I guess she can stay." He leaned closer. "I will protect you, try not to worry so much."

She nodded and exhaled a heavy sigh. Lately, it was disturbing how many times her stepmother seemed to show up in the same places that Cassie found herself.

Zach turned back to her, his jaw still clenched in determination. He seemed to force himself to relax.

Without warning, his rogue smile returned and as his blue eyes peered intently at her, he kissed the back of her hand and whispered. "I could dance all evening with you. But that will have to wait until next time."

"I look forward to it." A thoughtful smile curved her mouth and she was very afraid that her husband could see the deepest longings of her heart in her eyes.

Needing a moment's break from the emotional rollercoaster she was feeling this evening, she whispered. "I need to go to the little girls' room. But I'll meet you back at the family table soon."

"Alright, Cassie. Don't be gone long." Zach squeezed her hand before she walked away.

Cassie's skin prickled pleasurably as she walked towards the washroom.

Being close to Zach was like a drug, lulling her into euphoria that she never wanted to end.

She was still sighing happily as she stepped into the washroom, but stopped suddenly when she came face to face with the one person she had hoped to avoid.

Her stepmother.

"Here you are Cassie." Larissa's dark eyes looked up and down her outfit, landing on her face. "Well, I must say, if you were hoping that new designer dress you're wearing would help you fit in with the Stevenson family, I'm afraid I must be the one to tell you, that plan completely failed. Personally, I think you looked better in those baggy, frumpy clothes you used to wear."

Cassie's back stiffened and suddenly she was desperate to get away. "If all you want to do is criticize and insult me, I'm leaving."

Larissa quickly moved to block the exit door. "Not yet. There is one more thing we need to discuss."

Her stepmother gave her an icy stare. "Zach Stevenson and I are both competing for that waterfront property zoning permit. You need to tell your husband to back off."

"Why would I tell Zach to do that? He's wanted to expand his great-grandfather's Marina into a resort for years."

Larissa leaned closer, and spoke in a soft menacing tone. "Because if you don't, you'll be very sorry."

Suddenly, terrible memories of living under her stepmother's thumb came flooding back.

She wondered what horrible things Larissa was planning this time. But now that she was older and married to Zach, Cassie told herself she was going to stop cowering in fear.

"Don't start making threats again like you used to, Larissa." Cassie spoke with determination, even though her legs felt weak from fear.

Even though a familiar fear tried to force her to cower at her stepmother's threats, she was determined not to give in this time. "This time I'm not going to listen."

Unexpectedly, a woman pushed her way into the washroom despite Larissa's effort to hold the door.

Cassie saw her way of escape and took it.

Larissa called after her. "You'll be sorry, you didn't do as I asked, Cassie. Real sorry."

Despite her stepmother's threats, Cassie left the washroom and made her way back to the Stevenson family's table.

Still shaken from her stepmother's threats, Cassie sat down and forced herself to breathe normally.

Zach leaned closer giving her a probing look, but she

simply gave him a small smile. He reached over and held her hand, rubbing his thumb along her soft skin. The gentle circular motion had a calming effect on her.

Cassie decided she would tell Zach about Larissa's threats later on. Right now, she would do her best to enjoy her evening.

Zach's brother Gabe was introducing the next person to speak. Cassie recognized Cindi standing behind the podium.

She remembered Cindi was one of the girls that had been taken by Sloane and his gang when she worked at the homeless camp with Razelle trying to help free them from Sloane's influence.

Tonight, Cindi stood with the microphone in one hand, sharing her story of how she was rescued from human traffickers.

"So, once they took me from the homeless camp, they blindfolded me and put me in a windowless van." Cindi shuddered and paused for a moment before continuing.

"After a few days we finally arrived at our destination — which I found out later was Detroit. The hotel they took us to was a run down, dingy sort of place in the seediest neighborhood in the city."

Her hand shook as she continued. "There were many teenagers and even some children in the hotel and everyone was forced to do what amounted to slave labor."

"Long hours working grunge work and whoever didn't do something right would go without food for a day. The group of teenage girls that I was part of were also forced to do unspeakable things with our jailers and their friends."

She shuddered and swallowed back emotion. Her voice was raw when she continued. "I was rescued by a police raid at the hotel a couple weeks later."

"I discovered later, the reason I was found is because my friends didn't give up on me. I was lucky enough to be able to stay at the Stevenson Safe House where understanding doctors helped me heal from pain and trauma."

Cindi looked at Razelle and Luke and at Cassie and nodded. "I'm so grateful. Because some people helped to free me from the hands of oppressors, now I get to spend a bunch of time speaking up for others who can't speak for themselves."

"Tonight, I hope everyone will donate something to this very worthy cause of freeing helpless and innocent people from human trafficking."

As the crowd broke out into applause, Cassie was proud of Cindi for being brave enough to share her story.

There were a few more speakers sharing their stories and then the evening was over.

After Cassie and Zach said goodnight to the rest of the Stevenson family, they walked to his car.

While Zach opened the door he turned to her. "You look worried. Did something happen tonight?"

She sat in the passenger side of the care, her fingers tensed in her lap as he sat down on the driver's side.

With one hand he reached over to cover her clammy hands with his warm one.

"Talk to me, Cassie."

At his urging, she told Zach what happened with her stepmother. "She told me if I didn't somehow convince you to back away from your plans to expand the Marina into a Resort — and thereby making it real easy for Larissa to get that area rezoned for what she wants — that I'd be real sorry."

To her dismay her voice broke slightly. She was so tired of always needing to find a way to evade her stepmother.

"Hey, look at me." Zach put gentle fingers under her chin and turned her head so she was looking his way. "Don't be afraid. I will do everything I can to see to it you are safe."

Cassie chewed on her lower lip and stole a look at him. "I told her I wasn't playing her game, but I can't help but be afraid. What if she hurts someone we care about?"

"I'll admit to being concerned about that myself. But, I have a retired Navy SEAL friend who is also my Private Investigator. I'm going to call him and ask him to investigate your stepmother and her boyfriend. If anyone can find some answers, it's Zeke Forrester." Zach took charge with a quiet assurance.

Her husband's confidence and determination encouraged her not to give up. Somehow this time her stepmother and boyfriend's evil schemes would be stopped.

"Thanks, Zach. I feel better knowing that." She looked up, flashing a smile of thanks.

An easy smile played at the corners of his mouth as he leaned close. "You're welcome."

Then Zach's lips brushed against hers. The kiss only lasted for seconds, but it was a delicious sensation that overwhelmed her senses. When he suddenly lifted his lips from hers, she was left wanting more.

As her husband drove home, she couldn't help but think of the evening with Zach and his family.

A delicious warmth flowed through her veins. She felt so happy surrounded by Zach and his family. She felt accepted, safe and loved.

All the things she yearned for she'd found in the Stevenson family.

She longed for the love of family. She longed for the love of a mother and grandparents. She longed for the love of her husband.

A small sigh escaped her lips. Would it ever happen to her for real? She loved being with Zach, but she knew their agreement was only for one year.

He kissed her and whispered wonderful sweet words in her ear, but none of that was real or was it?

She couldn't seem to get a true sense of where she stood with her husband. How did he really feel about her?

It seemed that he gave her too much of everything but himself.

She yearned for more. She longed to be truly loved by her husband.

Cassie was astonished at the depth of her own feelings for Zach. It was an awakening feeling that left her reeling.

She truly did love him.

Knowing that meant that when the day came for each of them to go their separate ways the pain would be all the more difficult to bear.

CHAPTER TWELVE

ach

ZACH TURNED into the driveway of Walker's Cove Marina the next morning, his thoughts still on last night's benefit gala and dancing with his lovely wife.

As he parked his truck and started walking towards the large building that held the store and offices, his gut tightened as he recalled Cassie's stepmother and her threats.

Enough was enough. There had to be a way to stop whatever horrible scheme she had planned.

Taking out his smartphone he dialled his Private Investigator.

"Hey Zeke, this is Zach Stevenson."

"Good to hear from you. How are things?" Zeke's voice sounded out of breath.

"Good, but I do have a problem I need your help with." Zach grinned at the short breaths on the other side of the phone line. "Did I catch you at a bad time?"

"Nah. Just working out. Gotta keep in shape so I can catch the bad guys."

Zach chuckled. "You are one of the most fit people I know."

"Good. I aim to stay that way. So, you were saying you had a problem that needed to be solved. What's the trouble?"

Zeke had a way of getting straight to the point. Being a former Navy SEAL, he was a man who took action right away. That was a character trait Zach appreciated.

"Well, my wife's stepmother has started to threaten her and I'd like her to stop. But I thought it might be prudent to do a little digging first."

"Yeah, that is a good idea. What's the stepmother's name?" Zeke questioned and Zach could hear scratching sounds in the background.

Zach was troubled by the boyfriend as well, even though he wasn't as outspoken as Larissa. "If you could also do a little digging into the background of her boyfriend, Emery Jakes, that would be helpful."

"Sure thing. I'll let you know soon what I find out."

"Thanks, Zeke. Talk soon." Zach disconnected the call and walked into his office at Walker's Cove Marina.

With that phone call out of the way, Zach felt relieved. Hopefully, any new information Zeke uncovered would finally put an end to Larissa White's bullying tactics against his wife.

Sitting down at his office desk, he pulled out the large

pad of paper he'd been using to sketch out ideas for the upcoming Fourth of July celebration at the Marina.

Scanning the paper, he noticed the family friendly games they had planned for the children. Then there were the sailboat races scheduled for the morning and the fireworks for late evening.

Without warning, a memory flashed across his mind of racing with Koda in their motorboats during the Marina's annual July fourth celebration. Without fail, the next image that hit his subconscious was seeing his best friend's boat explode.

Zach's belly clenched in a fist and the pain in his heart became a sick and fiery gnawing. The same torment he had every time he thought of how his friend died.

Regret and guilt twisted and turned inside him. He still believed he was at fault for Koda's death.

Zach had stopped participating in all motorboat races at the Marina years ago because of his friend's accident.

Those motorboat races used to be the highlight of every Fourth of July celebration at Walker's Cove Marina.

When Zach had turned eighteen, he had become an active part of planning the annual Fourth of July event.

He had asked the manager of the Marina to organize the motorboat races, without including him. He didn't want any part of it.

He recalled the new insights he'd learned last night as he began reading Koda's journal.

At Cassie's urging, he had finally begun to read the very personal story his best friend had penned all those years ago.

Rubbing his forehead, Zach recalled Koda's words.

My mom just passed away from breast cancer. I can hardly believe I'm writing these words. She was sick for three years. I watched her go through too much pain, but now her suffering has ended. I'm relieved about that.

Even though in the end my Mom died way too early, the part I'll always remember about her was that she didn't let fear beat her.

She didn't let the Doctor's prognosis define who she was.

Instead, she lived her best life everyday in spite of all the problems she faced everyday.

I want to live my life that way too.

And that's why I'm going to do my best to talk Zach into racing our motorboats in the Marina's Fourth of July celebration.

I know the boat Dad gave me is old and needs a lot of work — but once the mechanic cleans and fixes it — it should be ready to go.

Being on the lake and racing my motorboat makes me feel alive like nothing else ever has. I feel closer to my mom as I fly across the water and feel the wind in my hair. And I'm determined to do that again.

Even if Zach doesn't go along with my idea — I'm still going to race. I have to, because of what I learned from my Mom. She told me: Son, don't let your fears stop you from living life. Even if something painful happens along the way. Learn from it. Sometimes the best thing you can do is get on the horse again after you've been thrown off.

That's what I learned from my Mom who had been kicked down by life more times than I can count. She kept getting back on that horse... and I will too.

Zach sighed heavily.

Makoa Lightfoot had been right when he'd handed him the tattered journal. *"Read my son's journal, Zach. Do it for Koda, Zach. Read it, simply because he would want you to understand him better and to give yourself the opportunity to heal."*

Reading the journal had reminded Zach of how much wisdom his best friend had even at sixteen years old. He'd always seemed more knowledgeable and wiser than any of their other teenage friends.

After reading Koda's journal, Zach realized belatedly that most likely the wisdom found in those pages had been gained from facing so many difficult life situations at such a young age.

He also realized from Koda's words that his friend had been as determined as ever to race his motorboat during the Fourth of July event years ago.

Was Cassie right when she'd said if Zach had stopped Koda that day, his best friend still would have found a way to race his motorboat?

Could it be true that perhaps he wasn't to blame for his best friend's death?

As he ran a shaky hand through his hair, Zach stood up from his chair and began to pace back and forth.

He needed time to think.

Only one thinking place came to mind. It was the one spot hidden from the world, where he'd always gone ever since Grand first brought him to the Marina as a little boy.

Today, he needed it more than ever.

"UNCLE GUS, are you sure you don't need me to stay?" Cassie looked at her beloved uncle, her worry about him creating deep grooves between her brows.

"My dear, I'll be fine. I'm already doing so much better since the surgery a few weeks ago. You don't have to worry about me." Her uncle walked slowly towards where she was painting in the sunroom.

"Besides, Nurse Connor will be here soon and in only a few hours all the guys will be home too. So, you see? I'll be fine."

Cassie rinsed out her paintbrush and set it down, her violet blue eyes gazing intently at her uncle trying to assess whether he was being completely honest with her.

"You'll rest until they arrive home?" Cassie wasn't about to leave anything to chance. She simply couldn't lose someone else she loved. She didn't think she'd survive it.

"I will." Uncle Gus stepped beside her and pulled her into a warm embrace. It was one of those healing kinds of hugs where all the love he had for his niece spilled out of Uncle Gus and into her.

She squeezed him tightly for a moment before finally letting go. "Alright then. But, I want you to know I'll be nearby. I'm just going to my favorite place to paint. I wanted to catch the morning sun in just the right way for this piece."

Cassie had started the painting, but soon sensed that for this particular art piece, she wanted to be in the exact location. "So I won't be far away if you need me."

"And I appreciate that, dear niece." Uncle Gus smiled at her indulgently. "But, selfishly I want to see the final result of this particular painting of yours. I have a feeling this one will be extra meaningful. So, you just go and don't worry about me."

Cassie grinned and gave him one last kiss on the cheek and stepped back. "Alright, I'll go."

Grabbing her paintbrushes and easel she walked to the door. Turning she said. "I'll be back in a couple of hours."

Uncle Gus eased himself into his favorite easy recliner and waved with a smile on his face. "Have fun, my dear."

Cassie whistled for her dog who came eagerly running towards her. She hurried away from the cottage and down the trail that led to the Marina, Cocoa at her side.

As she walked, her thoughts drifted back to dancing in Zach's arms at the charity gala.

Even now, she could still feel his strong arms around her, holding her close. Her lips tingled as she remembered his kisses.

He'd been so attentive and so lover-like she couldn't help but fall a little more in love with her husband.

But falling in love hadn't been part of their agreement for this marriage of convenience.

It was frustrating because she wasn't certain where she stood with him. Zach had never told her he loved her, even though his actions — his passionate kisses and tender embrace — seemed to show he cared for her.

But to be fair, she hadn't told Zach she loved him either.

Sighing heavily, she decided she wasn't going to focus on that right now.

She looked at how the morning sun shimmered across the lake and onto the hidden cove where she stood.

Setting up her easel, she got excited. This was exactly the picture she wanted to paint.

Cocoa was busy pawing in the sand by the lake, while she got things ready.

For a minute she looked around this secluded part of the shore that was farther away from the real busy place where the boats were at the Marina. It was a sheltered and sandy inlet on Paradise Lake that served as a private haven.

Since coming to live with Uncle Gus, there had been many times she would come here and sit for hours on this rocky crag overlooking the lake.

She watched the boats on the lake and loved the sound of the white-capped waves as they hit the rocks below.

Reaching for her paintbrush, she got out her palette and began to mix the paint with just the right color of blue she wanted for the sky.

Cassie had a picture in her mind of what she wanted this picture to look like when it was done.

Her plan was to give this painting to her husband after the Fourth of July celebrations ended at Walker's Cove Marina.

When he looked at the painting, she hoped it would inspire him.

She hoped he would find more of who he was. She hoped he would find the healing and peace he longed for.

Most of all, she hoped he would be aware of how much broader the scope of his safe harbor really was — that it included all the people who loved him… including her.

Just as Zach was about to leave his office, he was jerked back to reality with the loud ringing of his phone.

"Zach Stevenson here." He answered in short sentences, impatient to be gone.

"Wanted to call to let you know I found some photos of you and Cassie." Zeke Forrester was on the other end of the line.

"I discovered the pictures in a few of those shoddy online magazines that publish smear campaigns against celebrities and influential or wealthy people."

"What?" Zach's heart hammered in his chest and his thoughts raced dangerously.

Zeke's discovery of photos of him and his wife, brought back memories that haunted him of his ex-girl-friend's betrayal.

Felicity Kingston had been swayed by the promise of quick cash when she handed over photos of the two of them to a couple of online magazines months ago.

His ex-girlfriend had then tried to lie about it to him.

Along with Felicity's betrayal, came the memory of his dad's death and the woman that spread vicious lies about his Dad and Mom.

Zach's cheeks burned in remembrance of that day and the effects of that day in the weeks that followed.

His mom was too humiliated and embarrassed to be seen anywhere in town for weeks afterwards.

The reminder of that pain still seemed fresh in his mind today. Never again would he allow another person to deceive him or cause hurt to people he loved.

Zeke's findings proved there was another person now who had decided to make money from photos of him.

"What did the photos look like?" He was numb with increasing anger as he waited for an answer.

"Looked like they were mostly pictures of your wedding and maybe one event you attended recently." Zeke replied, his voice calm.

Zach's breath burned in his throat. "I guess that's not a big surprise."

"Not surprising, but I don't know yet where the photos originated from or who sold these photos to the magazines. I'll do some more digging. Just thought you should know." His private investigator was worth his weight in gold for always staying on top of the details.

As Zach thought about who could have taken the pictures, he realized only one person other than himself and their photographer would have access to those wedding photos.

"You can keep digging, but I'm fairly certain I know who is responsible." He replied in a low voice, taut with anger. "Thanks for letting me know, Zeke."

After hanging up the phone, Zach's heart hammered wildly in his chest.

Marching out of his office, he hurried outside knowing he needed time to calm down.

His steps led him to the trail that led to the private rocky crag that overlooked Paradise Lake.

It was the one place where he could think without being interrupted and right now he needed time to think before he did something rash.

As he approached the small inlet, amidst the sound of waves crashing against the rocks he heard humming.

Coming into the clearing, he stopped in his tracks.

Cassie was there busy cleaning her paintbrushes. Her back was turned so she couldn't see him.

His wife stood next to an easel that held a canvas. Try as he might, Zach couldn't see the painting.

Doing his best to control the anger burning inside of him, Zach spoke in a monotone voice. "Do you often come here, Cassie?"

Cocoa ran to meet him, the dog's tail wagging at Zach's familiar voice.

She turned suddenly, a rose colored blush staining her cheeks. Her beautiful face held an innocent charm to it. From past experience he knew looks could be deceiving.

"I do." She smiled one of her inviting smiles and it almost pulled him in again. "I love this quiet inlet, hidden away from the world. This morning, the way the sunlight was shimmering across the lake, this place called to me."

"What are you painting?" Zach stepped forward so he could see the painting, but Cassie quickly moved it so all he saw was the back of the canvas.

A swift shadow of anger swept through him at her actions. "Keeping secrets, dearest wife?"'

Cassie turned to look at him with a puzzled look. "You'll need to wait a few days before I show this particular painting to you."

Zach frowned and crossed his arms over his chest. She was

Ever since that recent conversation with his Private Investigator, he knew better.

"Since you feel the need to hide this painting, it makes me wonder if there are other secrets you've covered up." His voice was quiet, yet held an undertone of cold anger.

Turning swiftly, she stared wide-eyed at him. "What are you talking about?"

The innocent hurt he saw in her eyes, caused him to pause for a moment. But no, he was sure he was right on target from what his private investigator had recently discovered.

Zach went on, heedless of what his wife was saying as memories of his ex-girlfriend's betrayal haunted him. "I honestly thought you were different from any of the other women I've dated. "

"I believed you were innocent of the tawdry deception and lies other women had in spades. But I'm sad to see, I must have been mistaken. Now I know the truth about you. All you are is just another pretty face."

Her body jerked as if he'd struck her.

"Zach, why are you angry? What did I do?" Cassie sputtered, bristling with indignation and her features contorted with shock.

"You know what you did. I guess the million dollars you'll be getting from this fake marriage isn't enough for you." Zach's voice was cold and lashing.

"Well, I'm going to have my lawyer get those photos removed from those magazines. I got rid of them last time this happened and I'll do it again."

He watched as Cassie's face turned pale and her arms wrapped around her middle as if she was going to be sick.

For a moment Zach hesitated at the pale look on his wife's face. No, he wasn't wrong. He couldn't be. This time, he knew better. He was convinced Cassie was a better actress than he gave her credit for.

Zach continued. "But as for the two of us, anything

remotely personal between us is over. We will fulfill our agreement of the marriage of convenience we started with and be civil to each other until the year comes to an end."

"However, anything more than that between us is over and done." Zach's cold voice was laced with contempt.

He glowered at her one last time before he spun on his heel and walked away.

CHAPTER THIRTEEN

assie

THE SKY GREW dark with rain clouds.

Loud thunderclaps echoed in the air around Cassie as she hurried back to Uncle Gus's cottage.

Her dog ran ahead, eager to return.

Tears streamed down her cheeks, mingling with the raindrops falling from the sky.

A deep unaccustomed ache pierced her heart.

Her misery was so acute that it was a physical pain.

Her hand shook as she pushed open the door, nearly dropping the canvas, paintbrushes and easel.

Quickly she cleaned Cocoa's paws with the clean dry cloth.

Then, closing the door behind her, she closed her eyes, reliving the pain of her husband's hurtful words.

I honestly thought you were different from any of the other women I've dated. I believed you were innocent of the tawdry deception and lies other women had in spades. But I'm sad to see, I must have been mistaken. Now I know the truth about you. All you are is just another pretty face.

Hot tears rolled down her cheeks as she remembered. She was confused when Zach accused her of putting photos of the two of them onto an online magazine.

Cassie had never — and would never — do something like that. But, he'd been so angry, she'd never had a chance to tell her side of the story.

Why would Zach assume she'd do something like that? He'd said something about the million dollars not being enough.

Did he think she would betray him like that simply to earn money from the sale of photos of the two of them?

The pain in her heart became a sick fiery gnawing.

The worst part was the finality to his parting words. *As for the two of us, anything remotely personal between us is over. We will fulfill our agreement of the marriage of convenience we started with and be civil to each other until the year comes to an end. However, anything more than that between us is over and done.*

Her sorrow was a huge, painful knot inside. All her dreams of Zach loving her and of the two of them being a family were crushed.

A heaviness centered in her chest from the weight of all she'd lost.

Cassie swallowed hard and bit back more tears from flowing down her cheeks.

Angrily, she wiped the remaining tears from her

cheeks. She needed to try to get her mind off of Zach. Deep inside, she realized there was nothing to be gained from rehearsing her heartache, but it was so very difficult to accept Zach's rejection of her.

"Cassie is that you?" Uncle Gus called from the sunroom. Wiping the tears from her eyes and cheeks, she picked up her easel, canvas and paintbrushes and carried them to the cozy sitting room with the large windows.

"I'm here, Uncle." Cassie forced a smile and placed the easel in the corner of the room with the canvas facing the wall.

It was much too painful to look at the painting she'd poured her heart and soul into right now.

She set everything down and turned to look at her uncle. Cocoa lay resting near Uncle Gus's feet.

"How are you feeling Uncle Gus?" Impulsively, she bent down to hug him as he sat on the recliner, feeling a desperate need to feel loved.

"Ah, that feels better." Her uncle smiled at her warmly, until he got a good look at her.

"What's going on, Cassie?" Uncle Gus put a wrinkled hand on her cheek, looking at her closely. "Your face is pale and your hands are shaking. Are you not feeling well?"

Cassie couldn't tell him the truth of what happened. Uncle Gus believed her and Zach were in love.

Instead, she latched onto her uncle's suggestion that she wasn't feeling well, because the reality was she did feel sick to her stomach from all that had happened today.

"Yeah, I am feeling a little under the weather, uncle." She spoke quietly, her voice strained.

A worried crease formed between her uncle's brows. "Will you be alright driving home?"

Home. Her uncle meant Zach's home. It certainly wasn't her home — at least it seemed like her husband wanted to make sure that she knew this was temporary.

Cassie sighed heavily.

She really wasn't looking forward to returning, but she had made the fake marriage agreement with Zach and was determined to see it through.

Also, she didn't want Uncle Gus or Zach's mom or grandparents to begin to doubt the fact that they'd married for love.

Although, perhaps they were already seeing signs that theirs was a fake marriage.

"Yeah, I'll be fine, Uncle Gus." She grabbed her purse and kissed him on the cheek. "But I should get going. I'll drive slowly, I promise."

"Call me when you get home."

"I will, worrywart." Cassie grinned and blew a kiss. As she headed out the door, she whistled for her dog.

Cocoa followed and eagerly got into the car for the drive home.

She drove home slowly through the driving rain thankful that it was only a few miles from Uncle Gus's to Zach's home.

Parking the car in the garage, she hurried into the house, her dog at her side.

As she cleaned Cocoa's paws, she remembered seeing Zach's truck in the garage. But, now it was quiet in the house.

Going to the kitchen, she noticed that Mrs. Beale had already gone for the day.

It was just as well. She didn't feel hungry anyway.

Once again Zach's angry words came back to haunt her. *We will fulfill the terms of our agreement until it's over. But, anything personal between us is over and done.*

She had opened her heart to love Zach, only to be rejected. She had loved and lost and her heart was broken.

Tears blinded her eyes as she walked quietly to her bedroom. Closing the door, she fell onto the bed yielding to the compulsive sobs that shook her.

Cocoa lay beside her on the bed and licked her cheek trying to comfort her, but nothing helped.

She cried until she finally fell asleep.

"WHAT'S GOING on between you and Zach?" Lydia grabbed her hand and pulled her away from the crowd that was arriving at the town hall meeting.

"He's been giving you some chilly looks, yet he can't seem to keep his eyes off of you even now."

Lydia peered across the room, before turning to her. Cassie nodded, knowing that to be true. Her husband had hardly spoken to her in the past couple of days.

However, he continued to be ever the gentleman, opening the car door for her and making sure she was taken care of.

She had even caught Zach watching her a few times and had been startled by his long lingering looks – however chilly -- that sent shivers through her even now.

But, Cassie knew the truth. Her husband was simply waiting until their fake marriage was over, so he could finally be rid of her.

"Yeah, Zach is upset with me right now. Something about some photos of us he found in a magazine." Cassie replied in a low, tormented voice.

"Zach doesn't know you very well if he thinks you would do anything to hurt him or the relationship between the two of you." Lydia frowned. "Do you want me to talk to him?"

"No, it's okay." Cassie shook her head and straightened her tense shoulders. "I'm still hoping that he'll let me explain. But, if not and he's determined to believe the worst of me, then I guess we didn't have much of a relationship anyway."

Lydia nodded and was about to say something when Mrs. Anderson interrupted.

"Welcome everyone. As you all know, we're here for the final time to hear from a few more people who wanted to share their thoughts on the waterfront properties in Paradise Lake."

Mrs. Anderson continued. "First we will hear from a new community member, bestselling mystery author Nate Spears."

Cassie whispered to Lydia. "I should go. Zach is waiting for me to join him."

She hurried to sit on the empty chair beside Zach, smiling warmly at his mother and grandparents who sat next to him.

Cassie turned to look at Zach and forced a smile. His

piercing blue eyes stared at her like she was a puzzle to figure out.

Swallowing, she turned to listen to the speaker. "So, I think that condos are really the way of the future. In my opinion, Paradise Lake should move with the changing times and not against it."

As the author walked to his seat, Zach's arm curled around the back of her chair and his hand touched her shoulder.

Her skin tingled where he touched her. She knew Zach only put his arm around her for appearances sake, but still his touch stirred the longings of her heart.

She swallowed nervously, hoping the evening would end soon so she wouldn't be tortured by his touch any longer.

Her stepmother took the opportunity to reach for the microphone. "I'm very grateful to our small town's mystery author Nate Spears for sharing his vision for the future."

"And as you know, it's something I've been saying for some time." Larissa brightened as she went on to talk more about her ideas for the Condos and the Yacht Chartering services she had planned.

"And speaking of boats, I would like to invite everyone to join us on our Yacht, *The Violet Diamond*, for an evening of cocktails and appetizers. We would like you to see for yourselves how fun and exciting having the yacht services on the waterfront would be. Join us at six in the evening on July the third. We hope to see you there."

Cassie knew her stepmother wasn't all that excited to

have a bunch of people on the yacht Larissa had inherited from her father.

An uneasiness flooded her. She knew with certainty that her stepmother couldn't be trusted, but was this only about winning the competition against Zach for the waterfront area?

After a few more people spoke, Uncle Gus walked slowly to the podium and took the microphone.

Her eyes widened in surprise. She hadn't even seen him arrive at tonight's meeting.

"You all know me in this small town for decades. I've got to know most of you and your children and even grandchildren in some cases. The stories I could tell."

Folks chuckled at the man they all knew as Doc White. "However, some of my proudest moments were when my lovely niece came to live with me and recently when she married Zach Stevenson."

Uncle Gus looked at the two of them with a big smile. Heat stained her cheeks when many of the townsfolk turned to look in their direction. "Zach Stevenson's ideas on expanding his great grandfather's Marina into a peaceful Resort for families to come vacation, is just what this town needs."

"The small towns that have become tourist spots have turned towards building tall condos and strip malls. I think we have enough of those kinds of buildings. But, a quiet and safe harbor for folks to come when they need peace and to enjoy God's creation, we definitely need a place like that here."

"I believe Zach will create one of the most sought after resort areas in the nation. With my beautiful and kind niece Cassie by his side helping him, I don't see how that plan could do anything but succeed."

Uncle Gus winked at them both as he walked by.

"That was quite an endorsement from Doc for both of us." Zach whispered in her ear as he drew circles with his fingers on her shoulder.

She nodded and turned to him. "Uncle Gus does believe the best of both of us. I'm glad he stood up for you tonight, Zach."

"You've worked hard to fix and build the Marina to where it is today. Besides, you've also been doing the difficult task of drawing out plans for the Resort. You deserve the endorsement."

His hand stopped its movement and he gently tucked a loose tendril of hair behind her ear. The focused intensity of his blue eyes on her, made her shift uncomfortably in her chair. "How is it that you always know exactly what I need to hear?"

She shook her head, looking down at her hands that twisted together on her lap. "I don't. I'm just telling you what I believe."

He didn't say anything else, but his hand moved possessively to her shoulder as the evening drew to a close.

Cassie's heart fluttered wildly in her chest at his touch. Just one touch from Zach and she melted in his arms.

Tonight she wished he wouldn't be so close to her. After all, he'd made it perfectly clear that anything personal between the two of them was over.

Already her heart was broken from losing the man she loved.

❦

"So, it looks like that's the plan for the Fourth of July Celebration here at the Marina." Zach spoke to his workers at the Marina.

Remember we have less than a week to get everything organized." His gaze swept over the smiling faces.

"Well then, let's begin." Andrea stood to her feet, the first among his team of twenty-four staff to do so. The rest of the workers soon followed, ready to get to work.

Zach gathered his papers and started to walk back to his office when he spotted Cassie.

She stood by the door to his office, her face pale. Her hands fidgeted with jeans that looked loose on her.

He frowned as he walked towards her. She looked like she was losing weight. To his eyes, she looked far more fragile than usual.

Placing his hand on the small of her back he said. "Join me in my office, so we can have some privacy."

She nodded and walked ahead of him.

He followed, closing the office door behind him.

"This is an unexpected surprise." Zach sat on a corner of the desk, his gaze roaming appreciatively over her comely face and form.

Cassie looked over at him and her cheeks blossomed pink under the intensity of his gaze. "Sorry, I realize I didn't have an appointment, but there was something important I needed to ask you."

He frowned as he saw her hands nervously toying with the denim fabric of her jeans. "Cassie, you don't need an appointment to see me."

She looked at him and nodded, but seemed unconvinced.

"What did you want to ask me?"

Cassie started pacing as she explained. "While I was walking to Uncle Gus's place today, I saw that my stepmother's yacht was gone. I'm worried about Addy and Olivia."

"They're the teenage girls I was telling you about that quit their jobs at the restaurant to work as servers on Larissa's yacht. But now the yacht is gone, and I can't stop thinking about those girls."

Zach walked over to her and grabbed his wife's slender hands, holding her small cold hands in his large warm ones. Finally, her hands stopped fidgeting. "You're really worried about those girls aren't you?"

A worried crease fell between her brows. "I am. I just don't know what to do."

He squeezed her hands before letting them go. Just touching her hands affected him deeply. But he didn't want her to know that.

"Well, Larissa invited everyone for a cocktail party on her yacht the day before the Fourth of July celebration at the Marina. So we can be assured that your stepmother and all those working on the yacht will be back in a few days."

Cassie nodded, quickly wiping her wet cheeks. "Yes, that's true." She seemed to ponder that. "Well, maybe I am worrying needlessly if they will be back in only a few days."

A half grin turned up the corners of his mouth. "Maybe. But, I'll keep an eye out for them."

"Okay, thanks." She walked to the door, before turning she asked. "Did you ever hear back from your Private Investigator about what he'd found out about Larissa or Emery?"

"I did ask him and so far Zeke hasn't found much. But he's doing some digging. I'm sure I'll hear from him soon." Zach walked towards her noticing for the first time her thin shoulders and how the belt around the waist of her jeans defined its smallness.

"Alright, that's good."

His brows creased together as his concern grew. "Is your worry for the girls the reason you haven't been eating or sleeping properly?"

"I get enough of both." She swallowed convulsively and looked down for a moment tucking a loose tendril of hair behind one ear.

Leaning closer he whispered. "That's not what Mrs. Beale's been telling me."

"Well, your cook shouldn't be telling tales about me." Cassie's grip tightened on the leather strap of her purse.

She looked up at him, unspoken pain alive and glowing in her large violet eyes. "You don't need to worry about me. I'll be fine."

She stepped closer to the door, placing one hand on the door handle. Turning she spoke softly. "Thank you for talking with me. I won't take up any more of your time."

With that, she opened the door and walked away. She was definitely keep her distance from him and it bothered him.

Zach's gaze followed Cassie as she hurried outside. His

conscience pricked at him as he was reminded of her worry about the missing teenage girls.

His wife had a soft heart towards others. She'd come to see him because she was worried about them.

Memories came back to him of that day he'd found her painting by the quiet inlet.

He'd been too harsh with her.

Maybe he had misjudged her too.

Why would a kind and compassionate woman like his wife be willing to sell photos of the two of them to a magazine?

It made no sense.

Maybe, it was time to ask Zeke to do some further digging as to where those photos originally came from… *or who.*

CHAPTER FOURTEEN

assie

CASSIE'S FINGERS tightened nervously from the place where they curled around Zach's arm.

Mini-lights shone from the wood ramp that led from the pier towards the connecting gangway and up onto the deck of the large boat.

The tiny lights were also wrapped around the railing and windows along the upper deck of the yacht.

It was quite beautiful and a fresh reminder of Larissa's talent of making things look good on the outside, even though deception and corruption weaved their way throughout the inside of things.

Cassie hadn't wanted to come to her stepmother's yacht party tonight, but Zach had insisted. Keep your friends close and your enemies closer, he'd told her.

It was good to be reminded of the truth of that.

However, it still seemed strange to once again be aboard the same boat that her dad had loved so much.

A wave of loneliness swept over her as she remembered her beloved father and the wonderful childhood memories she had with him.

However, time went on and things changed.

Now, this was her stepmother's boat, inherited from Cassie's father. It was also the same boat that had been christened in honor of Cassie's birth mother.

Her father had loved to tell the story of how this yacht, *The Violet Diamond*, was named after her mother.

Dad said whenever he looked into her mom's eyes, he was captivated. Violet blue he called them. Every so often he'd remind Cassie that her eyes were the same beautiful color as her mother's.

Now, this same yacht that had been one of the best memories of her mother and father, had been inherited by Larissa.

For Cassie, it seemed like a gut punch. Another beautiful memory that had been turned into ashes by the actions of her selfish stepmother.

Zach patted her hand in the crook of his elbow as they stepped onto the deck and walked into the Main Salon area.

Shaking off the painful memories, she looked around.

Her gaze roamed the room, noticing that most of Paradise Lake's town council was here as well as most of the folks who had spoken up at the town hall meetings.

She spotted her stepmother talking with the TV

actress Autumn Sommers and the mystery author Nate Spears.

Larissa had always had an insatiable need to be adored by the beautiful and popular people in the crowd. She'd never understood that need, but remembered well her narcissistic tendencies.

Her husband squeezed her hand again.

Cassie presumed Zach touched her, to reassure her that she would be fine tonight. She only hoped that was true.

But, she couldn't help but have her doubts. She was afraid there would be another scene created by her stepmother.

Looking back to her teenage years with her step-mother, most of what she remembered were going to events with her stepmother and being made to feel small and unwanted in front of the guests.

All she'd wanted was to be accepted and loved by the only mother she'd ever really known. But, that wasn't to be. Instead, she was belittled and insulted.

She did not want to experience that again.

Looking up at Zach, she could see the tense lines in his jaw. His blue eyes settled on her, cool and assessing.

Cassie pulled her hand out from the crook of his arm. Ever since her husband had spoken those hurtful words, unconsciously she had erected barriers around her heart when it came to their relationship.

She tried to stay out of Zach's way as much as possible. He continued to act the gentleman towards her, but the warmth was gone from his eyes and his words.

Cassie really missed the old Zach. But, there wasn't

much she could do, so instead she distanced herself emotionally from him.

Forcing a smile she spoke softly. "I see Lydia over by the food. I think I'll join her."

Zach nodded. "Sure. I'll catch up with you later."

"Alright." Cassie nodded quickly aware that what he was really saying was they needed to be seen together to keep up appearances. Turning, she walked toward Lydia, happy to have a friendly face in the crowd of people.

Side tables were filled with specialty foods like caviar, veggie rolls, cheese balls, meatballs, pasta salads, Caesar salads and many kinds of dips and large platters of assorted meat, veggies and fruit.

"All this food looks so delicious." Cassie stood beside Lydia with a grin on her face.

"Yeah. I couldn't resist. You know how I love food, and especially specialty food." Lydia sighed. "I'm glad you came. I know you didn't want to be here tonight."

Cassie sighed heavily. "No, I didn't. There're too many painful memories. Hopefully, this evening will be short."

Lydia turned and really looked at her. "Yeah, I hope so too. But meanwhile there is all this great food." Her friend tasted some caviar, savoring the flavor. "Cassie, fill a plate and join me."

"I'm not really hungry." She looked around and noticed Addy and Olivia walking over to the table with another platter of food.

Cassie stepped closer and whispered to Addy. "I'm glad you girls are back. I didn't know where my stepmother had taken you to and I was worried."

Addy looked around, watching people around her

before she looked at Cassie. "At first I didn't know where we were either until I saw familiar landmarks that the yacht had arrived at the port in Seattle."

The teenage girls continued to methodically add food to the table as they talked to Cassie. "I don't know what happened, but our friend Brynn, who worked as a server with us, was no longer with us when we left Seattle to return to Paradise Lake."

Cassie decided to put some veggies on a plate and spoke in low undertones so they wouldn't be overheard. "She simply disappeared?"

Addy nodded. "Yeah. It was after Mrs. White and Mr. Jakes had a party on the yacht at our usual port in Seattle. I remember there were a lot of people there, but it was mostly the men and women wearing expensive clothes who would stare at all of us servers. Then all I remember is the next morning, I couldn't find Brynn anywhere."

Cassie swallowed as fear and anger knotted inside her. "Did she say anything to you that she planned on leaving?"

"Nothing at all. That's why I'm worried about her. Maybe she got lost and missed the yacht when we left." Olivia spoke up.

"Or something else happened." An icy fear twisted around Cassie's heart. "When you girls finish with this party, I want you to come home with me tonight."

"What?" Addy looked at her puzzled. "No, we can't. Mrs. White asked us to stay the night on the yacht, because she said they had folks coming for brunch and they needed us to be ready early in the morning, to help serve food."

Cassie shivered, watching these innocent girls with

acute and loving anxiety. She didn't know what was going on, but the hairs on the back of her neck prickled from fear for them. She was desperate to do whatever she could to protect them.

"I really don't think you're safe here. I need to tell you…" Cassie was about to tell them more when she was interrupted.

"So, the beautiful Cassie White has joined us tonight." Emery Jakes' silky smooth voice echoed from behind her.

Cassie turned at the sound, a cold knot forming in her stomach.

Larissa's boyfriend was as slick as ever. His dark wavy hair glistened with the expensive hair product he used and reeked with cologne.

She remembered the familiar smell from years ago, and it made her nauseated.

Forcing a pleasant expression on her face, she spoke. "Hello, Emery. My name is Cassie Stevenson now. I came tonight with my husband, Zach Stevenson."

Emery stepped closer to her. "Ah yes. You're husband. I heard you moved up in the world, my dear. But, hopefully you still have time to dance with me, for old times sake?"

Cassie heard the band playing a slow song in the background. Emery held out his hand and reluctantly she placed her hand in his. For the sake of appearances, she felt like she had no choice.

As Emery moved her onto the middle of the dance floor, he whispered. "And I was convinced that I'd never have a chance to dance with you again, Cassie. I'm happy I was mistaken."

She shuddered, hating every moment near him. His touch alone was so repulsive to her.

Memories came back of those months after her father died. From what Cassie remembered of that time, Larissa had only truly mourned for her husband for a few weeks before she started seeing Emery Jakes.

But the worst part was yet to come.

When Larissa began inviting her boyfriend to their home, he would sometimes force her to dance with him when her stepmother was on the phone or busy in the office.

The one time he tried to kiss her, she had pushed him away, desperate to escape. Just at that moment, her stepmother walked into the living room and assumed she was encouraging Emery to kiss her.

Her stepmother sent her to her room without food for a day as punishment.

She had kept a great deal of distance between her and Emery Jakes ever since that day.

Cassie shivered as the unwelcome memories came back to haunt her.

Emery tried to pull her closer as they danced, but Cassie resisted.

Suddenly, a large hand tapped Emery on the shoulder. Cassie looked up to see Zach standing next to her stepmother's boyfriend, his jaw clenched in determination.

His low voice was firm, final. "I believe I would like to exercise my privilege as Cassie's husband and cut in."

Emery looked at the taller man, and with one look at Zach's blue eyes blazing down at him, he shrugged and stepped away from Cassie. "We'll dance again sometime, darling."

"Not if I can help it." A muscle flicked angrily at Zach's jaw as his cold eyes met those of the man beside him.

Emery stepped back as if stung and hurried away.

Zach turned to her and slipping one arm around her waist he pulled her close. Holding her other hand, Zach began to lead her in a slow dance as the bandleader crooned a love song. She felt safe in her husband's arms, instead of Emery.

His gaze traveled over her face and searched her eyes with a new intensity. "I really don't like him."

"I don't either." She shuddered visibly.

"Why did you agree to dance with him if you don't like him?"

Cassie sighed. "For appearances sake. I didn't want to cause a big disturbance."

Zach shook his head and sighed. "Well, don't dance with him again, okay? I don't trust him."

"Alright." Cassie agreed, relieved that he would care enough to protect her.

Pulling her close he touched her cheek with the back of his fingers. "You look a little pale. Are you feeling okay?"

His possessiveness over her and his sudden concern puzzled her. Her senses leapt to life at his kindness towards her, but she pushed those feelings down.

Zach had made it perfectly clear that he didn't want there to be anything personal between them anymore. Since that time, she'd done her best to put up the barriers around her heart, to protect herself.

It wasn't fair when he showed compassion and concern for her, because it caused those carefully erected barriers to fall down.

Forcing a steady voice she whispered. "I'm fine."

The song was just ending and Zach nodded. "Alright. Don't go far. I just need to talk to one more person and then I'll come find you and we'll go home."

"Alright." Cassie nodded quickly as he turned to go. She searched for Lydia, and spotted her in the corner talking with another friend.

She hurried toward her friend wanting the comfort only a best friend could give, when suddenly her step-mother stopped her.

"Cassie, I'm glad you and Zach decided to come tonight. Come with me and I'll introduce you to some important people that are new to Paradise Lake. I'm sure you'll want to get to know them." Larissa slipped her hand in Cassie's arm and walked forward with her.

She really didn't want to meet new people, but again she didn't want to make waves.

"I have someone to introduce to you both. This is my stepdaughter, Cassie White Stevenson. She recently married Zach Stevenson." Larissa continued. "Autumn Sommers is a TV actress and Nate Spears is a bestselling mystery author."

"Nice to meet you both." Cassie nodded, forcing a smile. "So, what made you decide to move to our small town?"

Autumn grinned and waved a perfectly manicured hand in the air. "Oh, sometimes I just need to get away from all the hustle and bustle of city life. Paradise Lake seemed like the perfect place to live."

"I will be right back with our drinks. You all continue chatting." Larissa interjected and quickly left.

Cassie listened as the TV actress explained how she liked the quaint little town and that it was a breath of fresh air from the usual noise and congestion of the big city.

By the time Autumn finished talking, her stepmother was back with a clear wine glass for each of them.

Handing a small wine glass to Cassie she said. "This is our best house white wine. I saved the best for last." Larissa waited until everyone had a glass then she raised her glass. "Cheers. Here's to unexpected surprises."

Cassie shrugged and took a sip of the wine.

Larissa again. "Tell us about your latest mystery novel Nate."

The author explained a little about what he was writing. "This small town has been just the change of scenery I've needed to help inspire my writing."

Cassie could feel herself feeling extra tired as Nate continued to talk about his book.

"I'm sorry, I need to excuse myself. Suddenly, I'm not feeling well." Cassie started to turn away to walk toward where her friend sat when her vision blurred like she was seeing double.

"Cassie, wait. Let me help you." Larissa's voice sounded in her ears, she was too weak to resist her stepmother's offer for help. "We'll need to find some place for you to sit down. Luckily, I know just the place for you."

She felt her legs weaken and then another hand grabbed her other shoulder.

Her stomach churned with anxiety and frustration at her helplessness. Why was she feeling so dizzy and disoriented? What was happening to her?

"I CAN'T HELP but be impressed by your tenacity in trying to expand Walker's Cove Marina into a Resort, Zach." Mayor Al Riggs grinned, his mustache twitching with the movement. "But, I really don't think this decision will come out in your favor."

Zach was irritated by the Mayor's overly confident tone and responded with a soft voice that had a steely edge to it. "Well Mayor, I guess we'll both know by the end of the Fourth of July celebrations tomorrow, when the Paradise Lake zoning committee announces their decision."

"I guess we will." Mayor Riggs mouth spread into a thin-lipped smile.

At just that moment Larissa White stopped to join their conversation. "You are both still here, good. I was hoping to end the evening by sharing a drink with both of you." Larissa motioned for a server to bring the wine. She grabbed a glass of wine to hand to Zach.

He quickly spoke. "I don't think I should indulge, but thanks anyway. I need to find Cassie."

Zach worried that he hadn't seen Cassie ever since he'd finished dancing with her. He had felt very protective of his wife, especially when he saw her dancing with Larissa's boyfriend.

Her face had looked pale as she danced with Emery and he worried about her. Even now, he was concerned about her and was eager to find her and take her home.

His gaze swept the room once more.

"Don't worry about Cassie, Zach. Last I saw her, she was talking with her friend Lydia, so you've got time for a toast." Larissa handed the Mayor a glass of wine and then reached over to give Zach the other full wine glass.

When he hesitated, she urged. "I saved my best wine for the end of the evening. I wanted you to taste it. Let's celebrate together."

Zach sighed and reached for the wine glass. "Alright."

"Good. Cheers to everything lining up just the way it should." Larissa clinked her wine glass together with theirs.

After he finished it he spoke again. "I really need to find my wife. If you'll excuse me."

He started walking towards where he had last seen Cassie, but couldn't find her anywhere in the crowd. He was beginning to feel light headed and a little dizzy.

When he saw Lydia, he started walking towards her, but got too dizzy to reach her.

He heard her voice. "Zach are you alright? What's wrong?"

It was the last thing he heard before all went dark.

CHAPTER FIFTEEN

assie

"ONCE AGAIN, *you've been a very bad girl, Cassie." Her stepmother grabbed her arm and dragged her down the back-stairs to the basement and shoved her into the small pantry-like-room.*

"I overheard you tell your little friends that you didn't like me. That I was a terribly mean stepmother and that you loved your father far better than you loved me. Now all your little friends will go home and tell their parents what an awful mother I am to you. Shame on you for telling such lies."

Her stepmother threw hurtful words at her like stones, her face a glowering mask of rage. Without warning, her hand swiftly slapped her hard on the cheek.

Stinging pain brought tears to her eyes. She looked up to see her stepmother standing there, looking down on her with a face twisted in white-hot anger.

Fear knotted inside Cassie's belly. She began to shake as the fearful images built in her mind of what her stepmother would do now.

Her stepmother's voice suddenly changed and became emotionless, sending chills up and down her body. "How do you think your dead father would feel if he knew his beautiful princess was telling such horrible lies about members of his own family?"

Cassie huddled in the corner of the small room, making no response. Her father wouldn't be happy with his daughter talking bad about her stepmother, but everything she had told her friends was true.

She swallowed hard, her stomach becoming more nauseous by the minute.

Her stepmother leaned closer and hissed at her. "Your father would hate it, that's what. He would hate you, his own daughter, for spreading terrible rumors."

Cassie jerked back at her words. Her father would hate her for saying what was true?

Her beloved father had always encouraged her to tell the truth and to speak for and help people who were less fortunate than she was.

She was taught to be honest in every conversation. So why did her stepmother insist that her dad would hate her for being honest?

A crease of worry formed between her brows and confusion swept over her. She looked up to see her stepmother watching her closely.

Larissa's face held a smug look as she crossed her arms over *her chest, before she spoke in a silky smooth voice.*

"Lucky for you, I'm not as horrible of a stepmother as you've made me out to be. So, your punishment won't be half as bad as I could make it."

"For the entire day and night you'll stay locked in this room with no food or water. That should give you plenty of time to think about how bad you've been and what you can do to change."

Stepping out of the tiny room, her stepmother slammed the door, turning the key in the lock to bolt the door shut.

As her stepmother's footsteps faded into the distance, Cassie cried out. "Please, don't leave me down here alone. I'm afraid. Help me."

Despite her tears and her cries for help, no one came to help her. Her shoulders shook and she wept aloud, rocking back and forth in the small room. She was alone, desperate for someone to help her but no one came.

"Help me. Help me." Cassie's repeated whispers continued as the nightmare took her ever deeper into her deepest fears.

She tossed and turned her mind desperate to escape.

Without warning, the familiar chilling tones of another voice spoke.

"I'm sorry, but you won't be receiving any help from me no matter how much you plead."

Cassie jerked awake, her breath coming in gasps. Her eyes opened wide as she stared into the cold black eyes of her stepmother.

Trying to jerk back, she couldn't move. Looking down she saw that her hands and feet were tied with tight ropes.

"What — er, where am I?" Cassie looked around the

small room, with the minuscule window located high above the single bed.

"What have you done to me?" Looking down at the ropes tied tightly on her hands and feet, frustration and fear bubbled inside of her.

Her head throbbed slightly as she tried to remember what happened.

Larissa stepped closer to the bed. "You and Zach came to our yacht party last night." Her stepmother inspected her long nails before answering. "But, instead of letting you go home, we decided to keep you here with us."

She could feel the gentle rocking of the boat against the waves.

"What have you done?" Cassie closed her eyes for a second as a dizzy spell made her headache even worse. She was also having trouble seeing straight.

"I simply added a sleeping drug to your wine last night. It didn't take long before you passed out. Which was just what I wanted."

Cassie swallowed the fear that threatened to overwhelm her. "Why would you want to keep me here with you? And what did you do with Zach?"

"My, aren't you full of questions." Her stepmother walked over to the tiny window, peering outside for a moment before turning to her with a frown. "It always comes back to Zach Stevenson with you doesn't it?"

"Well, he is my husband. I'm concerned about him."

Larissa shook her head angrily. "You're just like my mother. She was always trying to please my father, but never could. She simply accepted his harsh words and physical beatings as her just desserts."

"Your husband is fine. I told everyone he was most likely sick to his stomach, so your friend took him to see Doc White."

"You drugged his drink too didn't you?"

The corner of Larissa's mouth twisted with exasperation. "Of course." She sighed heavily and whispered in cold tones. "I can't believe how much you are like her."

Cassie looked over at her stepmother, confusion clouding her face. What was she going on about?

"My mother was beautiful too. In fact, that's why my father married her. There were two things he valued above all things: beauty and wealth." Her stepmother had a faraway look in her eyes as she remembered.

"Yes, I remember well. In fact, those were the two things that brought my bull-headed father to his knees. By the time I was a teenager and had enough of his verbal and physical abuse, I determined that I would do whatever it took to be beautiful and have a lot of money. I would not be like my mother and let some man control me. I would be the one in control."

Larisa lifted her chin, her icy eyes meeting Cassie's gaze head on. "By the time I was eighteen years old, I had enough money saved to have my first plastic surgery. I had four plastic surgeries by the time I was twenty-five."

"And it paid off, because I found a rich man who saw me as beautiful and wanted to marry me. He died only two years later, making me a rich widow. A little later that year I met your father."

Cassie shivered, sickened as she learned of her stepmother's plot to capture her father. "Who also made you a rich widow."

Larissa let out a crazed laugh. "Yes, that's exactly right." But her stepmother turned and rested her gaze on Cassie, her lips puckered in annoyance. "But, I hadn't counted on you. You ruined things for me."

Her stepmother pointed a long manicured finger at Cassie, her eyes narrowed in anger. "You were the chink in Edmund's armor. He loved his beautiful daughter to distraction."

"So, I had to tread carefully. I tried different ways to get rid of you. You finally went to Boarding School, but the problem was you always returned home."

Memories haunted Cassie of those years. She'd never once felt accepted or loved by her stepmother.

"Then, I finally got an idea. I ordered my bodyguard Jackson to take you to one of your father's charter boats. You were supposed to leave on that boat and never come back."

"Instead, I found out a few days later that you left on a bus to go somewhere. When Jackson wouldn't tell me where you'd gone, I fired him." Larissa sighed in frustration.

"But, now I have you exactly where I want you. And I'm going to get rid of you, for good." Her stepmother paused, her cold eyes staring pointedly at her.

Cassie's eyes widened in fear. "What — what do you mean?"

"It seems I've used up most of your father's money. But, there is a clause in your father's will where in the case of your early death I'll get your portion of the inheritance. It's perfect, really." Her stepmother smiled, her tone chilling.

"I just need to double check that Emery has everything set and ready to go with that explosive device. We wouldn't want that to go off until Emery and I can get off the boat."

Her stepmother's shrill laugh echoed eerily around the room. Cassie's body went cold with fear.

Larissa walked to the door and opened it, turning suddenly. "I'll admit that you are beautiful Cassie. But your real problem is all that compassion and gentleness that's part of your nature has made you weak. And I hate weakness."

"Your time on this earth is up. You have a few minutes to say your prayers — use them wisely." Larissa stepped out of the room and Cassie could hear the irrational sounds of her stepmother's cackling laughter as it faded down the hallway.

Cassie's eyes filled with tears of frustration and fear. She did her best to pull the ropes off her hands, but they were tied much too tightly to loosen.

Tears trailed down her cheeks and fear clenched her belly like a fist. Was she going to escape or was this truly the end?

Her thoughts went back to Zach. She had many wonderful memories together with him. Even though it seemed like he wanted nothing more to do with her, she still loved him.

Zach had even gone out of his way to give her that painting. She could still picture the details of it. The woman with her head slightly bent, looking down, pondering her life.

It was a picture of finding your identity and embracing who you truly are.

After listening to her stepmother go on and on about how she was so weak, Cassie realized there was some truth to Larissa's words.

She had chosen to be weak instead of going after life head-on. She had disguised herself for years in loose clothing, to make herself look as drab as possible so she wouldn't attract attention.

Hiding herself had become a way of life that she had chosen to make herself feel safe.

And yet while she'd been hiding, she hadn't been truly living.

It was time for her to choose life over death. It was time for her to choose embracing herself over losing herself. It was time for her to choose love over fear.

Cassie was still pondering her new discoveries, when the door opened. Addy and Olivia walked into the room and closed the door quickly behind them.

"Girls, thank God you're here. Do either of you have a pocket knife?" Cassie held up her roped hands for them to see.

Addy eyes widened for a moment before she quickly slipped a hand into a hidden pocket in her skirt.

"Clever girl." Cassie nodded her approval.

Addy hurried to cut the ropes loose.

Cassie spoke quickly. "We need to get off the boat as fast as we can."

"Why? What is going on?" Olivia burst into tears.

"It will be okay. It will take too long to explain right now, but I will tell you that my stepmother is determined to get rid of me and all of us on this boat. So we need to hurry." Cassie bit her lip to keep her composure in front of the girls.

"This is all our fault. We should never have agreed to this job, Addy. Look at Cassie all tied up." Olivia sniffled, wiping away tears from her cheeks.

"First of all, none of this is your fault, okay?" She eyed both girls needing them to understand that. "We'll be okay, as long as we work together."

"We can do that. Do you have a plan?"

"Yes, well sort of. This used to be my father's boat and I think I have an idea." Cassie thought through the idea that came to her.

Both girls nodded as Addy finished cutting through the ropes that tied her hands and feet.

Hearing loud sounds coming from the bow of the yacht, Cassie hurriedly yanked the ropes off of her and stood to her feet.

"Thanks. Not a moment too soon from the sounds of things." Cassie ran to the door, motioning for them to follow. "We need to hurry, girls."

Sitting up in bed, Zach pressed both hands against his forehead trying to get rid of the ache in his head.

Why was he feeling so horrible this morning?

Peering toward the window, he noticed the sunrise merging with the horizon line along the lake.

It was early. No wonder he felt groggy.

Seeing messages on his phone, he listened to one from

Doc White asking him to call.

Dialling his number, Doc answered right away. "How are you feeling this morning?"

"My head hurts."

Doc grunted on the other end of the line. "Not surprised. When Lydia brought you to see me last night after Larissa's yacht party I could tell your upset stomach and dizziness wasn't typical food poisoning."

So that's where he'd been last night. "I don't remember. Did Cassie stop by with me last night when I saw you?"

"No, it was just Lydia and you. What's up?"

Remembering Doc's bad heart, Zach was careful not to say too much. "Oh it's nothing really. I'm just not remembering last night too well, that's all."

"It'll come back to you."

"Hopefully." Pressing both hands against his forehead, he tried to stop the ache. "What's wrong with me then?"

"I'm not sure. Still waiting for those swab tests to come back. But, you'll be okay. Just take it easy today, Zach." Doc reassured him and hung up the phone.

Small moments from last night's party were coming back to him. Cassie had been on his arm, looking as beautiful as ever in her violet evening gown.

When Emery Jakes had begun to dance with his wife, he saw red. Marching over there he scared Emery away from Cassie and stepped in to dance with his wife, holding her possessively close.

He couldn't help it. He'd felt a burning jealousy seeing her dance with another man.

But, after the dance, he couldn't see her.

Getting dressed, Zach went down the hall to his wife's

room and knocked gently on the door, peering inside.

The bed hadn't been slept in.

Where was Cassie?

Hurrying to the kitchen, he stopped when he saw his cook. "Mrs. Beale, have you seen Cassie? Did you see her come home last night?"

"No, Mr. Stevenson. I didn't see your wife last night or this morning." His cook studied him over the glasses perched on her nose. She stood near the countertop, rolling the dough.

"I'm worried. If she calls, let me know okay?" At her nod, Zach turned to leave.

Suddenly, his phone rang.

"Zach here."

"I've got some news."

Zach expelled a breath, relieved to hear from his Private Investigator. "Zeke, just the man I wanted to talk to. Let me hear what's on your mind."

"After some digging, I've learned that Larissa White and her boyfriend Emery Jakes aren't on the up and up." The sound of documents rustled in the background as Zeke continued.

"I'm not surprised. What do you find?"

"For starters, Emery Jakes has a list of past priors as long as my arm. They include sexual assault, drug dealing and sexual misconduct with a minor. Oh, and the police have reason to believe he could be involved in human trafficking."

"I knew there was a reason I didn't like him." Zach expelled a breath. "And what did you discover about Larissa?"

"She too has a checkered past. For one thing, Larissa White, despite inheriting a lot of money years ago from Edmund White III, is now drowning in debt."

"Since her husband died Larissa has chartered her yachts as a source of income, but there is evidence to believe she has shady dealings going on. These include trafficking drugs and possibly being involved in human trafficking." Zeke explained.

Zach's voice was rough with anger. "Why am I not surprised?"

"There's more." Zeke continued. "During my investigation I found out a few more problems that Larissa White has been responsible for."

"Like what?" "Well, for one thing, I found out that Larissa hired someone to set that fire at the Marina."

Zach's jaw tightened in anger at the news. "She must have been desperate to either ruin me or get me out of her way."

"Looks that way." Zeke continued. "There's more. I found out who was responsible for selling your wedding pictures to those magazines."

"It was your wife's stepmother. Somehow, she must have had access to those photos." His private investigator was quiet on the other end of the line.

Zach felt the nauseating sinking of guilt at the pit of his stomach.

He'd blamed Cassie for selling those photos of the two of them to magazines. The terrible things he'd said to her that day when he'd talked with her at the lake.

She had been happily painting, looking so beautiful and innocent. When he found her there, he was angry and had already convinced himself that his wife was responsible.

Terrible regrets bombarded him as he remembered his cold words and actions towards her ever since that day.

Her violet blue eyes filled with hurt from that day he'd spoken so harshly to Cassie, haunted him.

How could he make things right between them? Could Cassie ever forgive him for judging her so wrongly?"

"Zach are you still there?" Zeke's voice on the other end of the phone broke through his inner torment.

He sighed heavily before replying. "I'm here."

"Good. I just have a couple more details to fill you in on." Zeke cleared his throat roughly. "So, this one is rather concerning."

"I talked with Cassie's best friend Lydia and learned that your wife's stepmother used to physically and verbally abuse Cassie after her father passed away." Zeke hesitated before continuing. "There's enough reason to believe that your wife's stepmother could be planning to harm Cassie."

A harsh gasp escaped Zach. "Do the police know? Is something being done to bring those two to justice?"

"Yes. It was your wife's friend Lydia who alerted the police to the fact that Cassie went missing last night at the party. In fact that's why I called this morning." Zeke hurried to explain.

"The police have found enough evidence to make an arrest. Larissa and Emery's yacht is missing from the Marina. The police have reason to believe *The Violet Diamond* sailed late last night right after their party."

"And they've taken Cassie with them?" Zach's breath came raggedly in impotent anger.

"The police believe Larissa and Emery have taken your wife along with a few others on that boat."

Zach felt as if a band closed around his throat.

"But, I believe we can catch up with the police boat and with Larissa's yacht." Zeke suggested and Zach leapt on the idea.

Impatient, Zach replied. "Let's do it. I'll meet you at the Marina."

"Sounds good."

Zach grabbed his sunglasses and hurried out to the waterfront of his property.

Hurriedly, he untied the rope that anchored his motorboat to the pier and turning on the engine, he gunned the motor and took off toward the Marina.

Seeing the former Navy SEAL standing on the pier, Zach slowed and pulled up next to it.

Zeke jumped on board and immediately Zach hit the accelerator and soon they were skimming across the lake.

"Keep going north. Hopefully it won't take long to find them." Zeke stood beside him at the bow of Zach's motorboat, the mist from the water catching their hair as they skimmed along the water.

Fear stabbed at his belly like a dozen knives piercing through his skin.

The worst had come true. His wife was now in the clutches of her desperate and depraved stepmother.

Since he'd learned the truth from Zeke about Larissa White's cruel and ruthless ways, Zach was now more determined than ever to stop her.

He wouldn't stop until both Larissa and her boyfriend were behind bars.

He couldn't allow Cassie to be hurt again by her step-mother. He increased the speed of the engine and clenched his jaw in determination.

Finally they reached the channel that led from the lake to a larger body of water.

"There it is. That's Larissa's yacht, *The Violet Diamond*." Zeke pointed to the large yacht with the purple and blue paintbrush design along the stern of the boat.

As they closed in, Zach noticed the police boat cruiser was just ahead of them.

"I see two people in a small boat leaving the yacht. Could you see who that is?" Zach pointed to a compartment on the motorboat. "I keep binoculars in there. Want to see what's going on?"

"Sure." Zeke pulled out the binoculars and described what he saw. "There's a small boat beside the large yacht, and seated in it are Larissa and Emery. I don't see anyone else. The police are closing in on them."

Zeke slipped the binoculars back into the compartment. "Hopefully this will be resolved quickly. We'll have to see what happens."

Zach nodded in agreement as he steered his motorboat closer. Fear and anger knotted in his belly. Questions burned inside him. If Larissa and Emery were in the boat beside the yacht, that meant Cassie was on the yacht along with a few other people.

What was going on?

They finally got close enough to see the people in the

boats at close range. One cop was holding a handheld blow horn to his mouth. He spoke firmly, issuing orders.

"Surrender your weapons." The cop called out, his voice loud in the megaphone.

"We won't surrender!" Emery Jakes yelled out and tried to accelerate their boat forward but suddenly the small motor their boat sputtered and died.

Zach shook his head and moved his motorboat forward, desperate to find a way to save his wife.

He moved the motorboat a short distance past Larissa and Emery's boat when Zach leaned over to Zeke. "You take over. I'm going to get Cassie off that boat."

"What are you…" Zeke called from behind him as Zach dove off the motorboat and into the cold water. He began to swim as fast as he could towards the yacht a short distance away.

He was determined to find a way onto the yacht no matter what happened.

There was no way he was going to let Cassie die.

As he continued to swim, he heard the officer's voice through the megaphone. "You're outmanned and outgunned, Mr. Jakes. It would be wise to surrender. This is your last chance."

Zach could see the yacht only a few yards away now.

Suddenly, he overheard Emery yell from behind him. "Do you know what my girlfriend is holding in her hand, officer?"

The policeman said. "Why don't you tell us Mr. Jakes?"

"It's called a dead man's trigger. If she lets go, it will cause the explosive device to go off and the yacht will explode."

Zach began to tread water near the yacht, looking for a way to climb aboard.

He glanced behind him and saw Emery waving Larissa's arm back and forth in the air to emphasize that he held the upper hand.

The cops on board the police cruiser talked quickly between themselves.

Zeke continued to move the motorboat towards Zach's location.

The police officer put the megaphone to his lips again, when arguing started on Larissa and Emery's small boat.

Zach overheard them arguing with each other as he spotted a rope that would get him onboard.

He started to swim towards the rope.

Larissa yelled at Emery. "Stop waving my hand. The remote is slipping. Let go, I said!"

"No! Here give me that thing!" Emery gripped the hand that held the remote and with his other hand began to pull the remote away.

"Don't do that! You'll take the pressure off the button and the boat will…" Larissa fought with him to stop, but Emery continued to struggle with her to take it out of her hand.

Suddenly, a deafening explosion filled the air. Fragments from the yacht filled the air and landed in the water. A small piece of wood struck Zach's shoulder and he went under the water from the impact.

He resurfaced just as another loud blast filled the air and more fragments from the yacht fell like hailstones around him. He ducked back under the water for a moment before resurfacing.

Shocked, he looked around him to see the wreckage of *The Violet Diamond*. What little remained of the yacht began to sink under the water.

Zach's heart stopped suddenly. *I'm too late. My wife is dead.*

Icy fear spread through his belly as shock and despair swept over him. It hit him hard like a tsunami wave drowning its victims.

In the background he heard the police officer tell Larissa and Emery they were under arrest, but it hardly registered as the pain of loss and heartache filled him.

Memories of losing his best friend in a boat explosion when he was a teenager swirled around and around in his head.

Now, another boat explosion had claimed the life of someone he loved.

It was his fault. He shouldn't have insisted Cassie come with him to Larissa's yacht party. If she hadn't come then she would have lived.

Terrible regrets filled him.

I loved her. I loved Cassie with all my heart and never told her. How could I have let her die?

Tears filled his eyes as raw and primitive grief overwhelmed him and he slumped over the helm of the boat, his head on his arms.

Zeke moved the motorboat until it was close to him. "Zach, look."

He was too deep in pain-filled thoughts to hear his friend.

Zeke spoke again. "Zach, you are not going to believe this."

Finally, his friend's words broke through his heavy thoughts. He looked up at Zeke.

"Take a look over there." Zeke was pointing near the stern of what remained of the yacht.

His breath caught in his throat.

Cassie, Addy and Olivia were seated in an inflatable boat paddling towards them.

"She's alive." Zach whispered in soft reverent tones. "I can't believe it. It's a miracle. How did Cassie and those teenage girls get off the boat in time?"

Zeke chuckled. "Looks like they must have figured out a way."

Zach watched Cassie, his body seemingly frozen as he stared at her in shock.

"Here, let me help you get in the boat Zach." Zeke grabbed his hands and pulled him onto the motorboat. "Now we'll get those three gals and bring them onto the motorboat with us. I'll drive Zach and you can take care of your wife."

It barely registered with him what Zeke was saying because Zach was so caught up with raw emotions of shock and unbelief at what he was seeing.

Zeke pulled the motorboat beside Cassie's smaller inflatable boat and Zach reached out to pull all three girls onto the motorboat.

"Cassie, I'm so thankful you're alive." At the last, he lifted Cassie into his arms, holding her tightly in his arms like he would never let her go. He rained kisses down on the tip of her nose, then her eyes, and, finally, he satisfyingly kissed her soft mouth.

He drank in the sweetness of her kiss, taking pleasure in the moment that he thought was lost to him forever.

Cassie pulled back, a happy smile on her face as she sighed. "Zach, you came for me."

"Of course I came for you. When Zeke told me what he'd learned about your stepmother and her boyfriend, I knew you were in trouble." Zach sighed.

"Larissa told me that she drugged my drink last night to force me to come with them. She wanted to get rid of me so she could get my inheritance money." Tears glistened in Cassie's violet blue eyes.

"But, she didn't count on the fact that those girls would help me get free from those ropes. And my stepmother also didn't remember that I knew where my father hid things on his yacht. So we found the boat and lowered it to the water and got into it before the yacht exploded."

"Thank God." Zach breathed into her hair, relief flooding him once again.

Zeke had turned the motorboat around and they passed by the large lake patrol boat. They both turned in time to see the police officer place handcuffs on Larissa and Emery.

"Looks like they won't be going anywhere for a long time." Zach turned back to see a lone tear trailing down his wife's cheek.

"Yeah. It's so sad about my stepmother's life." Cassie shook her head, wiping at the tears that fell down her cheeks.

"What do you mean?"

Cassie swallowed, remembering her stepmother's

story. "She told me how her own father had abused and controlled her mother and how she hated him."

"Larissa said I reminded her of her mother whom she saw as a weak woman. And she hated weakness. She said, people who are weak, deserve what they get. I don't mean to be weak, but I admit to being someone who wants to have peace and show compassion and kindness to others."

Zach was amazed that this woman in his arms could doubt how wonderful she was. He kissed the top of her head. "You are not weak. And compassion and kindness are your greatest strengths."

"Really?"

"Yes really. It took me a long time to realize that's only some of the many reasons why I fell in love with you." Zach whispered, toying with her wet hair as he gently helped her sit down on the seat at the back of the boat.

Her eyes widened and moistened as they clung to him. "You love me?"

"With all my heart, sweetheart." Zach tightened his grip on her waist, pulling her closer. "I can't believe it took almost losing you forever to make me realize how much I loved you."

He expelled a long breath. "I'm so sorry for keeping you at arms length. I'm so sorry for those terrible things I said. I realize now, that it wasn't you that sold those photos of the two of us to those magazines. It was your stepmother."

Sighing he stared into her eyes. "I am sorry for judging you so harshly -- and for believing for a moment that a loving and kind woman like you would do something so devious. Can you ever forgive me?"

CASSIE SWALLOWED. Her body trembled all over from the shock of barely escaping with her life.

Seeing the ravaged yacht beside the motorboat, reminded her of how close to dying she'd come.

She stared wordlessly at him for a moment, overwhelmed by everything that had happened to her.

Zach said he loved her. She smiled. Now, her husband was asking for her forgiveness. She exhaled slowly as a new warm glow started in her belly shooting upwards towards her heart.

Holding his gaze with her own she replied in a shaky voice. "How could I not forgive a man who chose to deliberately swim towards a ticking time bomb to try to save me?"

"But I didn't make it in time. The yacht exploded before I could get on the boat to save you."

Blinking back tears, she placed both hands on his cheeks and softly kissed his lips. "Thank God you didn't get on that boat, Zach. You were saved. And just so you know, it was the fact that you were willing to risk your life for me that has melted my heart. I'm undone."

Zach pulled her close, kissing the top of her hair. "I would have done anything to save you. I can't imagine my world without you in it."

His words wrapped around her like a warm blanket. He had unlocked her heart and soul and her love deepened and intensified beyond what she could ever have imagined.

She looked up at Zach as she felt his arms tremble as

he held her close.

"Your arms are shaking."

His blue eyes held a smoldering love. He released a chuckle that sounded strained. "I almost lost you my love. Of course I'm shaking." His eyes searched hers, a question lingering in his.

She knew what Zach was asking without him needing to say the words. "I know you experienced terrible betrayal and deception before from others in your life that you loved and trusted, Zach."

"I realize it's difficult to trust me, but I thank you for choosing to overcome your fears and to trust me with your heart anyway." She caressed his cheek with one hand. "Of course I forgive you. I love you, with all my heart."

"Thank you." Zach expelled a breath. "You are the woman of my dreams. I want to grow old loving you."

Cassie's lips spread into a wide smile. She loved that.

"Which brings me to my next question." Zach's eyes brightened and held a new sheen of purpose. "Will you become my forever wife, Cassie?"

"I will. I love you, Zach Stevenson." She kissed his lips lightly.

Zach turned quickly and looked at the others in the boat. "We have an audience, so I'll need to wait to kiss you like I really want to."

Heat rose up to her cheeks and she offered him a smile.

"And I love you, my beautiful bride." Zach wrapped his arms around her, holding her close.

How she loved this incredible man. She was so happy to pledge all her love to her real husband, *forever.*

EPILOGUE

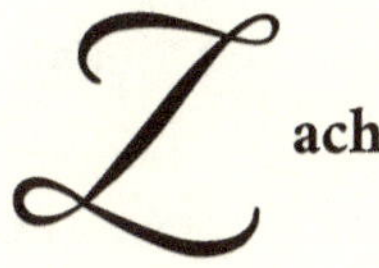ach

WALKER'S COVE *Marina ~ The Fourth of July Celebration*

ZACH HELPED Cassie out of the motorboat and onto the wood pier along the Marina's waterfront.

He had asked Cassie if she wanted to go home instead of coming to the Marina. He would understand if she needed to rest from the ordeal she'd just endured.

But, Cassie had reassured him. *I know how much this Marina celebration means to you Zach. I want to share this with you and be by your side.*

Zach grabbed his wife's hand as they began walking toward the sandy beach, more grateful than ever for his amazing wife.

Suddenly, loud clapping and cheers broke out.

The acres of grass along the Marina's waterfront were filled with folks from town who had gathered for the annual Fourth of July celebration.

Grinning, he waved at everyone and folks clapped in response.

Making their way down the grassy knoll to meet them, were his mom, grandparents and brothers and families.

Zach pulled each of them into a big hug.

"Thank God you're safe, Zach and Cassie." Misty eyed, his mom embraced him and Cassie, followed soon by his grandparents.

"We're fine, just a little shaken up." Zach grinned, pulling his wife close to his side.

Expelling a breath in relief, his gaze swept over the smiling faces of his family. All of his brothers stood nearby with their wives and children.

"Man, we heard what happened. We're thankful you and Cassie came back in one piece." Adam grabbed him into a quick embrace as did the rest of his brothers.

"It's definitely good to be back." Zach looked at each of them and then over at the large crowd where folks were having fun on the Marina grounds. "Looks like the Marina celebration is going well."

"Your workers took over and did a great job taking care of all the details of this day, Zach. But I think you should say a little something. Folks would feel a lot better hearing from you." Granddad slipped an arm around his shoulders, a warm smile lighting his face.

Zach nodded. "You're right." He looked at the podium

that had been setup just for this occasion. "I guess there's no time like the present."

He stepped up to the microphone still holding his wife's hand and began to speak.

"Well, we made it back, safe and sound." He held up Cassie's hand in his as the crowd cheered. "It was a little touch and go there, for a while on whether we would actually make it back here in one piece."

"We're thankful to be here. If you want answers about what happened, perhaps Sheriff Ritten has something to say."

Zach nodded to the Paradise Lake's man in charge of law and order.

Sheriff Ritten hurried up to the podium and grabbed the microphone. "I can't say too much because of legalities. But, I can tell you we have apprehended two people who we have reason to believe are suspects in criminal activity including allegations of drug dealing, human trafficking and attempted murder."

"More than that I can't talk about, as it is an ongoing investigation." Sheriff Ritten looked over at Zach and Cassie. "However, I will say I'm glad the two of you are back safe and sound."

Zach shook the officer's hand. "Thanks Sheriff. It's good to be back." As the Sheriff stepped off the platform, Zach spotted Koda Lightfoot's father standing in the crowd.

His thoughts tumbled from his lips as Zach saw his best friend's father. "Everyone of us has come to Walker's Cove Marina today to celebrate our freedom."

"The word freedom means something slightly different to each person, but I think most of us would agree it means to think, speak and act without any hindrance, coercion or constraints placed upon us." Zach looked at Cassie, who smiled warmly and nodded at him to continue.

"Many times, we think of our freedoms being denied us by other people, or those in authority in some way."

He cleared his throat and continued. "However, I've come to realize that we can be the ones that hinder our own freedom. Not long ago, I realized this was true in my own life." Zach's hand shook slightly, nervous as he shared his own story.

"You see, I remember another Fourth of July eleven years ago. I was sixteen and my best friend and I got our motorboats ready to race. We took our boats from the Marina to the starting place and when the guy brought the flag down for us to go, we each took off like a shot."

"It was exhilarating and fun, until we neared Rocky Crag Point and suddenly, I turned and saw the black smoke coming out of my friend Koda's boat. And I was too late to stop the boat explosion that caused the death of my best friend."

Zach bit his lips and swallowed back emotion as he recalled that day years ago. "You see, for years, I didn't celebrate life or freedom because I felt guilty that I lived and Koda died."

His voice was raw and hoarse. "Then, recently I read Koda's journal. His father gave it to me to read, saying that it would help me heal."

Makoa Lightfoot's gaze never left Zach as he shared

his story. "Reading his words has helped. Koda wrote that his inspiration was his mom who fought cancer for three years before it took her life."

"He wrote: *Being on the lake and racing my motorboat makes me feel alive like nothing else ever has. I feel closer to my mom as I fly across the water and feel the wind in my hair. And I'm determined to do that again.*"

"Even if Zach doesn't go along with my idea — I'm still going to race. I have to, because of what I learned from my Mom."

"She told me: "Son, don't let your fears stop you from living life. Even if something painful happens along the way. Learn from it. Sometimes the best thing you can do is get on the horse again after you've been thrown off."

Zach felt an indefinable feeling of rightness as he continued to share. "After reading Koda's words, I realized that I have been holding back from really living life because of misplaced guilt and fear."

"I realized my best friend wouldn't want me to live that way either. Instead of living in fear, we are going to embrace life and freedom."

He paused for a moment looking over the crowd and took a deep breath. "So, we are going to do something different for this year's Fourth of July celebration."

"For the first time ever, we will be starting motorboat races that will happen annually and I will join in the events."

"With every year's race, all the proceeds from the motorboat races will go towards helping struggling teenagers to overcome drug or alcohol addictions."

The crowd cheered at his announcement.

"However, I want to start this off by giving a gift to Koda's father." Zach waved his hand for the older man to join him at the podium.

"Makoa Lightfoot, you know your son was my best friend and I know you miss him as do I. Today, in Koda's memory, I want to give you the first motorboat in a new line of motorboats I designed and built — *The Koda Lightfoot Motorboat Series* — so named in honor of your son."

Moisture filled Makoa's eyes and a stray tear trailed down his cheek. He grabbed Zach in a big hug.

When Makoa finally spoke, his words came out raw and hoarse. "Zach, thank you. I will treasure this gift and the incredible reminder it will be to me of my son. And I am truly honored to learn that you designed a line of motorboats named after my son. He would be thrilled."

Koda's father reached out and put a hand on Zach's shoulder. "But, I believe he'd be even happier with your choice to not let your fears stop you from living life. I'm proud of you, son."

Zach swallowed hard trying to push back emotions that threatened to spill over. He grabbed Makoa Lightfoot and gave him a big hug.

The crowd clapped loudly, enjoying the meaningful moment.

Mr. Lightfoot left the podium, and Zach spoke. "Well, I think that's all…"

Cassie stepped close to him, and took the microphone from his hand. "We're not quite done yet. Mrs. Anderson and the rest of the committee have an announcement."

Zach stepped back, curious about this new announcement. Cassie grabbed his hand and smiled a new excitement in her violet eyes.

"We've come here today to announce that the decision has been made about the zoning for the Paradise Lake waterfront properties." Mrs. Anderson turned to Zach and smiled.

"We've come to an unanimous agreement in favor of the expansion of Walker's Cove Marina into a Resort. Congratulations Zach."

Joy bubbled up from deep inside of him at the announcement.

He walked over and shook Mrs. Anderson's hand. "Thank you."

The crowd clapped again and Mrs. Anderson and the rest of the committee stepped down from the platform.

"There's just one more item that I wanted to add to today's celebration." Cassie spoke softly into the microphone.

She looked at her Uncle Gus who walked slowly toward them, carrying something in his hand. Handing it over to Cassie, Doc winked at him and grinned.

He wondered at the happy glow he saw in her violet eyes.

"This is a little something I made, that I hope inspires you everyday. I hope this will help you discover more of who you are. I hope you will find the healing and peace you long for."

"Most of all, I hope your awareness will grow of how much bigger the scope of your safe harbor really is. Because it includes all the people who really love you." Cassie handed the tall package to him with a shaky hand.

Zach pulled off the brown paper and saw the painted canvas beneath it.

His eyes widened and he couldn't help the emotion that flooded him.

His lovely wife had painted a picture of him as a little boy sitting on a large rock by the inlet. Blue water was lapping gently against the rocks below.

He held a fishing rod and his great grandfather sat nearby looking at him with a smile. The title of the painting spoke to him: *Safe Harbor.*

"I can't believe you painted the vision that Grand talked about whenever he talked about his dreams for a Marina and Resort. It's beautiful. It's perfect my love. Thank you so much." Zach kissed her cheek and with one arm, held the painting high in the air for the crowd to see.

"May we as the people of Paradise Lake, make this a safe harbor for everyone who comes here." Zach spoke with conviction into the microphone.

The folks around him, clapped and whistled at his words, in full agreement with his declaration.

Zach grinned, happiness and contentment flooding him all the way down to his toes.

He turned to his wife, still not quite believing he had been fortunate enough to be married to a woman as beautiful and kind as Cassie.

Cassie felt a warm glow flow through her at Zach's gaze as he studied her.

His compelling blue eyes riveted her to the spot.

Vaguely, she overheard Zach ask some of his workers to take over the details of the rest of the announcements.

She felt the movement of his breathing as he stepped closer to her. Her heart hammered in her ears as he gently held both her arms.

Zach whispered his voice full of emotion. "Somehow you knew just the perfect gift. And even more amazing, you made it yourself. I'm going to put it in the big room at the Marina, to inspire everyone who walks by. We'll always remember to stay focused on our vision."

"Thank you again." Zach slipped an arm around her waist and pulled her close, whispering in her ear. "We have an audience, otherwise I'd kiss you senseless."

Without warning his grip on her waist tightened and leaning down his breath softly fanned her face. "What the heck, I can't wait."

He drew her face to his and pressed his mouth to hers. She kissed him back, savoring his sweet kisses. She was just beginning to feel her knees weaken when Zach raised his mouth from hers and gazed into her eyes.

"I definitely want to do more kissing tonight." His eyes were full of promise and she blushed at the thought.

Her husband's renewed ardor and passion for her ever since she narrowly missed dying in the yacht explosion, was a heady feeling.

Just when she had been convinced that their relationship was over, he had asked her forgiveness and confessed his love.

All that love wrapped around her like a warm blanket.

Reluctantly he released her and reached for her hand, turning to her with a curious expression in his eyes. "What inspired you to title your painting, Safe Harbor?"

Cassie breathed deeply, looking at him with vulnerable eyes. "I remembered one of our first conversations where you shared your great grandfather's original vision for this Marina."

"However, the name is also taken from my own personal experience, as this place has been a safe harbor for me."

"Ever since I escaped my stepmother's home and came to live with Uncle Gus here in Paradise Lake, I've felt safe and cared for." Moisture welled in Cassie's eyes and she quickly blinked them back.

"I think for me, the name Safe Harbor perfectly describes the feelings I've had since living here. It means, no longer needing to hide who you really are, and choosing to push past your fears and embrace new freedom so you can fully live."

"Sounds like you've gone through a metamorphosis, like I have."

"Yeah, that's a good word for it." She nodded, swallowing the emotion that clogged her throat.

"I'm glad for you, Cassie. May this place and our lives with each other always be a safe harbor for both of us." Zach pulled her close to his side.

"Yeah. I want that for both of us, Zach." Her heart swelled with a longing for a true home and a family of her own to love.

Zach nodded at the people sitting on the grassy knoll, laughing and having fun together.

Her gaze followed Zach's to his family and her uncle and his friends enjoying spending time together.

"Looks like, my mom, grandparents and my brothers and their families and your Uncle Gus and his friends are waiting for us to join them."

Cassie smiled. "Yeah. It's wonderful to be surrounded by so many friends and family who love you."

"It is." Zach slipped his arm around her waist as they walked together towards those that they loved.

Cassie sat near Uncle Gus and kissed him on the cheek. "My dear girl, I'm so thankful you are safe."

Her uncle squeezed her hand.

"I am too, Uncle Gus. And I'm glad to see all of you guys, too." Cassie smiled warmly at her uncle's six housemates.

Drummond grinned. "I saved a piece of your favorite chocolate cake for you, Cassie. I knew you'd come back home."

Cassie was touched by the gesture. Drummond didn't say much, but when he really cared about someone, his actions showed it.

"Grumpy, you love chocolate cake. Yet, you saved me a piece?" Cassie shook her head and grinned.

A toothy grin turned up the corners of the Scotsman's wide mouth. "Aye. Thought you could use some cheer."

"That was so thoughtful, thank you." Cassie eyed him thoughtfully. "Since you continue to be so kind to me, I've decided I'm going to change your nickname from Grumpy to Cheerful. What do you think?"

Drummond grinned. "Aye, I like it. Cheerful, it is."

"I'm glad." She sat there with her uncle and his housemates enjoying her chocolate cake until Zach motioned for her to come join him.

She excused herself to join her husband.

Cassie looked at Zach who motioned his head towards his mother.

"Mom has something to say to all of us." Zach reached for Cassie's hand. She loved sitting close to Zach and being part of his big family.

Looking over at Eliza Stevenson, she noticed the handsome older gentleman sitting next to her.

"It is so wonderful to be together with my family today. As I listened to Zach give his heartfelt speech today, I couldn't help but think of how proud I am of all my sons, their wives and our grandchildren."

"I'm convinced your father is looking down from Heaven so pleased with each one of you." Eliza's blue eyes misted for a moment, a faraway look in her eyes as if remembering her late husband.

"I am so pleased that each of my sons have married lovely wives — lovely inside and out I might add."

Cassie's heart wrapped in a silken cocoon of euphoria as Zach's mom looked at her and smiled warmly.

A mother's love was something she'd always truly longed for and Eliza Stevenson was everything she could hope for in a loving mother.

"Well, because each of my sons are settled so nicely, it makes what I want to tell you, a little easier to say." Eliza breathed deeply, looking a little nervous.

A telltale blush made its way to Eliza's cheeks as she turned to the distinguished looking man who sat beside her.

"I want you all to meet the man I've begun seeing. This is Henry Wyndham." She paused a moment before continuing.

"His wife died fifteen years ago and they never had any children. So, go easy on him. He's not used to a family this large." Eliza smiled over at all her adult children and their families.

"It's nice to meet you, Henry." Adam spoke with a grin. "I think I can speak for everyone and say that if you make our mother happy, we're thrilled to have you as part of our family."

"Hear, hear." Jack lifted the drink he had in his hand and all four brothers followed his lead.

Henry chuckled as his gaze roamed the faces of the family gathered. "I'm very pleased to finally meet all of you." He looked lovingly at Eliza before turning back to the family.

"And I couldn't agree more with you, Adam. It took me a long time to find a beautiful, gentle and compassionate woman like your mother. Now that I've found her, I don't ever want to let her go. I'll do whatever it takes to see to it that your mother is happy."

"Well said." Gabe grinned and nodded at the older man.

Each of the brothers and their wives nodded and smiled warmly at the gentleman who had captured their mother's attention.

They all talked for a long time getting to know Henry, before Zach announced they were going to take a walk on the beach.

"We'll be back soon." Zach reached for Cassie's hand

and helping her to her feet, they started to walk along the beach.

"Where are we going?" Cassie grinned, secretly loving the spontaneous side of her husband.

Zach sighed contentedly. "Seeing Henry look so lovingly at my mom, made me aware that I haven't taken enough time to do those things that make you happy. And I really want to do whatever it takes to put a smile on your face, sweetheart."

Cassie's heart lurched with a delightful shiver at his words.

"Zach, it means the world to me to hear you say so." They reached the small inlet they loved so much, hidden away from the world.

Cassie stopped, and turned to him. Reaching upwards she placed both hands on his cheeks, her gaze intense with emotion.

Lifting her heels up, she stood on tiptoe and gently touched his lips with her own. "I'm already so incredibly pleased. I'm happy you married me. I'm happy you chose to save me. And most of all, I'm happy you love me."

"I love you too, with all my heart." He wrapped his arms around her slender waist.

Pulling her close, he reclaimed her lips, and crushed her to him.

She gave herself freely to the passion of his kiss.

Their kiss was like a soldering heat that joins metals -- joining their lives and their hearts forever as one.

❧

**Thank you for reading Zach and Cassie's story.
Are you ready to read some Cowboy Clean Romance?
Begin reading Wyatt and Abby's love story today at:
https://memorablefictionbooks.com**

ALSO BY MELODY ARCHER

Clean Billionaire Fake Marriage Romance Series

Book 1: The Billionaire's Marriage Bargain

Book 2: The Billionaire's Marriage Contract

Book 3: The Billionaire's Marriage Promise

Book 4: The Billionaire's Marriage Barter

Book 5: The Billionaire's Marriage Pledge

7 Brides for 7 Cowboys, Small Town Sweet Western Romance Series

Book 1: The Forgiven Cowboy's Best Friend

Book 2: The Redeemed Cowboy's Secret Baby

Book 3: The Honorable Cowboy's Convenient Marriage

Book 4: Pre-Order The Wounded Cowboy's Beauty Bride

Books 5, 6 & 7 *Still to Come...*

Find your favorite Sweet Romance series on my New Author Website. *Grab your book at a discount when you buy direct(use code: MFB10)*.

www.MemorableFictionBooks.com

ABOUT THE AUTHOR

Melody Archer lives in Alberta with her husband and their four young adults.

Recently, her oldest son married his wife from Brazil. Their family has been enjoying getting to know their new daughter-in-law.

She loves new and classic romantic movies, green smoothies and going on adventures with her family.

Connect with Melody below :)

Copyright ©November 2022 by Lorna Faith Kopp

All rights reserved.

No part of this publication may be reproduced, distributed, or transmitted in any form or by any means, or stored in a database or retrieval system, without the written permission of the publisher.

The only exception is brief quotations in printed reviews. The reproduction or utilization of this work in whole or in part in any form whether electronic, mechanical or other means, known hereafter invented, including xerography, photocopying and recording, or in any information storage retrieval system, is forbidden without the written consent of the publisher and/or author.

Thank you for respecting the hard work of this author. This edition if published by Lorna Faith Kopp. First eBook Edition: ©December 2021 by Lorna Faith Kopp. First Paperback Edition: ©November 2022 by Lorna Faith Kopp.

This is a work of fiction. Names, characters, places, and incidents are either the creation of the author's imagination or are used fictitiously, and any resemblance to actual persons living or dead, business establishments, events or locales is entirely coincidental.

www.ingramcontent.com/pod-product-compliance
Lightning Source LLC
Chambersburg PA
CBHW051129190726
48290CB00006B/1759